TWISTED

REASONS

(First book of the 'Twisted' trilogy)

by

Geza Tatrallyay

Deux Voiliers Publishing

Aylmer, Quebec

First Edition

Copyright © 2014 by Geza Tatrallyay

All rights reserved.

Published in Canada by Deux Voiliers Publishing, Aylmer, Quebec.

www.deuxvoilierspublishing.com

Library and Archives Canada Cataloguing in Publication

Tatrallyay, Geza, 1949-, author
        Twisted reasons : (first book of the 'Twisted' trilogy) / by Geza Tatrallyay.

Issued in print and electronic formats.
ISBN 978-1-928049-12-8 (pbk.).--ISBN 978-1-928049-17-3 (Ingram Spark-pbk).--ISBN 978-1-928049-15-9 (smashwords-epub).-- ISBN 978-1-928049-10-4 (kindle).--ISBN 978-1-928049-18-0 (Ingram Spark-epub).

        I. Title.

PS8639.A875T95 2014   C813'.6

                                                            C2014-908011-5

                                                            C2014-908012-3

Legal deposit – Bibliothèque et Archives nationales du Québec, 2014

Cover Art and Design – Lin-Lin Mao

Red Tuque Books distributes *Twisted Reasons* in Canada. Please place your Canadian independent bookstore and library orders with RTB at www.redtuquebooks.ca. For outside Canada, please order through Ingram.

To the many who died and are still
dying as a result of the Soviet Union's
reckless pursuit of the atom bomb.

Human nature too has curious twisted reasons that the heart certainly knows nothing of.

Graham Greene, *The Third Man*

If only it were all so simple. If only there were evil people somewhere insidiously committing evil deeds, and it were necessary only to separate them from the rest of us and destroy them. But the line dividing good and evil cuts through the heart of every human being. And who is willing to destroy a piece of his own heart?

Aleksandr Solzhenitsyn, *The Gulag Archipelago*

Prologue

András watched the scarlet ooze seep through the crystals of the newly fallen snow crunching beneath his feet. This was the third time he had vomited blood that day, and on this occasion, he did not even make it to the latrines. *Just as well*, he thought, as he spat more blood, *at least out here I can breathe—* although the short gasps of bitter cold air stung his lungs. The dizziness, and the fatigue too, returned, and all he wanted to do was to lie down and fall asleep right there. He leaned against the building for a moment to gather strength and kicked snow over the bloodstain to cover it. Looking up, in the Siberian twilight, he saw a guard with a huge dog pulling at a leash, both staring straight at him.

András struggled against the freezing February wind and slowly made his way back to Block 12, which he shared with a hundred or so other prisoners. Escaping from the cold through the flimsy door, he paused for a moment by the wood-burning stove to thaw out, then made his way to Row 6, where he had the top bunk on the right side. He used his meager reserves to climb up and stretch out his exhausted body to rest. Concentrating hard to fight the drowsiness clouding his mind, he turned on his side, raising his head so he could see as he used his blistered fingers to pry out a small notepad and the stubby remains of a pencil hidden between two wooden slats of his bed.

*****

The day before, as he and the others on his shift were scrubbing themselves after their work inside the reactor, András had asked Efim Pleshkov whether he could get him some paper and a writing implement so that he could compose a letter to his wife, and whether he would be willing to get it to her in the event that András did not survive.

Pleshkov had been a friend before the War; they had studied together under the great Otto Hahn, the discoverer of nuclear fission, at the Kaiser Wilhelm Institute for Chemistry in Berlin. Now he was one of the Russian scientists overseeing the work of the convicts.

Supervisors like Pleshkov only stayed inside the reactor for a maximum of one hour each, whereas the prisoners' shifts lasted six grueling hours. And with each hour he worked, András felt his condition deteriorate. First had come the nausea and vomiting, then the diarrhea, now several times during each shift, turning each six-hour spell into unrelenting agony. The fever and the headaches made it that much harder to concentrate, and over the last couple of days, the intensifying dizziness and disorientation brought him to the realization that he would not be able to work much longer at this task. The pitiful look that Pleshkov had given him at the end of the last shift only seemed to confirm this.

Where had the sickly looking convicts in his Block from the previous shift been taken to just a couple of days ago? After five days, he and his fellow shift workers now looked equally wasted. He hoped they would all be moved to the camp infirmary; they were in desperate need of medical attention. But he knew enough of Soviet inhumanity during and after the War ...

What was this debilitating chore they were performing? András had studied chemistry and physics; his specialty had been nuclear fission. He was one of many prisoners here at this gulag near Chelyabinsk—many thousands— and their charge was to construct what he concluded must be some kind of reactor complex. When he first arrived, the guards had questioned him—and this is when he had again met Pleshkov, who was present at some of the interrogations—to see whether his knowledge could be useful, but since he was relegated to the drudgery of laying brick and pouring cement, he surmised that the Soviet scientists by now knew much more than he did. No doubt from their spies who were stealing American and British secrets and from the many scientists they had captured across the occupied countries. They did not need him. He was glad not to be forced to contribute his knowledge to what he concluded must be the Soviet effort to construct a nuclear bomb.

Early in the morning, nine days ago, half the prisoners in his Block were suddenly given orders to assemble outside and were led off towards Unit A, which András suspected was the one completed reactor. When he got back that evening from construction labor on another building, those same convicts were lying motionless in their bunk beds, visibly weaker and more spent than usual. All he could get out of the one or two who would speak to him was that they had been taken into the reactor and told to remove some rods and extract metal blocks from them, and that they had felt sicker and sicker during the day.

Three days later, András' shift was ordered to perform the same terrible task. Inside the reactor, they had to haul, one by one, ten-meter long, vertical black rods—András was sure there were more than a thousand of them—out of the coolant water, open them up and manually remove forty or so pellets from each. The anxiety among the Soviet staff was palpable, and at one moment that first day, he was surprised to see the legendary Igor Kurchatov—who András knew from Pleshkov had been placed in charge of the entire Soviet nuclear effort by Stalin—inside the reactor chastising several convicts.

On the way out that day, he had asked Pleshkov what it was they were doing, but he either did not know or, more likely, just did not want to tell his friend. András, though, was convinced that something had gone terribly wrong in the reactor, and that he and the other prisoners were being used to help put it right. It was only on the third day of feeling very ill and weak that he dared admit to himself that the blocks they were handling must be some highly radioactive material.

*****

András could barely stand up by the time the head guard blew the whistle to end the shift. He and his working partner, Grigor—a Russian soldier who had been captured by the Germans, liberated by the Americans and sent back to the Soviet Union—had just managed to complete the dismantling and emptying of one rod between them, but he was glad to be ushered towards the washrooms. He looked around for Pleshkov; he was nowhere to be seen. András made his way to the toilet—a bit more civilized than the latrines behind the Block—and, as had been the case over the last few days, blood came out from both ends. He felt faint and dizzy as he struggled to get up, and went to wash himself thoroughly with the block of lye provided for the purpose. As he dried himself with one of the sandpaper-like communal towels, Pleshkov appeared in the doorway. Their eyes met. András went over to the Russian, pulled out the sheets of folded notepaper and said, "Would you be kind enough ..."

"I can't promise, but I'll do what I can." Pleshkov quickly took the letter, glancing around to see if anyone was watching and tucked it into the inside breast pocket of his jacket.

*****

Two military trucks were waiting outside the door, with a line of guards toting machine guns every few meters delineating a path toward them through the snow. The prisoners were ordered aboard. András wearily climbed up the back of the second vehicle and sat down on the cold and slushy floor along with twenty-five others.

"Thank God. Finally, they're taking us to the hospital," he heard one of the prisoners say in the rear.

Three guards climbed in; two others closed up the back. The trucks sped away, motors grinding, wheels sliding on the snowy road. András tried to see out, but they were traveling away from the camp. He had the sense that they were going toward the periphery of the complex. The prisoner next to him threw up, mostly blood; he stared dispassionately at the red slime, as the jostling of the truck caused it to flow toward him.

The vehicle stopped and there was some shouting, then it started again. A turn to the right onto a small, unplowed road: the engine struggled as it forced the rough treads of the large tires through the thick snow. András glimpsed the icing sugar-capped conifers of the Siberian forests march by, as the trucks made their way deeper and deeper into uninhabited territory.

Finally, they came to a halt. Motors turned off, and for a moment, there was only the silence of the taiga. Then yelling—two guards opened the back, and they were ordered to dismount. András was shoved forward into the deep snow by one of the soldiers and when he struggled to his feet, he saw that the prisoners from the first truck were stumbling along a sort of dam or spur that led across a large frozen lake, with the machine guns of their guards pointing at them.

He was prodded onto the spur by a Kalashnikov-carrying soldier. He looked around and down on either side, but it was a good four meters to the ice. And he was so, so tired. Even if he were able to jump and not break a leg, what then? Escape was not possible; there were too many armed guards, and he was much too weak to run or fight.

The rat-tat-tat of machine gun fire suddenly violated the stillness of the forest, and András saw those furthest out on the dam fall to the ground or down onto the ice of the frozen lake. Prisoners dropped in rapid succession, like a row of dominoes. András tried, but could not move, and the last sensation he had was that the crimson paint spilling across the canvas of white snow and ice was rapidly advancing toward him and would soon envelope him.

Lily, I love you …

4

Chapter 1

February 2016

This was Anne Rossiter's favorite part of the day. After finishing her hour-long, after-work routine of stretching, weights and the elliptical, she was ready to start the evening. Time to relax, play, read. She relished these few moments of transition in her daily routine: the winding down, the recovery, the cleansing.

Still breathing hard, elated from the rush, Anne peeled her top and shorts from her sweat-soaked body and caught a glimpse of her radiant cheeks, shapely torso and long, well-toned legs in the full-length mirror on the bathroom door. She was in terrific shape. She had to be. As an Interpol agent, she had to undergo an annual test for physical conditioning. She prided herself on being number one or two each year among female officers in the region. Buying the second-hand machine and a cheap set of barbells for use at home had made it just that much easier.

Anne was now in her third year with Interpol in Vienna and she had been glad to accept the posting to the former Imperial capital. Vienna's mix of high culture and underground activity made it interesting both personally and professionally. Fluent in both German and Russian, she was equally at home watching a play by Grillparzer in the Burgtheater or eavesdropping on the Russian mafia laundering money through real estate purchases in Kitzbühel.

For all its rediscovered elegance, Vienna had retained its seedy side. It was still an *entrepôt* for trade in everything from women to weapons. As it had been in the immediate post-war years, it was still a hub of espionage and intelligence operations.

Anne took longer than her usual five minutes in the shower, relishing the sensual pleasure of water flowing over flesh, until she heard the first notes of the *Radetzky March* from her mobile. She rarely got calls after hours. She grabbed a towel, and wrapping it around her torso, scurried across the bedroom to her night table where she had left the phone.

"Hello. *Guten Abend*. Anne Rossiter." A small pool was starting to form around her feet.

"Anne, it's Adam." The familiar but unexpected American voice blasted excitedly into her ear. "Sorry to disturb, but I'm glad I caught you." Adam Kallay was her contact at the IAEA, the International Atomic Energy Agency, charged with securing nuclear material across the former Soviet Union.

"Why, what's up, Adam?" Anne was getting cold. She pressed the speaker button and rested the mobile on the night table.

"Anne, I just had a call from Fazkov. You remember Andrei, the physicist from Mayak, your blind date at the IAEA ball a couple of years back?" Anne recalled the entire embarrassing evening only too well. How could she forget?

"Yes?"

"He just called to say that another fifty pounds of highly enriched uranium cannot be accounted for at Mayak. He didn't want to say any more over the phone."

"That's enough for half a bomb, isn't it?"

"Yes. I asked him to come to Vienna so we could see where we go from here. He'll try to get a flight tomorrow. Luckily, his visa's still good."

Anne heard Adam clear his throat and hesitate before he continued: "Anne, could I come by now to discuss this?"

To gain time, Anne coughed several times. "Adam, no. It's not a good time. It's late." Though tempted, she did not want to get into another awkward situation with him.

"Well, how about tomorrow morning?"

"Tomorrow's good. Café Central at nine?"

"Okay, nine it is."

Anne turned the speaker off and went back to the bathroom. This was serious. Two weeks ago, just less than ten pounds of uranium had disappeared. Again, it was Fazkov who had noticed the discrepancy. And two Chechens had been caught crossing the border into Abkhazia. After some persuasion, they admitted that the nuclear material had come from Mayak.

And now, this. Someone, somewhere, was trying to get their hands on enough highly enriched uranium to make a bomb. There were going to be more thefts, that was for sure.

Tomorrow, first thing, she needed to reread Adam's report on the earlier robbery. The two had to be connected.

*****

Brushing her teeth, Anne thought again of Adam. Maybe she should have let him come this evening. But no, she had to keep to her resolution not to mix the personal with the professional.

She had liked him in the beginning, when she had hoped that their work relationship might develop into something more. He had good genes and great prospects. He claimed to be descended from Hungarian nobility, was in his thirty-fifth year and strikingly handsome with blond hair and piercing blue eyes. An undergraduate degree from Harvard and a doctorate in nuclear physics from MIT, a well-paid job in an international organization—not bad at all. Yes, she had entertained notions of a possible relationship right up until that evening, the night of the IAEA ball in the Hofburg, two Februarys ago, just a few months after she had started her job in Vienna …

Chapter 2

Greg Martens had not felt this upbeat for a long time, perhaps since just after his divorce. *Yes,* he thought to himself, *this is the right thing for me now*, as he clicked on the send icon to expedite the email to his friend.

He had come up with the plan to visit his best friend after receiving an invitation to attend a conference on the modern American novel in Vienna, hosted by the Austrian English Literary Society. Greg had been asked to present a talk on emerging trends in American fiction. They must have had a cancellation, he reasoned, or perhaps no other member of the New York literati had volunteered. He would only have to make a short speech about a topic on which he could happily talk for hours. As a struggling writer, living alone in New York and with unpaid legal costs from his divorce, he was not about to pass up a short break with some of his expenses covered.

Greg hadn't seen Adam since his friend visited New York soon after his appointment to the IAEA. If anybody, Adam would be able to provide the kind of companionship Greg now so sorely lacked in the Big Apple.

Adam was his dearest childhood friend. They shared Hungarian roots—Adam's grandparents were Magyar and Greg's mother had been born in Budapest. They had grown up together in Cleveland, played in the same sandbox and shared a babysitter, gone to the same kindergarten, camps, schools and even Hungarian balls. Rather than brook separation after high school, they both applied to Harvard, celebrating together when they received notification of acceptance. They tried out for the fencing team. Greg, the *sabreur*, was elected captain, although Adam proved to be the bigger star, losing only three epée bouts all season. The next three years, they shared a suite in Dunster House—one of the upperclassmen dorms—and led the Varsity team to both All-Ivy and All-American honors in two of those seasons.

Greg majored in creative writing and literature, with a minor in modern languages, Adam, nuclear physics and international relations. After graduation, Adam went on to study for a doctorate at MIT while Greg followed Laurie, his college sweetheart, to New York: she, to intern in investment banking, he, to work on his first novel.

Adam was best man when late the next year Greg and Laurie got married. But Greg could not make it to Boston when Adam graduated with his Ph.D., as he and Laurie were in California visiting her father who was recovering from a heart attack. After working on nuclear security for the U.S. Government for several years, Adam had just been appointed Deputy Director of the Department of Nuclear Safety and Security at the International Atomic Energy Agency in Vienna at the time he visited Greg and Laurie in New York. This was a huge job for a thirty-year-old.

*****

Five years had passed since he'd seen Adam, the longest they had ever been separated. A get-together was definitely overdue. And Greg's life needed a boost, a new direction.

Just two weeks earlier, Greg had finally submitted the revised draft of *The Bedroom Thief* to his publishers, who had given up on ever seeing the manuscript. He had turned to writing these formulaic crime novels when he had found himself unable to replicate the success of his only serious novel, *Wintertime,* written straight out of college.

And did Adam even know about the divorce? Had he been in touch with Laurie? They had all been such good friends back in college. Maybe too close. Adam's visit had seemed to bring Laurie a little nearer for a while, but they barely communicated, and slowly, a poisonous atmosphere of rancor and mutual recrimination had set in again. There was no way back. A definitive, final separation had been the only option. This was followed by the drawn-out divorce, the terms of which had only been finalized recently.

He guessed that Adam had no idea about the turns his personal and professional lives had taken. If he had, he may have had a good chuckle, never one to resist the dark temptation of a little *Schadenfreude*.

Plus, a trip to Vienna would give him the chance to hop over to Budapest and finally do the research on his family that he had been promising himself to do since college. With Adam, if he could tempt him.

*****

Adam responded enthusiastically to Greg's email.

"Greg, great idea. It's been too long. I will rearrange plans to be here. Vienna is fabulous—you will love it. We will go to the Staatsoper and the Musikverein. We'll take a trip to Budapest, as you suggest. And travel around. We always wanted to go back together and discover our roots. See where our grandparents came from."

So Adam was on the same wavelength. "Terrific," Greg emailed back. "Will look into flights. Thanks and see you soon."

Greg would finally make progress on his long-term plan to write a novel about his mother's family. He knew that the obvious place to start was with his Hungarian grandparents and he needed to find out a lot more about them. Maybe this was the occasion. Was fate giving him direction? This could be his next serious book.

Greg thought of his grandmother with affection and respect. Omi had been one of those *grandes dames* of Central Europe, who could converse in five languages fluently and always had an opinion about everything. Though now in her nineties, she was still living in an old-age home in Cleveland, and yes, he needed to visit her. Maybe when he came back.

He had fond memories of her, growing up: the late summer afternoon sessions on the front porch, when he—often with Adam—would listen to her tell about life in Hungary, the terrible War and post-War years, and the escape with her two children and second husband during the Revolution in 1956. Greg had always listened with interest. He had never met his maternal grandfather and Omi did not say much about him, although on occasion she would open up with tantalizing tidbits. This trip could be an opportunity to do some research, maybe even talk to some of his distant Hungarian relatives.

*****

A careful search for the cheapest flight available yielded one with Lufthansa, with a connection in Frankfurt, leaving on February 10. He could not help but think how good it would be to leave his empty life in New York behind, if only for a couple of weeks.

Mostly though, Greg was determined to enjoy the trip. He deserved to have some fun. He'd get to do five years of catching up with his old buddy. He'd get to explore Vienna, a city he and Laurie had visited in their student days. Kärtnerstrasse, the Stefans Dom, the Burg, Grinzing and the *heurigers* ... They were good memories.

He relished the prospect of what lay ahead. It would be an adventure. Greg realized that for the first time in a long while, he felt optimistic, energized. He was happy.

Chapter 3

Anne arrived at the Café Central just before nine. She was glad to come in out of the wet snow, still falling in big flakes that now covered the hood and shoulders of her coat.

She smiled at the statue of Trotsky sitting by the entrance, reminding her that in a previous era, the café had been a hotbed of revolutionary intrigue. She sat down on the upholstered bench at one of the round tables in a corner. The Central was her favorite café in Vienna, with its Italianate arches and ceiling, its white-aproned, black-tied waiters, and Emperor Franz Joseph and Sissi staring at the patrons from their brilliant, life-sized portraits on the back wall. A reminder of the paternalism of the Empire, but with Trotsky there too, of the social turmoil that it had spawned as well.

Anne had just ordered a *mélange* and toast when Adam came through the door, shaking his head with its mop of wet blond hair, and stomping his feet to get rid of the snow. He spotted Anne and came over, bending down to give her a peck in each cheek before he hung his coat and scarf on one of the racks. As always, he was immaculately dressed in a blazer and gray slacks, and a crisp, two-tone striped shirt open at the neck. Waterproof Merrill hiking boots replaced the black loafers Anne had seen him wearing the last time they met at his office, a concession to the falling snow.

Anne got straight to business. "So, is Fazkov coming?"

"Yes. He should arrive around three this afternoon. He'll come straight to my place for a debriefing. Easier there than in the office, where I would have to sort out security."

"Good. You'll call and let me know what he says?"

"Of course." The waiter arrived with Anne's coffee and toast and took Adam's order.

Adam cleared his throat before coming to the point. "Anne, I think we may be able to catch these thieves … *in flagrante delicto*." He smiled, relishing his own turn of phrase, before adding, "But we do have to move fast."

"How do you mean?"

"Fazkov made a strange comment on the phone yesterday. He was talking about Kolchakova, the director of Mayak. He thought that she must be involved. Or that she must at least know about the heist. He couldn't see how that much highly enriched uranium could be taken from the site."

"So, a classic inside job, you think?"

"Must be. Fazkov's right. Otherwise, how could the stuff just disappear like that?"

"I see your point."

"You know, Anne, I've been thinking. I've gotten to know this Kolchakova pretty well. If Fazkov really thinks she's involved, maybe I could infiltrate the gang somehow. Pretend I'm in it with them. I could let her know that I know and that, for a decent share of the profits, I would keep the disappeared material out of the inventory. So it would never appear as missing."

"That could be dangerous …" Anne trailed off as the waiter brought Adam's coffee.

"Anne, I know it's risky, but it would allow us to catch the bad guys. And it would be hard for them to say no, especially if I promised to look the other way. Not just this once, but for future heists as well."

"Why would they trust you?"

"Kolchakova knows me."

"Hmm …"

"I don't know. The money for one. I would ask for a big share of the profits and not just for this time. But leave that to me."

"Adam, it sounds crazy. Downright suicidal." Anne was thinking about the risks, but couldn't help being distracted by thoughts of just what Adam

9

meant by getting to know Kolchakova 'pretty well'.

"We need hard evidence. I have no proof that this fifty pounds even exists. Fazkov just knows because he's been around those warehouses for so long. He has a sixth sense about the stuff."

"Let's see what Fazkov says. Maybe he's got something more tangible that we can work with."

"I doubt it. It'll be just his word against everybody else's. Including the director's. If she's involved, then their denial looks pretty good. And that's the beauty of my plan ... we're playing to their desire to cover their tracks."

"And then?"

"And then we expose them. I'll wear a wire and we'll have all the evidence we need."

"If they catch you, they'll kill you."

"Kolchakova can't be the only one, Anne. There must be others involved. We don't even know about them."

"Hmm. Maybe. But let's wait till you talk to Fazkov."

"Fine. I wanted you to think about this though. I've got to run. Here, let me contribute," Adam said, pulling out his wallet as he stood up.

"No, no. My treat. Business expense. Thanks, and do call after you talk to Fazkov." Anne stood up as Adam reached across the table for a two-cheeked kiss, grabbed his coat and was out the door.

She sat back down to finish her breakfast and to mull over what Adam had suggested. Perhaps it did make sense; it would be a way to catch the entire gang. However risky, the wire would provide irrefutable evidence.

*****

As soon as she got to the office, Anne put in a request through Interpol headquarters to the FSB, the Russian state security forces, to see what information they would release on Irena Kolchakova, Director of Mayak. She didn't expect much to come back, certainly not any time soon.

Next, she searched the Interpol files. All she found was a brief résumé that gave Kolchakova's age as forty-one, her place of birth as Chelyabinsk and some details of her education and career. She had studied at the prestigious Institute of Nuclear Physics at the Lomonosov Moscow State University before doing research on high energy nuclear physics at the L.D. Landau Institute of Theoretical Physics of the Russian Academy of Sciences. Kolchakova was later

10

decorated—by Vladimir Putin, when he was President the first time—for contributions to the state and was assigned the post at Mayak after successfully running a smaller nuclear facility at Zheleznogorsk. But the high-flying career meant that she had paid her dues to the *siloviki*—the ex-KGB protégés of Putin —in some form or other.

Anne was just going into the file on the recent uranium theft when she got an urgent call relating to another big case: the trafficking of Russian girls to the West and the Middle East. The Austrian police officer on the other end of the line asked her to come to their headquarters for a briefing on the investigation.

It was only when Anne came out of this meeting close to the end of the working day that she had time to collect her thoughts and check her cell phone messages. She hoped that there might be one from Adam. But nothing.

She started to scroll through her missed calls. The very first one took her by surprise. Fazkov. Why would he call her? *Strange, Fazkov's contact is Adam.* Even though he knew Anne worked for Interpol and they had exchanged phone numbers the evening of the ball, he had never approached her directly. This would be a first—so it must be important, Anne thought as she pressed the call button. *Maybe Adam was just late and Fazkov couldn't reach him?* After all, she was the only other person he knew in Vienna. *Or had he misdialed?* She let it ring a long time and then redialed, but still no answer.

Walking back home along Porzellangasse, she called Fazkov's number again. In vain. She figured it was possible that his flight had been delayed and that he and Adam were in the middle of their debriefing by then—it was just now approaching 6:30 p.m. This thought reassured Anne and so she turned her mind to her evening routine of exercise and unwinding, followed by a light meal and the next chapter of *Agent of Love*.

Chapter 4

When he finished the mediocre airplane dinner and was on the fourth small bottle of the Languedoc red the stewardess plunked down on his tray table, Greg felt sufficiently lubricated to take out the notes he had written after each time his grandmother had delved into her memory to talk about the past. He had diligently jotted these down in the first person; so that rereading them was like hearing her recount her story for the first time, back there on the porch in Cleveland ...

*****

"It was April 1947. Late April, the eighteenth, I think, but it doesn't matter. I was very pregnant with your mother, close to term. I remember the little devil was already very active in my stomach. She kicked a lot and moved around, wanting to get out. Like we did.

Your grandfather came home from work and said, '*Virágom*,'—my flower, that's what he called me—'would you like to come to a football match with me?' He took me by surprise, because I knew he did not really follow the game, and he knew that I certainly didn't care. But then he continued, 'You know the Soviets are finally letting the Hungarian national team compete against the Austrians. Our great rivals. And the game will be played in Vienna.'

It was not hard to see what he had in mind. Vienna was then a divided city, like Berlin, with each of the victorious Allies controlling a sector. The stadium was in the Russian zone. Your grandfather thought this would be a great opportunity to escape to the West.

We were desperate to leave. Ever since the War destroyed the country. But even more so after, when there was no hope, no food, no money, only oppression and terror and misery. Stalinist Hungary was not fit to live in and we wanted to escape, get to the West. To America. Away from war-torn Europe. We did not want to raise our child in hunger and fear.

Somehow, we thought that if we managed to get to Vienna, we would surely be able to slip across to the British or American zones. Your grandfather had many contacts in the former Imperial capital, who we thought would help us.

But there were a few obstacles to overcome first. How to get tickets? And the *laissez-passer* for the game. Both, we knew, would be very difficult.

Fortunately, my father, Apa, who despite being of the wrong cadre, had been reinstated by the Communists to his pre-War position as director of the fight against tuberculosis in Hungary. After the War, an epidemic was ravaging the country, the medical profession was in disarray, the sanatoriums had been damaged by the fighting, and they needed someone to organize the fight against this dreaded disease. The authorities turned to your grandfather and he agreed, but only because he saw that otherwise many people would die.

I knew from Apa that some of his patients were well connected. So I went to him and told him of our plan. He said it was crazy and very dangerous, especially for a woman in late pregnancy, and that the secret police would see through it. Also, it broke his heart that he and my mother would lose me and their future grandchild.

But I pleaded and pleaded and I knew he could not refuse me, and despite the risk for him, the day before the big game, Apa came through with the tickets and the passes.

The night before, we packed a little bag. I put out my traveling clothes and all the jewelry my mother had given me to wear underneath to help us start a new life in the West. We went to say good-bye to our parents with mixed feelings; we knew that we might never see them again, but if we did, in just a few days, then our mission will not have succeeded.

We barely slept that night. The next morning, we got up very early to catch the bus to the train station. It was crowded, but since I was pregnant, I got a seat, with your grandfather standing right next to me. As the vehicle shook its way down Hegyalja utca, a few stops later, I felt a wetness between my legs. Devastated, I turned my face up to your grandfather and in a hoarse whisper said, 'My love, my water has broken.'

So instead of the train station, a thrilling soccer match and lifelong freedom, your grandfather took me to the nearest hospital to give birth to a healthy girl. Your mother.

And your grandfather listened on the radio, there in the hospital with the sick and the doctors and nurses, as the Hungarians walloped the Austrians 5:2 in a historic match.

So we didn't escape in 1947 and it would be another nine long years until an opportunity came again."

Chapter 5

The airport at Schwechat is an easy one to navigate and Greg's baggage came quickly. As he had gone through passport control in Frankfurt, he was out through the blue-starred EU corridor within fifteen minutes of landing. He checked his cell phone for the time and messages. Eight twenty. No one had called or sent a text message. Only T-Mobile Austria to welcome him.

Out in the arrivals area, he scanned the faces for Adam. How differently these people looked and dressed! Mixed with the well-turned out Viennese wives, waiting impatiently for husbands returning from business trips to Kazakhstan or beyond, were the less chic friends and relatives of Eastern Europeans or Turks living either in Vienna itself or in neighboring countries who used Schwechat as their airport. The winds from the East had not abated since the demise of Communism; they had just changed in character and temperament.

Greg was sure he would know Adam, but he felt a tinge of doubt when he could not find him. He still pictured the Adam he had last seen in New York City: the blond head of hair, the aquamarine eyes, the California tan and the trademark grin on top of the broad muscular form sheathed in immaculate, preppy Polo wear. He could already hear the friendly words of greeting—no doubt with some sarcastic, loudly verbalized afterthought—in Adam's easy-going manner. But Greg did not recognize a soul.

In their email exchange, they had agreed that Adam would pick him up on his arrival at five after eight. Not seeing him in the arrivals lounge, Greg walked outside, onto the slush-covered platform from where the buses left for Bratislava, Schweden Platz and the Westbahnhof, but no sign of his friend.

Strange, Greg thought to himself, as he scrolled down on his cell for Adam's number, strange to invite someone, saying he will change his plans, insist on picking him up and then not show. He pushed the green button to dial, letting it ring several times. After eight beeps, he heard Adam's voice say, first in German and then in English, that he was not available and could the caller please leave a message.

"Damn," Greg said aloud. Maybe he is delayed or there is a traffic jam on the Autobahn, he mused. He went back inside, still looking around at the faces in the lounge. Best just to sit at the bar for a while and wait.

*****

After a couple of glasses of *Zweigelt*—an Austrian red he remembered liking on his first visit—and a half an hour later, still no Adam. Greg looked up his friend's address and went out into the cold night. There was no one waiting in the taxi line, so he climbed into the first white Mercedes.

"*Guten Abend. Jaurèsgasse dreizehn, bitte.* In the Third District."

*****

The building where Adam lived was from the nineteenth century, the golden era when Franz Josef had overseen the expansion of the city outside the former walls, which he had replaced with the eclectic architecture of the Ringstrasse. Across the street were the German Embassy and staff residences—an eyesore, infill on a bombed-out site from the much poorer, post-Second World War era of Vienna—while on the northeast corner opposite stood the stately, imposing former palace that was now the Russian Embassy.

Greg pressed the bell again and again beside the dimly lit name plaque marked 'A. Kallay.' No answer. He tried the massive, carved wooden doors, but they did not budge. After seven or eight minutes of standing around and periodically ringing the bell, he was just starting to contemplate his fall-back options when he heard what he thought was shuffling inside the gates.

An ancient little man in slippers, with a huge craggy nose and tousled white hair, opened the door a crack and asked, somewhat angrily, "*Ja, bitte, was wollen Sie denn?*"

16

Greg had trouble adjusting his ear to the singing Austrian accent, but he understood enough to ask, "Herr Kallay. *Ist nicht da?*"

The porter said something rapidly that Greg did not catch. Greg asked him to repeat it in English.

"You too late," the little old man said. "Herr Kallay, he *tot*. *Kaput*. Dead."

The news at first did not sink in, just flashed by Greg's consciousness like the crawlers on CNN. It took him a moment to gather the strength to blurt out the questions: "When? How? What happened?"

The porter pulled up the sleeve of his tattered, rust colored sweater to look at his watch. "Hmm. Before four hours. Auto has killed him."

"What auto?"

"*Ein* … What was it? … *combi*. A van. Going very fast, like race car. Hit him, bang, die right away," the porter said, slapping his two palms together. "Body in the street. Very big mess. Terrible."

It was only when the porter compared the van to a race car that it all started to hit Greg; he saw again the once-vibrant Adam laughing behind the steering wheel, he in the passenger seat, plowing through a field of bashed-up mini cars at one of those silly dodger races at the state fair that Adam so loved. Now he was no more. Suddenly, Greg felt faint as the blood drained from his head and had to steady himself by putting one hand on the faux-marbled wall of the dark hallway.

"Police *ist gekommen*. Taken body."

"Where? Do you know?"

"Maybe Stadtleichenhaus."

Greg's German was just good enough to figure out that the last big word the porter had uttered meant the city morgue.

*****

The gate closed. Wet snow had started to fall; now it was coming down in big flakes, illuminated by the glow from the ornate, cast iron streetlights. Greg was glad for the silence and the darkness of the Viennese winter evening. There was no traffic; only a woman bundled in furs walking her Vizsla across the street. He just stood there on the sidewalk with his bags, trying to fathom what the little old man had said.

"Dead? Adam?" Greg muttered to himself, shaking his head. "I can't believe it." A few tears formed in the corners of his eyes and blended with the

17

melting snowflakes as he wiped his face with his sleeve.

After several minutes, his body started to shiver; the wet snow, the darkness and his jet lag were getting the better of him. He shook his head once more in disbelief and then set off for the Hotel Sacher.

*****

By the time Greg got there, he and his roller bag were wet and covered with the sticky snowflakes. The receptionist gave him a disapproving look when he said that he had arrived a day early and would like a room. It took several minutes, because a rude little man interrupted in a Yorkshire accent to ask the clerk for messages. Finally, the receptionist gave Greg a keycard and pointed him to the elevators.

Although he wondered whether this extra night—for which he was sure he would end up paying—would bring his Visa card very close to his credit limit, Greg was glad to clean up and take a shower in the luxurious quarters. He was exhausted, but—not having had a bite to eat since the meager snack of pretzels on the flight from Frankfurt—he was also hungry, and with the devastating turn of events, too distraught to go to sleep. So he put on his jeans and a turtleneck to go down to the bar for a drink and a late night snack.

Greg settled into one of the plush red chairs and ordered a glass of *Zweigelt* and a goulash soup. He was about to start collecting his thoughts on Adam, when a man who was sitting at the bar came over to the table.

"Excuse me, but are you not Gareth Martens, the writer? I overheard when you were checking in." Greg recognized the face with its longish nose, protruding eyes and oversized, translucent ears, reminding him of a weasel, as the rude little man who had butted in at the check-in desk. As the guy leaned over his table, Greg took an instant dislike to him.

"I loved *Sensation*. We are so glad you were able to free yourself up from your busy schedule in New York to come and talk to our group."

Greg had to force himself not to laugh out loud, as it dawned on him that his invitation to be a speaker at the conference had been a colossal mistake: this silly man had confused him with the other New York writer, G. for Gareth Martens, his almost namesake, who had written eight highly acclaimed novels, including his latest, *Sensation*, now on the New York Times Bestseller List.

"My name is Crabbe," the weasel of a man continued. "I am the organizer of the conference. Very pleased to meet you. We—that is, the Austrian English

18

Literary Society—are looking forward to your talk the day after tomorrow, in the Marble Room here at 4 p.m. More than a hundred people have signed up. We were expecting you to arrive on the twelfth, but I am so glad you got here early. It will give you a chance to rest up before the talk. And look around this lovely city. Of course, no need to worry—we will cover your costs for today as well."

Greg was vaguely toying with the notion of correcting Crabbe, telling him that he wrote trashy crime thrillers, but then the Austrian English Literary Society might have been less keen to pay his expenses. And he was sure that he could give a perfectly adequate lecture on emerging trends in the American novel. More importantly, he did not want this diminutive, talkative man to sit down. Responding only with a curt "Thank you," he willed him to go away, and, after an awkward minute or so of silence, Crabbe eventually did, respecting the wishes of the famous G. Martens.

Greg needed to think about Adam. His best friend from college was dead. He couldn't believe he was gone and he needed to figure out what to do next.

Chapter 6

Anne ran for the phone. Must be Adam, she thought to herself. Reporting on Fazkov.

It was an Austrian voice though, that greeted her. "*Hallo. Guten Abend. Fräulein Rossiter?* Haffner here. Sorry for disturbing so late." Anne, surprised, recognized the voice of her contact at the Austrian police.

"Why Rudolf, what's up?" Anne knew it was something important if the Lieutenant called after hours.

"I thought you should know as soon as possible. Adam Kallay. He was in an accident an hour or so ago. No, less. I am just coming from the site. A vehicle—a white van—hit him in front of his building. As he was crossing the street to meet some friends."

"But I saw him just this morning. He was supposed to call me. Is he okay?" Suddenly, Anne felt faint.

"Sorry. But I am afraid he is dead. A man ... a friend called the police." Haffner went quiet for a moment, probably to consult some notes, before he continued: "Hetzel was the name he gave. The *Bezirkspolizei* called us to the site. The upper part of the corpse was mutilated. Terrible ... we sent it to the morgue. There was another man there at the time of the accident—another friend, this Hetzel said. Let's see ... He had a Russian name. Yes, here it is. Sidorov. Sergei Sidorov. He was gone when the police got there. Hetzel also confirmed there was no family in Austria. We are checking both these men."

"Are you sure it was Kallay?"

"Yes. Hetzel saw Kallay being struck by the van. He said he had called him on his cell phone to get him to come down. They wanted to have a quick drink at a local café on their way to a business dinner and were running late. We have ordered DNA tests though. Routine."

"The van? Anything on the van?"

"No. They did not know the make, or see the license plate. Just that it was white and badly dented."

"Rudolf, thank you for letting me know."

"Of course."

"Could you spell those names for me?" Anne grabbed the pen and notepad she kept on her night table and wrote down the two names as the Lieutenant spelled them. "And which morgue did you say?"

"The city morgue. You know, it is now out by the Zentralfriedhof. We use a facility there in a double container. Temporarily, since they stopped taking bodies to the Institute for Forensic Medicine."

"I will go there first thing. Good night. And Rudolf, thank you."

*****

Anne was shattered. She placed the mobile on the night table, sat down on the bed, put her face in her hands and wept. What a shambles this had become. Adam, vivacious Adam—that was one of the things she had liked about him, that he was always full of life, always on the go—now dead. She had a coffee with him that very morning! And what of Adam's plans to infiltrate the nuclear heist ring?

Could the thieves have known that he knew?

Could it be murder?

Of course, that was it, her suspicious mind immediately jumped ahead: Fazkov's phone call—the one to Adam from Mayak—could have been tapped. The uranium thieves killed Adam because they wanted to stop him from telling the police. Best to get rid of the American IAEA representative whose job it was to foil their plans. But if that was the case, then Fazkov must be in danger too. Or perhaps even dead. But maybe he did make it to Vienna, maybe he's there. And he did try to call her. Perhaps when he couldn't find Adam …

Anne scrolled down to the F's and pressed the call button when Fazkov's name appeared. No answer. She then thought to try Adam's phone—maybe one of his killers took it and might answer. But again, no one picked up.

Anne felt frustrated, wondering how she would be able to catch the uranium thieves without Adam, the one who had told her about the heist. And it looked like Fazkov—Adam's contact at Mayak, who had brought it to his attention in the first place—was also nowhere to be found. Fazkov may be the only person other than the thieves who knew about the HEU.

Or could it simply have been an accident? Possible, but given the circumstances, she had to investigate the likelihood of murder.

The rest of the evening, while she prepared and ate her supper, these thoughts went around and around in Anne's mind. Unusually for her, she decided to take a sleeping pill. She needed to rest; with all this churning in her head, she was sure she would be up all night.

Tomorrow was shaping up to be one hell of a day: a visit to the morgue in the morning and then checking out Hetzel and that Russian, the small amount of uranium that went missing two weeks ago, more on the Mayak Director, Kolchakova—and there was the human trafficking case she was working on. She may even have to find a flight to Chelyabinsk, the closest big city to Mayak, to try and trace Fazkov herself or find someone who might know about the uranium. An impossible task, Anne knew, one she dreaded. Plus, Adam now gone, Fazkov missing … Then it dawned on her, what about the danger to herself? Fazkov had tried to call her and they—whoever they were—must know that she was Adam's contact.

Chapter 7

Greg rose at six, ready for a vigorous workout, followed by a steaming shower and a quick breakfast before the gruesome task of going to the morgue in search of his friend's remains. He was the first one in the Sacher gym and flicked on the remote to surf the channels. He stopped on CNN, where the picture that appeared and then the headline, made him stare at the screen in shock. He could only mutter, "No, no, not again."

"Live from CNN. Terrorist bomb annihilates Grand Central Station." Heart racing, Greg read the crawlers as he pressed the volume button urgently. "Hundreds feared dead or wounded. Security tightened across the U.S. Curfew in Manhattan. President whisked to a safe place." And then he finally heard the reporter's voices repeat the grim news: "Last night, at 8:47 p.m. Eastern Daylight Time, a suicide bomber detonated a powerful explosive device in the main chamber of Grand Central Station, leaving a gaping hole full of twisted metal, broken glass, torn slabs of asphalt and the charred flesh of victims." The reports went on to claim that the carnage would have been much greater a few hours earlier when commuter traffic was still at its peak.

Instead of doing his routine on the treadmill, Greg sat down on its edge, sank his face into his hands and fought to keep the tears back. *Good God, when will all this killing end? What is the point?*

He was near there just three days ago. Having lunch at the Harvard Club. He could have been one of the victims ...

The reports of the anchors were like muted voices from far away. They recapped history: the terrible destruction of the Twin Towers, the unsuccessful March 6, 2008 attempt in Times Square, and all the other minor and major terrorist bombings internationally and in the U.S. The journalists made allusion to the most recent failed tentative, just that year at the Rose Bowl, when Brother Bartholomew, member of a new home-grown group in the U.S., calling itself 'The Sons of Jesus', was caught trying to detonate an explosive device tied around his thigh. The police couldn't prevent him, though, from swallowing the poison pill he already had in his mouth, so nothing more was gleaned about this secretive fanatical organization.

Twenty minutes passed and Greg, still in a state of shock, gave up on his good intentions to start the day exercising and went back to his room, knowing that he had to deal with his own loss, the death of his friend. The TV was turned on while he undressed, and talking heads were questioning who the perpetrators might be. Greg paused before going into the bathroom as they argued al Qaeda or ISIS versus the Sons of Jesus and a few other known terrorist groups, but most pundits were of the opinion that this had to be the work of the Sons of Jesus. Much more difficult to trace since they were home grown, easier for them to perpetrate violence inside the U.S. and they were clearly adept at not leaving any traces. With the Rose Bowl bombing attempt, police had followed Brother Bartholomew's tracks to his former family home back in Tennessee, but that's where they stopped.

Greg saw the time on the screen and knew that he needed to get on with the day. After a quick shower, he dressed and went downstairs to ask the concierge how to get to the city morgue. There was a queue, so Greg went into the Sacher café to have breakfast. He took yesterday's International New York Times off the rack, but found he had no desire to read old news with the shocking events of the night before. In sullen silence, he consumed the mélange and Viennoiserie, wondering if any of his friends—rather acquaintances, since he didn't really have any friends in New York—might have been victims. Probably not, although several of his classmates who had successful careers in the city did commute to and from Westchester and Connecticut. And then there was Laurie, but she was no longer his wife. Oh well, I'll find out soon enough. It was time to concentrate on Adam's demise and he shivered at the thought of what could be waiting for him at the morgue. Just death, death all around.

"Mr. Martens, you said your friend was taken to a temporary morgue outside the Zentralfriedhof, which is the main cemetery of Vienna. I will show you," the concierge said, taking out the standard tourist map. "Right here sir, this is where you will find two … what are they in English? … Ah, yes, containers," the concierge said drawing a big red X on the map.

"Thank you," Greg said, somewhat puzzled.

"The City of Vienna's provisional morgue."

"Okay."

"We are here. You take tram number seventy-one from Schwarzenberg-platz—here," and he again drew an X on the map, "straight out the Rennweg and then along the Simmeringer Hauptstrasse. The tram takes you right there."

Greg thanked the concierge, slipped him a five Euro note and went outside. It was a crisp, sunny winter day, so he decided to walk to Schwarzenbergplatz. Turning by the Hotel Bristol and walking along the bustling Ringstrasse, Greg wondered what he would find at the morgue. Would he recognize Adam? Many of the victims in New York would not be identifiable. He had never liked morgues and cemeteries. He did not like to be reminded of his own mortality. And everything now did just that.

Although—a memory from his Harvard courses—Anton Brückner, one of his favorite composers, used to visit the Vienna morgue for inspiration. Greg allowed himself to be amused by the thought that this expedition might inspire his next crime novel, even though it was not to the provisional morgue that the celebrated musician went looking for his muse. How odd to have a temporary facility in containers as the city morgue.

Greg knew he was approaching his stop because, out the tram window on his right, he saw the high wall of the Zentralfriedhof, while on the other side, were the outlets of the purveyors of the paraphernalia of death: tombstones, urns, coffins, candles and flowers. When he got off the over-heated streetcar, he was almost toppled over by the vicious wind howling along Simmeringer Hauptstrasse. He had to walk a couple of hundred meters to the containers, which had been painted a muted tone of gray, to get to the makeshift morgue.

The reception area was deserted; the keepers of the dead were not used to walk-in visitors. Greg rang the bell on the counter. After a few minutes, a bald man wearing glasses and starched white coat came through the double doors behind the desk. A faint whiff of formaldehyde—or was it death?—wafted through with the cold air as the doors swung closed.

"*Grüss Gott. Kann ich Ihnen helfen?*" the man in the white coat asked.

"I'm sorry, but do you speak English?"

The man nodded.

"A friend was brought here last night. His name is Adam Kallay."

"*Ja, ja.* You wanted to see him, no?"

"Yes. That's why I'm here. If I could …"

"Not possible. He was very badly mutilated. Not recognizable. There was no family in Austria, but the friend said to go ahead and dispose of the body. He agreed that there was no point to keep it. We have very little space here and must be … how do you say? … ruthless. We sent him over to the crematorium for burning during the night."

Greg was stunned, though relieved deep down that he would not have to view the gruesome sight of his friend's mutilated body. *How would they cope here in the event of a terrorist atrocity like the one in New York*? He felt faint, could not utter a word and leaned on the counter to recover.

"Are you all right, *mein Herr*?" the man in the white coat asked.

"Yes. Thank you. Were there any personal belongings? Anything in the pockets?" In his grief, Greg wanted some tangible evidence that his friend was truly dead

"No," the clerk answered. "The police will have all that. You can pick the ashes up at the crematorium. There, through the park. If you would like to take the remains to the family …"

"No. Thank you, but no," was Greg's response after a moment's hesitation while he considered the prospect of taking the ashes to Adam's parents. But he shivered at the thought of carrying his friend's ashes back to the Sacher on the streetcar, let alone in his baggage on the airplane to Cleveland. Adam's cremated remains would be better left unclaimed—in the care of the Austrian state. He would keep Adam's memory alive, ashes or no ashes.

Greg pulled his coat together and started buttoning it to go back out in the cold.

"Sir, could you wait here, please? There is someone who wants to talk to you."

The man placed a call on the telephone behind the reception counter, turned away from Greg and cupped his left hand over the receiver, so Greg did not understand what was said, but he was sure it was about him. The attendant put the receiver down and said, pointing to a wooden bench, "Please, sit over there," before disappearing behind the double doors.

Chapter 8

Sitting on the bench, Greg thought about Adam, how hard it was to lose a friend. He thought of Omi telling him about the loss of her one and only love, his grandfather, so soon after the birth of their child. And how she suffered in silence all those years, made a new life for herself and her daughter with a new husband.

*****

"Your grandfather and I were really in love. You, Greg, are too young to know real love," she had said, adding, "but I hope you will one day.

It was a few days after your mother's birth, the very same night my beloved husband took me and my darling daughter home from the hospital. We were living then on the Buda side, in a one-room apartment in the villa on Lejtő utca that my father used to own before it was nationalized by the Communists.

We were exhausted and happy as new parents, happy in spite of the miserable circumstances we and all our compatriots were living in at the time. I was just finishing feeding Klárika, ready to put her to bed and get some sleep myself, when I heard loud banging on the door. I yelled to your grandfather, who was in the bathroom, asking him to see who it was. He put on his bathrobe, cursing under his breath at whoever dared disturb at such an impossible hour. The pounding got louder and louder, and he finally opened the door. There, in front of him stood four tough-looking men all dressed in black, with Bozsik, that stool pigeon of a caretaker that the Communists had installed in the basement flat, cowering behind. They were from the AVO, the dreaded secret police in the control of the Soviets, come for your grandfather.

The leader of the pack, an obnoxious, tall man, pushed him aside and stepped inside; the others followed, leaving Bozsik behind in the staircase. I came out from the bedroom with your mother still at my breast. The officer, or whatever he was, had a cigarette in his mouth; he blew smoke in my husband's face and accused him of being a bourgeois intellectual, which in those days, was a serious crime in Stalin's empire. I wondered if they had somehow found out about our frustrated attempt to escape—the walls in Budapest were porous and the neighbors not very trustworthy.

The men ordered your grandfather to pack a few things and say goodbye to me and the child. I cried and cried and tried to plead with them, in the name of little Klári, in the names of their own children, in the names of their wives, mothers, daughters—but to no avail. My husband hugged me for a few moments, kissed me and the baby, and said, 'Don't worry. I will always love you and the little one. Take care of her and yourself.' And then he turned and was led away by the four gangsters.

I never saw or heard from him again. Your mother never knew her father, or you, your real grandfather."

Where are his remains, Greg wondered?

Chapter 9

Anne woke to the insistent blast from her cell phone. She grabbed it from the night table, checking the time on the alarm clock in passing. Five thirty-three a.m., much earlier than her usual seven thirty wake up.

"Anne, John." It was John Demeter, her boss at Interpol, a former CIA operative. "We need you in the office right away. There's been another bombing in New York."

"Oh, no! Casualties?"

"Yeah, but we don't know how many."

"Who this time?"

"No fucking idea, but get your ass over here ASAP."

*****

"Could've been a lot worse," Demeter said, "if the blast had been earlier."

"Still pretty bad though," her French colleague, Pierre Labrecque commented. "What is it now? Three hundred and twenty they think?"

"Plus the wounded."

"Do we know who?" Anne asked.

"Still no. A mystery," Demeter fidgeted. "Maybe some al Qaeda-linked group again."

Anne's mind wandered. Another terrorist bombing. Countless dead, wounded and dying. *When will it stop?* A lot of good she—and the rest of the security forces the world over—have been. At least these fanatics didn't get their hands on any nuclear material.

Then she remembered that she had not yet briefed Demeter on Adam's death. It was all happening too fast, much too fast. Just as she was about to, she glanced over towards the TV screen in the corner of the briefing room.

"John! A CNN feed."

Demeter pressed the volume on the remote.

"… This video was left at 8:50 a.m. local time at CNN headquarters here in Atlanta today. It is disturbing in its implications, and you will see it all live here on CNN."

A blurry image filled the screen. A man with a hood drawn over his head sat at the center of a table. He was flanked by others, all hooded, dressed in what looked like brown monk's robes. The one in the center, his voice digitally altered, addressed the camera in a solemn tone. "I am the Voice of God. We are the Sons of Jesus. Our mission is to carry out Acts of God. We will punish mankind for its sins. New York is our first target. It is a den of iniquity, where evil has been festering and has corrupted the rest of the world. Today, there is much rejoicing in Heaven because Brother Thaddeus has carried out his mission successfully."

The video was short and the anchor went on to comment on the known circumstances of the recording. "This much we know. The tape was left in the lobby of CNN headquarters in Atlanta marked 'Grand Central Station, February 11th'. It comes from a group calling itself the 'Sons of Jesus', whose leader refers to himself as the 'Voice of God', and who were the perpetrators of the failed terrorist attempt at the Rose Bowl last month. The group sees its mission as exacting punishment on the world for its sins. The scene we just saw was staged to resemble paintings of the Last Supper with Jesus in the middle and the twelve apostles on either side. There are eleven others besides the self-proclaimed 'Voice of God'. Brother Thaddeus, the presumed suicide bomber, must have been the twelfth and it seems that Brother Bartholomew, who killed himself after the failed attack in Hollywood, has been replaced. It is almost certain that the remaining Brothers were named after the other eleven apostles. If the tape is indeed genuine, yesterday's murderous attack on Grand Central Station is the first successful and significant act of terrorism by a radical Christian fundamentalist group. It appears that the Sons of Jesus are homegrown and U.S.-based. This is speculation, rather than scaremongering, but as there are eleven more Brothers, further acts of terrorism could be expected from the Sons of Jesus."

"Holy shit!" Demeter slapped his forehead. "It's not only al Qaeda and its off-shoots that we have to fear any more. It's also these fucking homegrown American terrorist assholes who are now taking up mass murder in the name of God."

"Unbelievable!" Labrecque agreed. "So far they have been quite successful at staying below the radar."

"John, there is something I need to tell you. Last night …"

"What's that?"

"Well, you know my contact at the IAEA? Adam Kallay? He was killed yesterday evening in a hit-and-run accident. He was working on securing the nuclear stuff at Mayak. One of his contacts there told him about some missing HEU."

"At least these shithead losers haven't got their hands on any of that."

"It could be nothing, John, but …"

"Get to the bottom of it and keep me posted. Labrecque, I want you to contact the CIA to see how we can help."

*****

Anne was sitting by herself in the Café Concordia on Simmeringer Hauptrasse, just a few hundred meters from the morgue. She had gone there straight from the office after the early morning meeting, but could not take her mind off the bombing. She was dismayed to note that the world seemed to be slipping into a state of fear and lawlessness and wondered what more she could do to combat crime, especially terrorism.

And then to the café, where she finished her second *mélange*, feeling quite wired, wanting action. Anne impatiently speed-dialed Lieutenant Haffner, her thoughts wandering while she waited for him to answer. Why doesn't he pick up? Or call? He had promised. Had the Austrian police found out anything more about Adam's accident? What progress had Haffner made on tracking Hetzel and that Sidorov? Also, had he been able to trace the van? As she pressed the red button to hang up, Anne resolved to start checking on everything through the Interpol network as soon as she got back to the office.

She thought briefly about Adam and his proposal to infiltrate the ring of uranium thieves. *God, that had been just yesterday morning!* The offer went well beyond his job. But maybe, he was one of those international bureaucrats who was as dedicated as she was. To fight evil, to do the right thing. To save the world. *We need more of us,* she concluded, and Adam went up in her estimation. She found herself once again feeling a tinge of regret that she had not allowed anything to evolve between them after the night of the ball.

Arriving at the morgue just after nine, she was stunned when told the body had been sent to the crematorium. The official said that a Herr Hetzel had assured him there was no next of kin in Austria and they could go ahead and cremate the remains. Besides, the corpse was a mess. Given the tight temporary facilities, they had a rigorous policy of disposing of bodies expeditiously, especially badly mutilated ones.

Another setback. Her task of finding the missing uranium had been made difficult first by Adam's death—and now his quick cremation. Although from what Haffner and the man at the morgue had said, the likelihood of gleaning any information from the body was next to nil. Other than through DNA analysis.

Frustrated, she decided to call Fazkov again. Fazkov, who might hold the key, if ever he could be found alive. And then Haffner, who may have unearthed some other leads through his investigations. Both calls just rang and rang with no answer.

As she was draining the last drops from her near empty cup, her phone finally came to life, but it wasn't Fazkov. Or Haffner. The attendant from the morgue was on the other end telling her that a man had come asking after Adam.

Good, Anne thought to herself: the decision to wait in case someone asked for Kallay, some unknown interested party flushed out by Adam's death, had paid off.

Was it Hetzel, perhaps?

Sidorov?

Or Fazkov?

Chapter 10

Less than ten minutes after the white-cloaked administrator made the call, Greg felt a cold blast of air as the front door of the makeshift morgue swung open. He slowly lifted his face from his hands, where, elbows on his knees, he had been many miles away, thinking first about Adam, Adam's aging parents— whom he would have to notify— and then his own grandmother. His thoughts now interrupted by an attractive woman approaching him, taking off her gloves. Athletic, a bright smile, raven black hair falling around her shoulders. Probably around thirty. Maybe a bit younger.

"Good morning. You're a friend of Adam Kallay?" Anne greeted Greg with what he took to be an Oxford accent. "Anne Rossiter. Interpol." She quickly flipped her ID card before his eyes. "I need to talk to you."

"Interpol? What about?" Greg asked, standing up. But he knew. "Kallay?"

"Shall we go for a walk? In the cemetery? It will be easier to talk there. I know it's cold, but the air might do us both good." Anne liked what she saw: just over medium height, strong of build, a pleasant, boyish face punctuated by big hazel eyes and topped with dark brown, faintly reddish hair.

Out in the cold, Greg introduced himself and explained his connection to Adam.

"We grew up together. Same schools, roommates in college. But I haven't seen him for several years." This must be the friend Adam had told her about after the IAEA ball.

"Mr. Martens, when did you arrive in Vienna?"

"Yesterday evening."

"What brings you here, may I ask?"

"I was invited to speak at a conference. And Adam Kallay. I came to see my friend."

"Why now?"

"We hadn't seen each other for a long time. We were planning a trip to Budapest. He and I both have Hungarian roots."

"This must all be very upsetting for you," Anne said, as they crossed Simmeringer Hauptsrasse to the main gate of Vienna's largest cemetery, flanked by two white Art Deco pillars.

"What do you do for a living, Mr. Martens?"

"I write."

"What, may I ask?" Anne shouted into the frigid north wind gusting down the avenue.

"Fiction." Greg was not sure how this attractive woman would react if he told her the entire truth, but then decided it really didn't matter. "Crime novels."

Greg changed the subject as they entered the park for the dead. "I've never been here before. This cemetery is much larger than I thought."

"Yes, there are more than three million buried here. But it's always a peaceful place to come." There seemed to be no other visitors of the departed on this icy morning. The only sound was the wind howling between the ornate tombs and the leafless trees.

"Let's go up here," Anne said, leading the way along the main alley towards an Art Deco church at the end. "Do you like classical music?"

"Yes. Why?"

"I'll show you Beethoven's tomb. And Schubert's, Brahms's and Johann Strauss's. They're all up here, to the left. This cemetery is full of famous composers. And of course many other celebrities."

On both sides of the alleyway, Greg saw tombs and family mausoleums of marble and granite, ornamented with snow-haloed statues of baroque saints and angels. Names, dates and poems were etched in fancy gold lettering on some, while others had urns standing guard, poised to hold flowers in the milder seasons.

35

Where will they place Adam's ashes, he wondered, and for a second, regretted not taking them off the Austrian state's hands.

And his grandfather, where was he resting?

*****

Anne followed respectfully a few paces behind, but she needed to get some information from Adam's friend.

"Mr. Martens, I would like to know what you know about Adam Kallay's work."

Greg marched ahead, entranced by the beauty of the snow-covered tombstones.

"Look, Mr. Martens," Anne said, catching up with Greg, assuming his silence was a sign that it was too painful for him to talk about his friend. "You may not have heard, but there has been another terrorist bombing in New York. Grand Central Station. Several hundred dead and wounded."

"Yes. Last night. I know. Shocking."

"My job is to prevent nuclear material from getting into the wrong hands. Fanatics like those suicide bombers. Kallay was my key contact." She moved closer to Greg. "I'm going to tell you things I shouldn't, but I need your help. We have to move fast if we're going to prevent a nuclear catastrophe."

Greg had vague notions that Adam was in a sensitive position at the IAEA, but did not know exactly what the job entailed. He learned from Anne that he was in charge of the department responsible for inventorying and monitoring weapons-grade nuclear material around the world, with a particular focus now on the former Soviet Union. Adam was supposed to have close ties to Interpol and a key part of his job was to report the disappearance of such dangerous material. Anne was his first point of contact in Vienna if anything went missing.

Anne realized she was taking a risk in confiding in this stranger, but she was confident in her ability to assess character. There was no time to have Martens checked out and the terrorist bombing the night before underscored the urgency of her task. She had to believe that what he told her about himself was true. And she definitely needed to have him on her side if she was going to make any progress in figuring out Adam's death, which was clearly connected to the disappeared nuclear material. From past experience, she knew he would be more likely to divulge the truth if she showed trust in him and gave out a few tidbits of information.

Anne turned into the wind to face Greg. "About two weeks ago, Kallay learned that some high-grade uranium from the Mayak nuclear center near Chelyabinsk had gone missing. Mayak is the largest facility in Russia, where nuclear material is extracted from warheads before being sent elsewhere for dilution. Kallay was leading the effort to set up a system to inventory and secure the uranium and plutonium there with the help of the Americans—the National Nuclear Security Administration. Your government has focused a lot of effort on upgrading Mayak. Improving security and implementing better accounting and monitoring methodologies."

"Didn't the Russians have a system to keep track of all that stuff?" Greg asked.

"Yes, of course. But it was always rather loose."

"How do you mean?"

"Well, at Mayak, for example, there are a number of storage facilities housing weapons-grade uranium in different forms and shapes: discs, ingots, hemispheres, powder—you name it. These are stored in steel containers that sit on racks. Or in some cases, just on the floor. Each warehouse has its own inventory of the number of containers and what's in them."

"Sounds complicated."

"Your friend and the NNSA were trying to verify the numbers and bring it all into one accounting system. During Communist times, the managers under reported what was being stored in order to give them leeway in case of missed production quotas. So it's a huge task—numbers are wrong, uranium thought to be in one place is no longer there, while other highly radioactive material is being found in random piles around the facility."

"Scary. It seems it would be pretty easy to make some of it disappear? Now, before it's all properly counted and monitored."

"Turn down this path. The composers are this way." Anne led the way. "Be careful. It's slippery."

Good, he is smart; he grasps the issues quickly, Anne thought to herself, carefully choosing where to plant her feet on the icy path. So far, she had not revealed anything top secret, but she was glad that Greg seemed to have no prior knowledge of this. Now came the sensitive stuff.

"Yes, and Kallay wouldn't have noticed anything missing if one of his Russian nuclear physicist friends who works there had not told him that almost ten pounds of uranium powder had been lost from one of the warehouses."

"Is that a lot?"

"Well, ten pounds of even the highest grade—or ninety percent enriched uranium—won't get you to a stockpile that could ignite spontaneously. You'd need ten times that much—maybe a little less—for a simple bomb, the kind we think the terrorists could easily build. They can even get blueprints off the web for such a bomb."

"Ten times ten pounds is a lot of uranium though, isn't it?"

"Yes, but not out of the question. And that's the real problem."

"What do you mean?"

"You're right, ten pounds is not a big deal. In fact, it was picked up by the secret police in Sukhumi just two weeks ago. In Abkhazia—the breakaway province of Georgia."

"Georgia?"

"That's the preferred route. And then into Turkey, across the mountains. Or by water along the Black Sea coast. It makes sense. Once they get the nuclear material into Turkey, it's easy to disappear with it. The big market for this is in Istanbul."

"And the uranium?"

"Two Chechen couriers had it with them in a metal briefcase. They were caught red-handed delivering it to some Turkish guys. One of these Turks has since also been captured, and we know he has al Qaeda connections."

Anne stopped in front of a tasteful white monument on the left, graced by the bust of a bearded man, snow-capped head pensively resting in his right hand, left holding sheet music in stone. Two naked figures frolicked on the frieze behind. The simple marking told Greg that this was the tomb of Brahms.

"They caught the thieves. And recovered the nuclear material. So what's the problem?"

"The Chechens were not the ones who took the uranium from Mayak. They were just the mules. The couriers."

"Hmm."

"We asked Kallay to probe further with his physicist friend how the disappearance could have occurred at Mayak. Two days ago—the evening before his death—Adam called to tell me that Fazkov—his physicist friend at Mayak—telephoned to tell him that another fifty pounds of ninety percent HEU—sorry, highly enriched uranium—had gone missing at the complex.

That is enormous! The largest theft ever of nuclear material. Whoever gets their hands on that will be halfway to having enough for a big bomb."

"Amazing."

"That's not all. Fazkov apparently had suspicions that it was an inside job. Mayak's director. If that's the case, it's just a matter of time before another heist. That could have been the first installment, with another of equal size possible very soon. Or several smaller ones."

"And then there would be enough for a bomb?"

Anne stopped in front of a simple white obelisk with a golden harp and letters in a gothic font. Beethoven. Out of the corner of his eye, Greg noticed two men in black leather coats strolling from the Brahms to the Strauss grave. Just then, Anne turned again to face Greg.

"Yes. And if all that gets into the wrong hands, we could see an explosion bigger than Hiroshima. That was equivalent to fifteen kilotons of TNT. Depending on how successful some terrorists might be with a simple bomb and say a hundred pounds of HEU, they could produce a blast of ten, maybe even twenty kilotons. If detonated at ground level, that would be enough to destroy much of Manhattan or Central London. Not just Grand Central Station. And claim several hundred thousand victims. Plus millions over time from cancers and other radiation-related illnesses."

"Do we know where this ... HEU is?"

"That's just it. We don't. Nor do we know who took it. But Kallay asked Fazkov to come to Vienna to report. And to plan what we do next. But now ..."

"You think my friend was murdered because he was onto something?"

"There is a good likelihood." Anne hesitated a moment. "But no need to jump to conclusions. We have no evidence." She calculated that it did not make sense to hold back. "Before the accident, Kallay offered to try to infiltrate the ring by suggesting to the director—whom he claims to know well —that he could keep the disappeared material out of the inventory. So it would never appear as missing. Clearly, for a share of the profits, to be convincing."

"And you think they decided that killing him would be a cheaper and better way of keeping the stolen HEU out of any accounting system. It would also get rid of a nosy American, of course."

Their path had taken them behind the domed Art Deco church and, passing a tomb marked 'Elchinger, 1913', Greg was surprised to see a young woman dressed all in black. She was standing at the foot of the next grave over, her face in her palms. It was a new grave, covered with a simple, unmarked slab of granite. So there was the odd new burial in this cemetery …

Greg again spotted the same two guys they had passed back at the Beethoven tomb. Were they being followed? No, these men were surely just visiting graves. No need to be paranoid, Greg told himself as he turned back to Anne, trying to remain calm.

"It's not that easy. The thieves would know that Kallay would not keep it to himself for long. Then there's also Fazkov. But I'm telling you too much." She looked around, and seeing the men, picked up the pace.

"How much would a hundred pounds of HEU go for?"

"You mean the ninety percent stuff? I don't know. The market has never seen such big amounts. My guess would be that in volumes sufficient to make a bomb, upwards of half a million dollars a pound wouldn't be out of the question. Even more, with clean delivery. Or in a bidding situation."

"Over fifty million dollars!"

"Yes. Maybe even a hundred. Depending on how much they want it. As I said, such a large amount has never, ever come on the market."

"But now Adam is dead."

"Yes."

Greg was suddenly overwhelmed. What had his friend gotten into?

"The nuclear material—all fifty pounds of it—is missing from Mayak. Fazkov, too, we cannot find."

"Well, what happens next?"

"Did Adam write you anything or say anything that might be relevant?" Anne avoided answering Greg's question. She did not know herself. Even if she did, she would not want to share it with this friend of Adam. She had divulged enough, perhaps too much.

"No. He encouraged me to come to Vienna."

"Has anything suspicious happened since you arrived?"

"Well, apart from Adam's death …"

"Yes, of course."

"No. I found out about the accident when I went to his place. After he didn't show up at the airport. By the way, are we being followed?"

"I did notice two men. But I don't think it's anything. Don't worry."

"All this talk of a uranium heist, terrorists and Adam's death. And then this place … Spooky."

"It's all right, Mr. Martens. Relax."

"That's easy to say."

"Did Kallay ever talk to you about a man named Hetzel? Or Sidorov? Sergei Sidorov? Supposedly friends. They saw him being run over."

"No, no." Greg was exasperated. He felt stressed and needed to be alone, to think. "Look, I'm tired and cold. You must be too. And I still have a speech to prepare for the day after tomorrow. The conference."

"Yes, of course. Where is that?" They had circled back to the main entrance.

"The Sacher. A conference on the American novel."

"Is it the Austrian English Literary Society?"

"Yes."

"I may try to come," Anne said with a smile. "If anything comes up, please let me know. Here is my card."

"Thanks."

"I'd give you a lift, but I am not going back into town."

Anne flashed a smile that made Greg regret bringing their talk to an end. They said goodbye, but Greg was quite sure that this was not the last time he would be interviewed by the police. As he walked away, he hoped it would be this pretty and intelligent Interpol officer.

Chapter 11

Back at the Sacher, as Greg passed the front desk, the check-in clerk handed him an envelope. Greg opened it on his way to the elevators. The note, written with neat letters, read:

> Dear Mr. Martens:
>
> I am a friend of Adam. We should talk soon. I will
> be at the Café Hawelka (Dorotheergasse 6) until 3:00
> p.m., reading one of your books. In case you cannot
> make it, my cell phone number is 0679113097.
>
> Respectfully yours,
>
> Hetzel

Greg glanced at his watch and decided he had time to go to his room. The man could wait a few more minutes. A friend of Adam—yes, Hetzel, that was a name Anne Rossiter had mentioned—one of the friends who saw him being run over. That put the meeting in a different light, for sure.

Greg remembered where the famous Hawelka was from his earlier trip to Vienna. It was a Viennese institution: the café run by an ancient couple from Bohemia, formerly a separate kingdom within the Empire, now a part of the

Czech Republic. A smoke-filled den where *Buchtel*, a jam filled, doughy pastry was freshly baked and served every evening after ten, it was the late night meeting place of choice for the literati, artists, musicians and philosophers of Vienna. Some of the pictures of former patrons stuck with thumbtacks here and there around the establishment were barely distinguishable from the peeling wallpaper.

Entering through the faded brocade curtains that kept the cold out, Greg saw a heavy-set, well-dressed, mustachioed man draped in clouds of smoke sitting at a rickety corner table, reading what Greg could tell from far away, was *Agent of Love*.

"Herr Hetzel?"

"*Ja. Grüss Gott.* Hetzel. Good to meet you, Mr. Martens." Hetzel stood up, stretched out his hand: the tone was haughty, the palm sweaty and Greg took an immediate dislike to the man.

"Adam was a very good friend. He told me so much about you. He looked forward to your coming. This … this accident was horrible. A terrible shame."

"Yes."

"Please sit down. May I call you Greg? Or is it Gregory? Adam always referred to you as Greg. What will you take?"

Greg ordered his usual *Zweigelt*, Hetzel another black tea.

"Adam loaned me the book. I love it. It is so … so well written." Greg never thought he would hear the formulaic trash he churned out to make a living dubbed 'well written'. The man was either stupid or insincere, but somehow, he doubted that it was the former.

"Adam mentioned that you will be speaking at the conference on the American novel at the Sacher, so it was not hard to find you. I feel so very responsible for you, now that he is no longer with us. If there is anything you need, please, will you let me know? Anything, during your stay in Vienna."

"Well, could you explain to me the circumstances of Adam's death, Herr Hetzel?"

"Certainly. My friend, Sergei, and I … we had agreed to have a quick drink with Adam on the way to dinner with some business contacts. We were running late so, just as we were getting close to his building, I called him on my phone to suggest that he come down. We came around the corner from Reisnerstrasse—right opposite the Russian Embassy—when we saw him. He saw us and waved. He stepped into the street … Oh, *mein Gott* … just as a

43

large van came fast around the corner and knocked him down. The van was white and in bad condition, if I remember correctly. It did not stop, but sped along Jaurèsgasse and around the corner. Sergei and I rushed to Adam, but my friend ... it was horrible."

Hetzel pulled out a carefully folded white handkerchief, just in case, before he continued.

"The upper part of dear Adam's body was totally crushed. His face, his chest. Very little left. Blood everywhere. He must have died instantly." Hetzel paused to blow his nose noisily. "There was nothing we could do for him. I was very, very shaken. I called the police. They came within minutes and took notes for their report. Sergei—who had left by then—and I were the only ones who saw the accident. Fortunately—or unfortunately—I was able to identify the body. Not from the remains, I must say, but because I had seen Adam being run over."

"Do you think it was an accident?"

"What do you mean?" Hetzel seemed offended.

"Could the driver have wanted to hit him? Deliberately. To kill him?"

"Surely, no. I never thought of it. But, I don't think so, Greg. No. No."

Greg absorbed the details, but could not react. Now that he had heard how it happened, the loss of his friend was even more painful. Adam was killed in this freak accident. Or worse still, murdered. But in either case, crushed beyond recognition.

They sat in silence. Greg breathed deeply and took a gulp of his wine. He wanted to be alone, to figure things out, but he also wanted to hear as much about Adam as this supposed friend of his could tell him.

"There was a girl," Hetzel continued, after taking a sip of his tea. "A girlfriend. She doesn't know yet." And then silence again, as if he wanted Greg to tease things out of him.

"Who? You mean someone here? In Vienna?" Greg finally collected himself enough to speak.

"Yes, Julia. Saparova, I think. Russian."

"Was it serious?" It dawned on Greg that Hetzel may want him to tell the girl about Adam's death.

"They were, well, friends. And Adam was helping her with money. He was also trying to get her a job. She is a nuclear physicist. A Ph.D. But now she dances at the Revuebar Rasputin. You know, exotic dancing. She is very

44

good."

"How did they meet?"

"That is all I know." Hetzel glanced at his watch; it was clearly as much as he wanted to say. "I must go. I promised to meet Sergei." He got up, plunked a ten Euro note on the table and, almost as an afterthought, added: "Here is my card. As I said, if you need anything, anything here in Vienna, call me."

Greg watched Hetzel disappear through the haze of smoke and the heavy brocade curtains, wondering why the man had really wanted to meet with him.

Chapter 12

When she got back to the office from her twice-weekly target practice at the Laxenburg training facility, Anne spent the rest of the day compiling the facts and writing a report on the unsolved murder of a dissident Chechen activist several weeks earlier in Vienna. Totally pointless, she thought to herself; it would just go into the files. Sometimes her job was too bureaucratic. She hated the paper work, much preferred to be out tracking international criminals. That was what she had signed up for, not writing reports.

Anne glanced at her watch, and saw that it was nearly 5:00 p.m. Not enough time to do the background research on the Adam affair, which she had wanted to get to all day. But at least she could figure out what needed to be done and how to tackle it most efficiently tomorrow. She mentally made note of the things she had to look into: the report on the heist two weeks ago, Fazkov, Hetzel, that Sidorov, a refresher on Mayak and security arrangements, known staffing and so on.

And then there was also Greg Martens. A likeable character. Surely there would be nothing on him in the police files. She could not believe that he would in any way be involved in criminal activities. *Maybe on Google*, Anne smiled to herself. *Or Facebook, or Twitter—no, no, surely he was not that type. Perhaps the Hard Core Crime site*—she had noted that they were his publisher. At least in the time left today, she would be able to check him out. *Oh yes, and call Haffner*—he still hadn't shared what he might have found out.

If anything.

Anne pressed the speed dial button for the Lieutenant. No answer. So she turned on her computer and opened the window for the Interpol search engine. Anne typed her name and security code in the required boxes and waited for access. She entered Greg's last name, then the first, into the boxes and waited again. This amazing search engine not only scanned Interpol's own extensive files, but also the archives of many police forces in cooperating jurisdictions. It allowed her to view available information up to her security level.

Entries on several Martens and one Gregory Martens Jr.—a Wall Street con artist who had defrauded billions of dollars from several hundred investors with a clever Ponzi scheme—came up on the screen, but Anne was relieved to see that 'her' Greg Martens was not one of them. She easily eliminated Mr. Gregory Martens Jr. since, according to the file, his education had been at Yale and Stanford.

Next, Google. Surely there would be some entries. Anne typed his name, followed by 'author' to narrow it down. The Google page came back with 97,374 entries.

The first 270 or so—the most recent ones—were dated several years ago and talked about the rancorous divorce of the crime novelist, Mr. Greg Martens, from the highly successful investment banker, Ms. Laurie Cheevers, Head of Fixed Income at Goldman Sachs, citing irreconcilable differences.

Scrolling down the pages, the next several thousand were about the two Hard Core Crime books Greg Martens had written: *Agent of Love* and *Explosive Bodies*, the former being considered by far the more successful. She too, liked that one, although she had found some of the scenes rather racy. Several of the earlier entries talked about Greg Martens' highly acclaimed inaugural novel, *Wintertime*, written shortly after he graduated from Harvard. Mature for his age, innovative use of language, strong characterizations, much promise. And there were references to his college years—All-Ivy and All-American honors in fencing, graduating magna cum laude from Harvard, year off to work for the Tarayana Foundation in Bhutan.

Anne clicked on one of the entries leading to the Hard Core Crime site. His author page featured his two previous novels, as well as a teaser for *The Bedroom Thief,* a provocative thriller to be published very soon, and mention of a planned fourth book: *Nuclear Heist,* the thrilling chase by the sexy Karla Priestley after international arms thieves and traders who make off with enough nuclear material to blow up Manhattan. *Hmm. No wonder Greg had been so curious about what Adam seems to have gotten himself into.*

Anne glanced at her watch and saw that it was already a few minutes after six. Time to call it a day; she would get into the more serious part of her research tomorrow. Nevertheless, this had been informative and fun: Greg Martens had an impressive start to life, but somehow seemed to have lost his way.

Chapter 13

Back in his room at the Sacher, Greg closed the curtains, undressed and lay down on the bed. He needed peace and quiet to sort things out.

What exactly did he know? Adam worked in a sensitive job, and if the Interpol agent was to be believed, he was on to the sale of some stolen Russian nuclear material. Adam had offered to work with Interpol to trap the sellers. But he died—or was killed—on the evening Greg arrived, in a car accident.

Also, Adam had a Russian girlfriend—a nuclear physicist, a dancer in some strip joint—and some Viennese 'friends'. That awful Hetzel and the other one with a Russian-sounding name—Sergei something—were to meet him briefly on the evening he died. It was they who had witnessed the hit-and-run accident and found his remains in the street. One of them called the police and gave the consent for a quick cremation of the destroyed body. There was also another Russian, a nuclear physicist who worked at Mayak whom Adam had asked to come to Vienna. The one who had told Adam about the missing uranium. And who had also gone AWOL now.

All plausible. If Adam's death was not just an accident, then he must have gotten involved in some affair that was well beyond him. But Adam had always been like that, even in college. The brilliant one, the one with the swagger.

He was the one who, in their freshman year, had carried off that Tarzan stunt: randomly, at midnight some nights, he would let out a spine-tingling, primordial scream, each time from a different point in Harvard Yard. No one knew from where and when the scream would sound. But as soon as it did, students rushed from their dorms or the library in the direction of the yell. By the time more than a few had congregated, the Tarzan scream had stopped and the phantom friend of the apes had disappeared. Adam told only Greg, vowing him to secrecy. The campus cops never caught him, though the university administration brought in extra forces and put up notices with a handsome reward for information. Tarzan became a cult figure around college.

In fencing—really, in everything he did—Greg had had the sense that Adam was competing with him: he always had to have more wins, higher marks, the prettier and greater number of girls. *In some ways, that is why I married Laurie; to get away from competing with Adam on the women front.* No, that was unfair, but there was something to it. He had tired of the intensely personal competition and that is maybe why he had been happy to allow the friendship to lapse over the last few years.

That was the Adam—Greg's drowsy mind came back to the present—with all his faults, charm and quick wit, his pranks and games, that he had loved. Now dead, in a freak accident.

Yes, it was all plausible. But some of it—the nuclear physicist, Russian stripper girlfriend—seemed hard to believe.

The circumstances, too—that Adam had uncovered the disappearance of some nuclear material just before his death, the quick disposal of the body … *Well, the police did their investigation. No relatives in Austria, just those friends—Hetzel and … what was the other one's name? Again that Russian connection.*

*****

Greg awoke with a start and still groggy, looked over at the bright red numbers on the digital alarm clock. Seven fourteen. It must be evening, since no light seeped through the tightly drawn curtains.

The idea to go and find Adam's girlfriend came to him in the shower. *Julia, with the Russian-sounding last name. Yes, the note!* It was on the back of the letter Hetzel had left for him that he had jotted down her name and the place where she worked. As he toweled himself dry, he went over to the night table where he had emptied the contents of his pockets, unfolded and smoothed out the crumpled note and read: 'Julia Saparova, Revuebar Rasputin'. That was it. Perhaps she would be able to shed some light on the circumstances

50

surrounding Adam's death.

The Revuebar Rasputin was in the Dorotheergasse, just around the corner, as the concierge informed Greg when he called down. He offered to make a reservation. Greg decided to have a leisurely dinner first in the Sacher bar, and head over around 10 p.m.

*****

Greg rang the bell on the subterranean, fake-leather padded door of the nightclub and after being observed through a peephole, was admitted by a giant with a Slavic accent. Once his eyes got used to the bright lights on stage and red-tinted darkness everywhere else, Greg went over to the bar, which ran along the entire back wall of the club. He ordered a glass of *Zweigelt* and settled on a stool to watch the show.

Two girls were performing on stage, wearing just G-strings and tassels on their nipples. One was a tall, platinum blond with silicone breasts, the other, a delicate Asian woman with glistening amber skin. They danced for a while, gyrating on a pole, simulating erotic contact. Greg was not one who frequented strip shows, but had been to a few late-night stags. In his extended bachelor state, he could not help but feel himself hardening.

"Is one of those girls Julia?" Greg posed his question to a passing waiter.

"Julia? No. No. Julia, she come not next act, but next." The waiter also had a Slavic accent. Without Greg asking, his glass was refilled.

Greg looked around the room. It was relatively empty, with only a few slimy looking foreign business patrons in pairs or being singly entertained by scantily clad girls in the discrete, red upholstered booths. An Amazon with exquisite coffee-colored skin, introduced as Ginger from New Orleans, was now performing a steamy striptease. Not such a bad way to spend an evening alone in a strange town, Greg thought. *Although, in the end, I'm probably no different than those sleazy patrons in the booths.*

Ginger's act ended and the announcer in silver dinner attire came on stage again. "Next, we present our beautiful Julia from Russia performing an enchanting dance from the steppes of Siberia."

Darkness, a drum roll, then bright lights. On stage, a tall, high-cheeked girl, with long and luminescent straight blond hair stood in a shimmering, low-cut, see-through dress. Her slender arms were stretched above her head and her slow movements, undulating to the music, only accentuated her curves. Greg

51

moved closer, to an empty table right under the stage. To Rimsky-Korsakov's barely recognizable *Scheherazade*, Julia sensually unzipped her long dress and cast it aside to reveal an exquisite body marked only by the line of a G-string. Greg caught sight of her shapely breasts before she turned around and danced with her long legs and bare back to the audience.

That lucky bastard, my friend, Greg thought to himself, as the lights dimmed and Julia disappeared into the all-enveloping darkness. And then, maybe not so lucky, now that he is dead.

*****

Julia's was the last act before a break and the live band was replaced with canned music, the lights brought up a notch. Greg made his way over to the door that led backstage, where a huge man in dark glasses and with greased back hair, seemingly the twin brother of the bouncer at the front door, blocked his way.

"I would like to see Julia," Greg said looking up at the pockmarked face. "She's a friend."

"Not possible," the giant sneered at Greg, crossing his enormous arms across his barrel chest.

"Could you please give her a note then?" Greg pulled out a pen and his little notebook from which he tore a page. He wrote: "I'm a friend of Adam and would like to talk."

"She busy now." But the giant did take the piece of paper and crumpled it in his pocket.

Exasperated, Greg went back to the bar, hoping that the bouncer would, in due course, give the note to Julia. He caressed his glass; it could be a while, he thought to himself, but as he was not tired and had enjoyed the first set, he settled in to watch the rest of the show while he waited for Julia.

*****

An hour and a half and too many glasses of wine later, the door to the back rooms of the club opened and Julia emerged in the same translucent dress she had on at the beginning of her performance. Greg saw her ask the goon something and the bouncer pointed with a jerk of his thumb to where Greg was sitting. He watched with pleasure as Julia approached him like a model on a catwalk.

"Hi, I'm Julia. You must be Greg. Adam told me so much about you. He was really looking forward to your arrival." She had a slight Russian accent, but otherwise her English was fluent. Just as well, because the Russian he had studied in college, though pretty good then, was too rusty to make conversation.

"Please, sit down. What can I get you to drink?"

"Look, I'm not allowed to spend time with friends here." As she said this, she glanced nervously over at the barman and then the goon by the door. "I don't want to lose my job."

"Could we meet after you finish?"

Julia hesitated, as if deciding whether he was trustworthy. "Sure. But it will be late. I finish at two in the morning."

"Perfect. I slept all day anyway. Should I come here or would you prefer to meet at my hotel? The Sacher."

"I will meet you at the bar in the Sacher. It's on my way home. At two fifteen." Smiling, she swiveled her body around and Greg's hungry eyes took in every movement as she made her way back to the stage door.

Chapter 14

Greg walked into the bar of the Sacher just after two. It was empty except for a couple of loud, drunken German businessmen. He steered himself to the plush sofa and winged armchairs in the farthest corner and ordered his usual *Zweigelt*. Although it was late, he did not feel tired.

Julia was a few minutes late and apologized. She was more covered up in her jeans and short, tight-fitting jacket than when he had first seen her, but Greg's eyes roved all over her.

"It's too bad Adam had to go to the U.S. just as you were coming," Julia said after the usual hellos. She sat down on the deep sofa and crossed her long legs. "But you know, his father is very sick. Dying ..."

"His father? The U.S.?" Greg interrupted and was glad the waiter came just then. His mind raced to try to comprehend what Julia had said and how it fit his developing view of what had happened to Adam. "What will you have?"

"A glass of *Mineralwasser*, please. Yes, to Cleveland. Didn't he tell you?" Now Julia was surprised. "How did you know where I work then, if not from Adam?"

"Julia, there's something I have to tell you." Greg took a sip of his wine to summon his courage. "When I arrived yesterday—no, the day before now—I could not find Adam."

"What do you mean? He was not at the airport? He left my place to go home, change, have a quick drink with some friends and then go for you. So he could spend at least one evening with you before flying to America."

"No. And when I went to his apartment, the porter told me there had been an accident. A van had run him over. Killed him. His friend, Hetzel, confirmed it. He's the one who told me about you."

Julia sat there stunned, not saying anything. Then, all of a sudden, the tears came in a torrent. She used Greg's paper napkin to wipe them away. He wanted to move over to the couch and put his arms around her, but he did not know how best to comfort her.

"He can't be dead. You're lying. That Hetzel is lying." Julia's sobs subsided.

"Julia, why would I?"

"He was so good to me."

"Yes, he was a great friend."

"You know, Adam was trying to get me a job." She stopped to fight back the tears. "So I could stay in Austria. Legally."

"Julia," Greg asked, trying to focus, "did Adam tell you anything about what he was doing before he died?"

"No. Just that he was going away for two weeks, to visit his parents."

"Yes, they still live in Cleveland."

For a second, Greg found it odd that Adam would have planned to go away just a day after his arrival without notifying him. He had been so enthusiastic about Greg's coming, even said he would change his plans. But perhaps, as Julia said, there had been an emergency Maybe he was hoping that he wouldn't have to go and when he finally decided, there was no time to communicate with him.

Adam was definitely dead. Hetzel and the porter had seen the accident. And the man at the morgue had told Greg that they had cremated Adam's corpse.

"Can I see him?"

"What? The body?"

"Yes. I would like to see him."

"Julia, I went to the morgue this morning and they told me they had cremated him already."

"What? So fast?"

"Yes. They could not find any family."

"Not even his parents? Who did they ask?"

"Hetzel, I guess."

"I never liked that man. He's strange. Dirty. How do you say … a lecher. And a liar."

"Did Adam ever talk about his work? Is there anything that might make you suspect that his death could have been intended?"

"You mean … that he … he was murdered? No."

"He was working on the disappearance of some nuclear material in Russia."

"Yes, he did go to Russia often. Last time, ten days ago. He only came back a few days before you arrived."

Just then the waiter came; it was almost three o'clock and the exhausted-looking man wanted to close the bar. Greg paid up and they went outside.

*****

Julia lived in the Fourth District, on Momsengasse, and Greg insisted on walking her home. The trams had stopped and the few taxis on the road were all occupied, but in spite of the lightly falling snow, it felt good to breathe the crisp, cold night air. Greg did not want to leave her alone with her grief just yet, but also, selfishly, he relished the company of this beautiful woman.

"So, how did you meet Adam?" Greg asked Julia as they passed by the Staatsoper and took the escalator down into the dingy Opernpassage.

"At a Christmas party. Shortly after I arrived." Julia paused to fight back the tears. "I came to Vienna as a tourist. But I wanted to get a job at the International Atomic Energy Agency. One of my university friends is a secretary in Adam's department, and I was staying with her. She took me to the party and that's where we met."

"Yes. Hetzel told me you have a doctorate in nuclear physics."

"I studied at the Institute for Nuclear Physics at Moscow State University."

"Why nuclear physics?"

"My father was a physicist. And my grandfather, too. They both worked at Mayak. You know, one of those closed cities during the Soviet era. All very secret. Near Chelyabinsk. I grew up there."

"Is your father still alive?"

"No. He died eleven years ago. At age fifty-three. Cancer."

"I'm sorry. That's very young."

"At Mayak, there were many accidents. A lot of radioactive pollution. My parents always wanted me to leave, come to the West. Get away from it. You know, the exposure ..."

"Yes."

"My grandfather died there too." Julia stopped for a moment to put her jacket collar up before they exited the relative warmth of the underground passage to plunge into the uninviting cold and darkness of Resselpark, deserted except for the busts of forgotten Austrian celebrities from another era, Ressel and Madersberg, and a modern statue of a naked mother and child. Greg looked over at Julia and saw the sadness in her eyes: was she thinking about her father and grandfather? Or how to escape their fate?

They walked fast, but in silence, Greg nervously looking around, not feeling safe in the desolate park.

"Adam is ... was a lucky guy."

"No, no. It's not like that. He was just trying to help me get a job at the IAEA. He was a good man."

Greg was relieved at Julia's denial, but wondered what it meant. Knowing his friend, he was not so sure that what Julia was telling him was true. The Adam he knew never kept relationships with women—especially one so beautiful—at the platonic level for very long.

"Now I really don't know what to do. I can only stay another month in Austria as a tourist."

This woman was a puzzle: gorgeous, intelligent, Russian. Working as a dancer in a high-class strip joint. How did she get here in the first place?

Could she be a plant? Greg wondered. A spy? And then he admonished himself for his paranoia.

"You know, I have a key to Adam's flat," Julia announced as they turned off Argentinierstrasse. "Perhaps we should go there tomorrow and see if we can find anything."

"Good idea. How early can you be there?"

"Let's meet at nine."

*****

When they arrived at Julia's building, Greg insisted that he go up and make sure she was all right and safely in her apartment. Julia assured him that she would be fine and just needed to sleep. She did not ask him in and Greg walked back down the four flights of stairs. He pulled the heavy gate open and came out in the cold night air. The snow had stopped falling, but the sidewalks were covered with a light dusting. Greg walked back to the Sacher in a state of turmoil. Although the streets were deserted, he could not help but look back every hundred yards or so; somehow, he had a feeling that he was being followed. Was he becoming paranoid? At the Zentralfriedhof, too …

Maybe it was just that so much had happened the last couple of days, his mind was overloaded and was starting to play tricks on him. But he could not get Adam out of his head. Dead. Why? And Anne, the Interpol agent, telling him about Adam discovering that uranium had been stolen and terrorists could get their hands on it … Secret Soviet cities where the stuff was being produced and stored, with weak security … And now this Russian woman, Julia, whom Adam had told he was going to see his parents in Cleveland. Why?

Chapter 15

Omi was talking on the porch. About her life.

*****

"My dear Greg, after the secret police took your grandfather away, I lost my will to live. I was despondent, ready to die. I did not get out of bed in the morning, did not bother to dress, did not eat. I just cried and cried, night and day. I did not feed Klárika. I often did not even change her. I just did not care about anything.

When my parents came from Györ to see their granddaughter, and saw what was happening, they were shocked and insisted that she and I go home with them. My mother took over looking after the baby. They took turns staying by my bedside and hovered over me like a sick child.

My father gradually managed to talk some sense into me, to rekindle the will to live. 'If not for yourself, then for little Klári's sake,' he said. 'For God's sake, pull yourself together girl.'

For the next six months, I stayed with my parents, and with their loving care, I gradually returned to a more or less normal life. I started to nurse the baby, to change her, to care for her and grew to love her like a mother should.

There is more to womanhood than just loving a man.

Just when I was starting to feel ready to go back to a life in Budapest, Apa and Mama introduced me to Kálmán, a former Hussar officer, the son of good friends. Kálmán was so gentle and so calm, nothing would faze him, and he had such a wonderful sense of humor. He treated me with respect, but how he could laugh and make fun of the world! It was impossible not to be enchanted by him.

It was Kálmán who suggested that Klárika would need a father, and I, a companion. At first I would have none of it, refused even to let him speak to me about it. It was still too early for me to give up on the love of my life. Deep in my heart, I still hoped that your grandfather would come back. The wound of his being taken away from me was still too raw.

I moved to a one-room apartment in Budapest with Klári and partially supported myself with a job translating English at home. The rest came from Apa. Kálmán took a room in a flat nearby, washing windows and doing handyman jobs for party officials. We saw each other every week or so and he respected my wishes, but every three months on the dot, he would ask gently whether I had changed my mind.

It took another two years before I was finally prepared to admit that your grandfather was not coming back and that for the sake of Klári, I did indeed want a partner. She needed a father. And I, an adult to share my life with. Of course, Apa and Mama were happy, but not as much as Kálmán.

So I married Kálmán in a small, quiet wedding in Buda.

Kálmán saved me. Kálmán loved me even though I could not return his love with the same intensity. As long as he was alive, every evening of our married life, he placed a single flower—a lily—on my pillow. Even during the biggest hardships and the coldest winters.

A year later, as you know, my dear Greg, I gave birth to a boy, your Uncle Péter. Kálmán treated both children with the same amount of love and was a perfect father and a model husband. He loved us very much and over time, I grew to love him too.

Not like your grandfather, though.

You know Greg, I have learned in life that there are many different kinds of love.

And more love in a person's heart than just for one person."

*****

But Greg knew that she often thought of his grandfather and of the life they might have had together, had her water not burst that day on the bus.

Chapter 16

Greg rose early. Again the first in the gym, he flicked on the remote and looked for CNN as he started jogging on the treadmill. He turned up the volume. The news from New York was grim—now the body count was up to 343, with 176 injured. They were rebroadcasting interviews of the hysterical wounded taken right after the event, as well as the policemen and medics who had rushed to the site.

There followed a panel discussion among four talking heads, who debated the claim by the Sons of Jesus of being the perpetrators. These so-called experts bemoaned the fact that so little was known about this group and discussed how active they might be in the near future. One of the pundits was quite erudite in his analysis, suggesting that the goals of the Sons of Jesus were, in fact, quite similar to those of Islam-based terrorist groups such as al Qaeda, the main divergence being positions on Israel. Both the Muslim fundamentalist terrorists and the Sons of Jesus were extreme in their anti-secular and anti-Wall Street-capitalist views and violently against the current régime in power in the US.

This was all very unsettling. No matter who was behind the bombing, the world had become a very dangerous place when a homegrown American terror group had the same aims as Muslim fundamentalists to destroy Western Civilization.

Arriving outside Adam's, from the other side of the street, Greg tried to imagine the tragic event as described by Hetzel. Just as he was picturing the van careening around the corner, he noticed Julia on the sidewalk opposite.

Lemongrass, Greg ascertained, as he did the two-cheeked kiss he was now becoming used to, again bowled over by Julia's beauty.

"Let's hurry," he said, looking around. "The police could show up any moment."

"Adam had this made for me," Julia said wistfully as she opened the heavy front doors with a key on a chain she pulled out of her coat pocket. "No one was supposed to know."

They rushed along the dark, ornate corridor to the elevator and waited impatiently. The turn-of-the-century, rickety *Fahrstuhl* was exceedingly slow, but eventually thumped to a stop on the fifth floor. Julia turned the key and pushed open the door to the apartment. They quickly entered, closed the door and found a light switch in the dark hall. Adam's was a classic Viennese flat with high ceilings and plaster moldings, several rooms joined by brass handled French doors and crystal chandeliers everywhere. To the right, Greg saw a small kitchen. Straight ahead, through double doors decorated with Jugendstil etched glass, was the living room. A corridor on the right presumably led to the bedroom.

Greg stuck his nose into the kitchen and smelled garbage. There were still unwashed dishes in the sink, a wrinkled brownish apple or two and a very black banana in a basket, empty wine bottles destined for recycling in a bucket in the corner.

Julia headed straight for a Biedermeier desk in the salon and by the time Greg joined her, she was starting up Adam's laptop. Greg looked around; the apartment was definitely a bachelor pad, with papers all over the desk, a burgundy cashmere sweater left inside-out on the back of an armchair, men's magazines on the floor by the sofa and a couple of goblets with dried red wine stains in the bottom, lipstick on one, still on the antique mahogany Chinese mahjong board that served as the coffee table.

"This is slow booting up." The laptop purred and the icons flickered on the screen.

"Shh ... shh. What's that?" Greg thought he heard a key being inserted in the lock in the front door. "Come, quick. Behind here." Julia rapidly disconnected the cables from the computer and slipped it under her arm as

Greg pulled her behind the heavy velvet drapes and held her close. He felt his heartbeat quicken.

They hid just in time, because in came a man Greg instantly recognized as Hetzel. He closed the door, took out his handkerchief to blow his nose and headed straight for the desk. Hetzel stared at the disconnected wires for a moment, shuffled the papers on top of the writing table, looked around the salon and then went into the bedroom. It dawned on Greg that he must be looking for the laptop. Hetzel came back into the salon and went over to the desk again with a perplexed look on his face. He touched the cables and quickly made his way out of the apartment, locking the door behind him as he left. Greg prayed that the wires had not warmed up enough for Hetzel to realize that someone had just taken the computer.

"That was too close," Greg whispered, peeling himself away from Julia. "Good you took the laptop."

He made his way over to the desk and started to rummage through the papers. On top of the pile was a calling card, the name 'William Crawford' on it.

"Who the hell is this?" he muttered to himself. "Sounds familiar. I can't quite place him." Below the name—Adam, probably—had written in pen, 'Hotel Imperial, Rm. 205'. He hesitated a moment, then put the card in his pocket.

Beside the card were two tickets to see *Don Carlos* at the Staatsoper. Tomorrow, February fourteenth. Great seats. He loved Verdi and *Don Carlos* was his favorite opera. Adam would have no use for them now. Greg took the tickets. He finished glancing through the papers but found nothing that might have been relevant to Adam's disappearance.

"Come on. We've got to get out of here. Hetzel may be back. Or the police."

*****

On the way down in the elevator, Greg had an idea. "Let's just ring at the caretaker's. Maybe he'll tell us more about how Adam died."

"Sure. Herr Pfaff is a funny old man. He can be a bit grumpy, but he was always helpful to Adam."

Herr Pfaff was still wearing his slippers and the rust-colored cardigan full of holes when he opened the door a crack. He was surprised to see Julia with

Greg, and Greg sensed an air of disapproval directed at her. The old man reluctantly came out into the corridor when she told him they had a few more questions.

"I'm sorry that Herr Kallay is dead. He was a good man. I have not seen the accident. I told the police everything. First I have heard a loud bang. I come out after. It was getting dark. Three men stand around the body. It was in very bad *Zustand* ... very bad condition." The caretaker paused and gave Julia a penetrating look, as if to size up the effect he was having on her. "Then police come. Lots confusion. I have seen only one man then. What is left of body taken to Stadtleichenhaus, I have heard police tell driver. That was it."

"Did you recognize any of the men?" Greg asked.

"No. It was already getting dark. But they have spoken Russian. They are terrible, the Russians. Vienna is now full with them."

*****

"One thing's for sure," Greg said as they left the building.

"What?"

"Somebody is lying. Hetzel said that he and that Russian were the only ones at the scene. And the Russian had left by the time the police came. Herr Pfaff said there were three men."

"It could have been anyone who happened to come along. Or just a mistake."

"Plus, Hetzel said nothing about a big bang."

"Do you think Adam was first shot and then run over?"

"I don't know what to think."

They walked in silence along Reisnerstrasse toward the Stadtpark.

"Julia, could we look at the laptop? We may be able to learn something. Let's go back to my hotel. I will buy you lunch after."

"Sure. Adam didn't use it for work much though. Other than to set up meetings."

"Well, still ..."

"Okay. I think I know the password. Adam let me use it a few times. But do you mind if we make a detour first? I have to pick up a letter at my girlfriend's. From my mother. My friend will be there just until two and then has to go back to work."

"Of course." Greg was happy to spend a couple of hours strolling through

64

Vienna with Julia. It would be a pleasant distraction for them both, from the pain and the mystery surrounding the death of the man who had brought them together.

Chapter 17

It was close to noon when Anne finally got back to her office. She had spent the entire morning meeting with the Austrian police, being brought up to date on the human trafficking file. When Demeter had asked her to be involved in this case, Anne had replied, "Delighted, John. I'm going to see that every one of those bastards has their balls lopped off."

Anne had been itching all day to do some research at her computer on the Adam affair. She knew she would need at least a couple of hours of quiet time, so she instructed Frau Huth, the matronly secretary she shared with Labrecque, to interrupt her only if it was very urgent. Nevertheless, she left her phone on and put it right beside the keyboard; Haffner, or for that matter Fazkov, could call at any moment. Haffner owed her a call on the van, among other things.

She opened the Interpol search engine. *I will start with Sidorov.* Anne had a hunch that the Russian was somehow at the center of things. She typed his last name and then the first into the boxes and waited.

Anne was initially surprised, and then disappointed, with what came back. There was only one entry for Sergei Sidorov: a serial murderer in New York City, apprehended several years earlier. Surely, this was not the Sidorov she was seeking. Strange that none of the intelligence services worldwide had anything.

She decided to try Hetzel next, even though she didn't have a first name.

She waited and waited, but nothing came back from any of the police files. She was just about to move on to see if anything more had cropped up on Kolchakova when the tune on her cell filled the small office. It was Haffner.

"Rudolf, I was trying to call earlier. We should meet. I've not been able to find anything on either Sidorov or Hetzel in the files. Are you sure you got the names right?"

"Anne, before we get into that ... there's been another death."

"Oh, no!" *Not Greg Martens, surely not. Please, no.* She had rather liked Adam's handsome and intelligent author friend.

"I was called by the police in the Third District. They know I am working on the Kallay case. The old janitor in his building was found dead just half an hour ago."

"Oh, God." Anne felt relief, then a tinge of guilt at having wished it to be anybody but Martens. "Do you think it's linked to Kallay?"

"Don't know yet. Don't know even if it is murder. He was last seen alive in the corridor talking to a girl—a beautiful blond—and a foreign man, probably American."

"Rudolf, we have to meet."

"Can you come down here? To Kallay's building. There are a few more things I need to finish, but after that, we can walk back to the station together."

"Okay. Thanks. I'll be there in fifteen minutes."

Anne went to get her jacket from the hook behind the door and then, almost as an afterthought, detoured over to the safe on the opposite wall. It was time to get serious. She did not like to carry a weapon, but there had been too many deaths already and she did not want to be the next corpse sent to the tacky provisional morgue out by the Zentralfriedhof. She dialed the combination, flipped the heavy door open and took out her Glock 29, a powerful, compact semi-automatic handgun. She quickly checked it, made sure it was serviceable, slipped it into the inside pocket of her jacket and turned out the lights.

Better safe than sorry, Anne thought to herself as she left the Interpol offices.

*****

"The old man's heart stopped beating. May have been suffocation. Or just a heart attack, with the tongue doing the choking. I can't tell, but we will do some tests and an autopsy. In any case, there are no visible signs of foul play anywhere on the body."

"You know, Rudolf, an American friend of Kallay arrived in Vienna a couple of days ago. He may have been the one talking to Pfaff."

"How do you know?"

"I met him. At the morgue. On second thought, maybe not. I doubt that he would know a blond here. He seems shy and doesn't know a soul in Vienna other than Kallay. And now me."

"What is his name?"

"Martens. Greg Martens. Staying at the Sacher. Here for a book conference and to see Kallay, his friend. But I'll talk to him."

"Thanks. We will check him out just the same." Haffner quickly entered the name and hotel into his iPhone.

They crossed the Stadtpark, and this was where their paths diverged. Anne remembered she wanted to ask Haffner about Hetzel and Sidorov.

"Rudolf, are you sure you got the names right?"

"Yes, yes, Hetzel gave me his name and address and Sidorov's name. But no address for the Russian."

"Well? Did you check out Hetzel?"

"I sent one of my men," Haffner answered, obviously embarrassed, looking down to avoid Anne's eyes, "and there was no Hetzel registered at that address. No one there has seen anyone like him. We have the place under surveillance though."

"Anything else come up?"

"Well, yes. It may be a coincidence, but a colleague in the First District sent in a report yesterday based on a tip from an informer that a Herr Hetzel is negotiating to buy the Revuebar Rasputin; the exotic dance bar on Dorotheergasse. The informer also said that this same Hetzel might be involved in trafficking women. But we have nothing concrete, just a rumor in the sex underground. We will follow this lead. It may give us a chance to pick Herr Hetzel up for questioning."

"The Revuebar Rasputin you said?" Anne took out her little notebook and wrote down the name.

"Yes. That was it."

Well, at least here was something on Hetzel. Something sordid. Anne could not help feeling again that Sidorov was the more important of the two. But it seemed unlikely to her that they were really friends of Adam.

Anne looked at her watch, thinking that she might try and get to Greg Martens before Haffner did, so she changed course towards the Sacher. The rest of the research would have to wait for another day.

Chapter 18

Back at the hotel, Greg was conscious of the disapproving stares of the receptionists as he headed for the elevators with Julia. He could just imagine what they were thinking, but didn't give a damn.

They went straight to his room; fortunately, he had had the presence of mind to take Adam's cables and the adapter, so within moments, Julia was typing the password and they were connected.

"Okay. Here's his Outlook. Some emails from me. Here's one from someone called Fazkov. Gives his itinerary. Arrived in Vienna on the eleventh, at 3:40 p.m. That was the day Adam died. Do you remember the time?"

"Hmm. Hetzel didn't tell me. But the porter said the accident happened a few hours before I got there. Which was sometime after nine. But not much. Maybe three or four hours earlier. It must have been sometime around six."

"Who's Kolchakova? Do you know? Several from her," Julia asked, perking up a bit. "Setting up meetings."

"Someone at Mayak. Oh yes, the Interpol agent did mention her. She's Director, I think."

"And some from a Levinson. Must be working on the project with Adam."

"Any from Hetzel? Or that Russian?"

"Nothing. There is one from a Polyakov. I recognize the name. He's come around the Revuebar several times with Adam and Hetzel."

70

"Open it."

"Let's see. It's in Russian. It just says see you this afternoon."

"Hmm... So he was going to meet with Adam that day too."

"There's another one from Fazkov."

"But nothing on the missing nuclear material?"

"I guess they wouldn't communicate about that. It would be too dangerous."

"So there's nothing here. Nothing that helps us. Other than that Fazkov was probably in Vienna when Adam died."

"Let's look at the files."

Just then the telephone rang. Greg picked up.

"Hello. Mr. Martens? This is Anne Rossiter. Interpol. I'm in the lobby. I need to talk to you. Urgently."

"What about?" As there was no answer, Greg continued: "Fine. I'll be right down."

He frowned as he put the phone down. "Julia, I've got to go downstairs and see that Interpol agent. If you can wait, we can go to lunch after."

"No, no, that's okay. I should go anyways. I want to read the letter from my mother, and I have a lot of things to do at home. Thanks. But go ahead. I'll just turn off the laptop and close the door."

*****

Anne, waiting in one of the plush armchairs in the lobby, stood up as Greg approached. Greg could not help but think how lucky he was to be going from one gorgeous woman to the next.

"Hello, Mr. Martens," Anne said with a smile," I hope I didn't disturb you."

"No, no ... that's fine. But let's go into the bar. Allow me to invite you for a bite of lunch." Greg had realized in the elevator how hungry he was and was damned if he was going to miss a meal and end up with a splitting headache, especially as the Austrian English Literary Society was picking up his tab.

Once settled at his usual corner table and the ordering out of the way, Greg asked, "So what's up? I didn't think I would have the pleasure of seeing you so soon."

"Well, not good news." Anne averted eye contact. "You know, the caretaker at Mr. Kallay's flat—Herr Pfaff, I think, was his name. He was found

71

dead just an hour or so ago."

"What?"

"I came straight here from the scene. I was called there because the Austrian police know we are investigating the Kallay death. Same building. Not sure yet whether it was foul play. Pfaff was last seen with a foreigner of your description and a blond woman. Mr. Martens, did you go there? And who is your friend?"

"Yes. We did talk to Pfaff. But we did not kill him." Greg hesitated a moment and didn't answer the second question since he remembered that Julia was working in Austria illegally and could get in trouble.

"The blond? Who is she?" Anne would not let it go.

"A friend."

"The Austrian police will want to question her. And you too, Mr. Martens. Although, if it's murder, it will no doubt be connected to Kallay's death."

"His murder you mean? You think the thieves who took the nuclear material killed him, don't you?"

"Don't know yet. Look, did Pfaff say anything to you that was … out of the ordinary?"

"Yes. He said there were three men at the accident before the police came. Hetzel told me that only he and some Russian were there. Pfaff said they all spoke Russian with each other."

"Hmm. We know about the two men, Hetzel, and Sidorov. We've been trying to find them. It seems that they are not nice people. Certainly Hetzel. But we didn't know there was a third man. Any idea of who that might be?"

"No."

Anne took out a notebook and scribbled something, before continuing. "You mean you met this Hetzel?"

"Yes. After our walk in the Zentralfriedhof."

"Can you tell me what happened?"

"He left a message at the hotel. To come and meet him, claiming he was a good friend of Adam's."

"Did he say anything that might be of help?"

Greg hesitated; he would have to keep part of the truth, again about Julia, to himself. "He described how Adam died and offered to help me while I'm in Vienna."

He suddenly remembered Hetzel's card in his wallet. "Here. He gave me this. There's a phone number too." Greg checked the card before he handed it over to make sure it was Hetzel's—he did not want to part with the other one until he got to the bottom of who William Crawford was. But he was glad he could offer Anne something useful, the tangible gesture somewhat expiating his guilt at holding back information.

"Thank you. That could be of help." Anne looked at the card and saw that there was only a name and a mobile number. She could tell from the first three digits that the carrier was T-mobile; she would check it out later. "Can you describe the man?"

"Rugged face, medium build, overweight. Sweats a lot." Anne quickly scribbled some notes again.

"And Fazkov. The physicist friend. Has he turned up?" Greg asked, wanting to move the discussion away from his meeting with Hetzel.

"No. Still missing. And has not been seen at Mayak for several days."

"Could he be the third man? I mean, at the scene of the accident?" Greg blurted out, the thought just coming to him then.

"But why would Hetzel not tell us about his being there?"

"Maybe because it was murder and Fazkov was really working with them. They were all part of the heist. They had Fazkov tell Adam, thinking he could help keep the disappearance of the uranium off the books, but then found him too unreliable. Too much of a risk. Maybe they found out that he told you. So they got rid of him."

"You'd make a good detective, Mr. Martens. But we need to go step by step."

"And the uranium? Has that been recovered?"

"No, not yet. Look, just make sure I can reach you in case Pfaff's death is another murder and the Austrian police want to question you. I want to be there, because they have a tendency to oversimplify."

"What do you mean?"

"Well, you are a foreigner and you were the last one with Pfaff. Plus you're also connected to Kallay."

"You mean they may try to pin Pfaff's murder on me?"

"Not necessarily. But you never know."

"Should I be worried?"

"Mr. Martens, this is a dangerous game. If both Kallay and Pfaff were murdered—which is a distinct possibility—then whoever did it is in serious trouble. And maybe ready to kill again."

"Of course."

"Mr. Martens, you should steer clear. Maybe even leave Vienna. I don't want yet another death to investigate."

"Thanks for the concern. But you could be in danger too."

"It's part of my job."

"In any case, I will not leave until I find out what happened to my friend."

"I can't make you go."

"Look, this is ridiculous ..." Greg was starting to get angry, but realized that this woman was on his side, so he controlled himself and switched the subject.

"So, tell me, how did you come to work for Interpol?"

"MI5 recruited me after Oxford. I fit the profile. Languages, sports ... you know all that. Then they trained me and handed me over to Interpol." Anne answered. Then she added, smiling, "In fact, I am reading one of your spy novels. *Agent of Love.* I rather like it. Though in reality, the life of an agent is less exciting. It's more lonely."

"You mean less ... coupling?" He almost said sex but didn't, thinking it would be too forward.

"Definitely," Anne answered with a little laugh.

"You're not married then?"

"No. Never really had the time for men."

"Well, you're making time for me now."

"That's all in the line of work." Anne said, looking Greg in the eyes. "I thought I would come to the Conference tomorrow. One of my favorite authors, Gareth Martens, is supposed to give a talk on the American novel. But I didn't see your name on the program. Was there some mistake? He does have the same last name as you ..."

Greg laughed. "You're the good detective. Yes, there was a slip up. The Society sent the invitation to Gregory Martens instead of Gareth and here I am!"

"That's funny."

"I suppose some members may be disappointed, but I can give a perfectly good speech on the American novel."

"I'm sure."

"Anyways, I'll see you tomorrow then."

They left it at that, since the waiter had cleared the dishes and brought the bill. Greg charged it to his room and silently thanked Crabbe and the Austrian English Literary Society for lunch.

Chapter 19

As Greg entered his room, he noticed the laptop was gone. Julia must have taken it. Also, the red light was blinking on the phone. A message from Hetzel, about twenty minutes ago, with an urgent request to meet. He left no number and Greg had given Anne Rossiter his card.

Fortunately, he remembered that the note asking for their first meeting had a mobile number. He looked for it on his night table and found the piece of paper he had crumpled on his way to the Café Hawelka.

"Hello, Herr Hetzel, I got your message."

"Yes, thanks for calling. I need to see you. I've a few things to tell you."

"What?"

"Not over the telephone."

"Where should we meet?"

"How about the Revuebar Rasputin? You have been there and it is a *gemütlich* place, no? Eleven o'clock, tonight, is that good?"

"Fine, see you there. *Auf Wiedersehen.*"

How did Hetzel know he'd been to the Rasputin? Was he there last night? Greg was angry with himself for not looking around, but glad that Hetzel suggested the Revuebar, so that he could walk Julia home again. He was concerned about her now, after what Anne had said. Not just because of the Austrian police, but also, if Adam had indeed been murdered, of the people who had killed him and maybe even Pfaff too. Plus, he would need to take a look at the laptop at her place afterwards.

*****

Greg headed over to the Revuebar shortly before eleven. He had never imagined that he would become a regular at a strip joint in Vienna, but consoled himself that tomorrow evening he would be doing something more highbrow. That reminded him to ask Julia if she could free herself up to come to the opera.

The goon at the door recognized him and let him in, no questions asked. Greg searched around for Hetzel and got cold looks from the customers being entertained by bare-breasted girls in G-strings when he peered into their private booths. No Hetzel. Greg wondered whether Julia had to service clients in this more intimate manner as well, but quickly put the thought out of his mind. He settled in at the bar, ordered *Zweigelt*—but this time, a bottle.

The drum roll, the announcer with the same silver tuxedo and introduction, and out pranced the lovely Julia in her translucent dress. *She is exquisite—am I falling in love with her?* Greg asked himself, as he took a large swallow of his wine.

Just as the dress came off, Greg felt a hand on his shoulder and a voice behind him pronounced the very words he was thinking. "A gorgeous woman, *nicht wahr*? Our friend was very lucky indeed."

It was Hetzel. He was with another man, slightly balding, smaller and younger, but very fit looking and square jawed.

"This is my friend, Sergei Polyakov. He was also a good friend to Adam. We are both very sad. Our condolences."

"Yes." Polyakov clicked his heels and shook Greg's hand, said something in rapid Russian to Hetzel, then made his way to join two men sitting at one of the front tables. *Polyakov—that was the name Julia had mentioned.* Yet another Russian friend of Adam—the one who had written the email saying he would meet Adam on the afternoon he died. But didn't Hetzel say it was a Russian with a different name who had been with him at the site of the accident?

Hetzel sat down on the stool beside Greg and ordered himself a Chivas.

"I see you speak fluent Russian," Greg remarked.

"I grew up in Russia. Russian was my first language and later, I used it in work."

"What were you doing?"

"Trading," Hetzel answered, his gaze avidly taking in Julia's dance on stage *"Mein Gott*, she is lovely!"

"What did you trade?"

Hetzel hesitated before answering, "Commodities. A good business. But you know, my friend," he changed the subject, putting his hand on Greg's knee, "Adam told me he was planning a trip to Budapest when you came. He wanted to see the land of your ancestors together with you. Rediscover your roots. He said you and he had talked about it a lot."

"Yes, in college. We planned to take a trip there one summer. Never did."

"He wanted to go with you now."

"Yes, he mentioned that."

"You know, Greg, I think he would really like you to go anyway. With Ms. Saparova. You should spend three or four days there together." Hetzel paused a moment to let the notion sink in. "Greg, you will be pleased. I have taken the liberty of making all the arrangements," he continued, reaching into his breast pocket to pull out a thick envelope. "Here are two first-class train tickets, a voucher for three nights at the Gresham Palace and five thousand Euros. You will have a good time."

"Why, Herr Hetzel …"

Julia was finishing her act and Greg again caught sight of her perfect body as she leaned down to pick up the discarded dress.

"Don't worry. Ms. Saparova will have the time off. And she does not need papers to go—Hungary is within Schengen. There is no border check anymore."

"Herr Hetzel, thank you." Greg was sorely tempted to grab the opportunity to have the vacation of a lifetime. All expenses paid. But why would Hetzel make such an offer? Surely, it wasn't a gesture of friendship towards the friend of his friend? No, could it be that he … they … someone wanted to get him out of the way? Off the trail of Adam's murder?

Had Julia agreed to this or was Hetzel going to force—or pay—her to go with him? And if she had, did that mean that she was part of the conspiracy?

However tempting the offer, he could not go. His priority was to find out what happened to Adam. And now there were all these other questions. *But any other time …*

"I cannot accept."

"Then it is your loss, my friend." Hetzel picked up his newly refilled glass of Chivas and stood up, even as he put the envelope back in his breast pocket. "Goodbye, Greg. Just be careful. Very careful. There are a lot of bad people here in Vienna."

Now that Julia was not on stage, Greg watched Hetzel make his way to join Polyakov and the two men at the table in front. He saw him shake his head from side to side, probably communicating the failure of his mission and then shrug his shoulders. The three got up and the party disappeared behind the padded door leading to the dressing rooms and offices with only a forced smile from the guard.

*****

Last call finally arrived, the announcer gave his good night speech and a few minutes later, Julia emerged, dressed in jeans and a T-shirt, carrying her sweater and jacket. She looked agitated. Angry.

"What's up?" Greg asked, getting up to greet her with the double-cheeked kiss. He felt a little woozy after the bottle and a half or more of wine.

"I'll tell you outside. Let's go."

Out on Dorotheergasse, Greg buttoned his coat quickly and turned his collar up to keep out the cold; Julia put her scarf over her head to protect her ears. Must get a hat, Greg thought to himself, but the cold air was bracing and he felt steadier than inside the warm club.

"Well, what happened?"

"That snake Hetzel showed up with his friend Polyakov. They were with the manager in one of the offices for a long time. Talking very loud. Then Hetzel strutted around as if he owned the place. He came into the dressing room, and started ... touching my body, feeling me up. I threatened him with scissors and he said something stupid, but scary. That it was just a matter of time."

"Julia, are you all right?" Greg noticed that Julia was close to tears. The wind howled along Augustinerstrasse, making conversation difficult.

"*Ja.* He's a real creep. I hate him."

"You know, Hetzel offered me two first-class train tickets to Budapest and three nights at the Gresham Palace. With you. Paid for by him."

"What? The bastard. How dare he! Did you accept?" Greg's news had just made her angrier. But he was relieved at her ire; at least she was not working with Hetzel or whomever to get him out of the way. He was a bit ashamed of his earlier paranoia.

"No. I must find out what happened to Adam." They were passing the Opera.

"I also want to know what happened. And I need to find a way to get a work visa."

They escaped down the escalator to the Opernpassage, where the bliss of momentary warmth fought with the unpleasant smells of the unwashed homeless seeking shelter from the cold.

"I haven't told you, but the Interpol agent who called earlier told me that Herr Pfaff is dead. The Austrian police think he may have been killed. You and I were the last ones to see him alive, so they will want to talk to us."

"Oh, no! That is all I need now." Julia was close to tears. "They will want to see my papers."

"I didn't give her your name, but it's only a matter of time before they find out."

They walked in silence for a while avoiding the few underground beggars still active at this time of night and the drunken or drugged-up youth sporting metal rings in ears, noses and lips. At the end of the passageway, they regrouped for a moment before plunging into the cold of Resselpark. They walked quickly past the towering, still-lit pillars flanking the Karlskirche, Julia's teeth chattering, and up along Argentinierstrasse.

"You know, it is becoming too dangerous here. Maybe we should have gone to Budapest," Greg mused, somewhat protected from the wind by the tall buildings on either side of the street.

"If the Russian mafia are behind all these killings, they could get us there just as easily. Maybe even more easily. They can't be stopped."

"Well, at least we would be out of reach of the Austrian police. Not that I've anything to hide, but for you, the visa will be more complicated."

"Yes, they will deport me."

They arrived at the gate of Julia's building. The dark corridor inside was just marginally warmer than the outside temperature. Adam again insisted on walking her up the stairs and, at the door to her flat, he held her hand a moment and said, "Julia, give me your telephone number. So I can reach you. And I'll give you my cell number too—although it's an American one and it's back at the hotel. In case of emergency."

"Come inside and I will write them down."

Julia went into the kitchen for pen and paper, but she did not invite Greg to take his coat off, so he just stood in the entrance, glad for the warmth.

"Oh yes, Julia, when can we look at the laptop again?" Greg shouted after her, hoping she would ask him to stay. He was getting used to these late nights.

"Why don't you come for lunch tomorrow?" Julia answered as she came back into the hall.

She handed him the piece of paper, Greg wrote down his number, and they said good night. Too stiffly, for Greg's taste.

*****

Greg checked his watch as he made his way down the dimly lit stairs. It was almost 3 a.m. He opened the heavy wooden door; outside, it was snowing again, a sleety, wet snow that the wind drove maliciously into exposed skin. He pulled his collar up and turned out of the gate along Karolinengasse in the direction of the First District. As he did so, across the street, underneath the lamppost, he thought he glimpsed the motionless figure of a man. But when he looked again, there was no one there.

Snow was accumulating on the sidewalk, several centimeters, and he wished he had worn more than just his loafers. Turning on to Argentinierstrasse, Greg had the sensation that he was being followed. Maybe there had been someone there on the sidewalk, shadowing him. But when he looked back along the long straight street, again he saw no one, no movement but the falling snow illuminated by the streetlights.

A feeling of loneliness overcame him as he thought about his best friend, now dead, possibly even murdered, his wife, long-since divorced, and the two beautiful women he had met recently, so near, yet so out of reach.

Passing through Resselpark, the sensation of being followed became stronger—maybe it was just paranoia, but he furtively looked around several times and picked up his pace. Greg literally jogged back to the hotel, driven by the wind through the empty, snow-covered streets. He was cold, wet and tired, but glad to arrive back at the Sacher.

The night watchman had replaced the doorman and greeted Greg with a "*Gute Nacht*." He hurried up to his room, undressed quickly and, on the spur of the moment, took a sleeping pill. He did not want to be up all night thinking about Adam. Or that his life might be in danger.

81

Chapter 20

Anne was running late, but could not pass by the Aida *Confiserie* without picking up a marzipan-filled croissant, her usual weekday breakfast. A few minutes later, she was in the elevator on the way to Interpol's fifth story offices in a turn-of-the-last-century building just behind the Börse, the former Imperial stock market along the Ring.

Anne settled in front of her computer and thanked Frau Huth, who brought her a steaming *mélange* to accompany the croissant. Booting up, she took a few sips and then went directly to her calendar to check the day's agenda. Good, she thought, as she relished a rich, almond-paste filled bite and quickly glanced down the page; most of it was empty, other than 4 p.m., where she had written 'Austrian English Literary Society—Sacher'. It would be fun to hear Greg Martens give his talk on trends in the American novel; that was something to look forward to. The rest of the day, she needed to make a few calls, pursue the research on the disappeared nuclear material and see if she could find anything more on Hetzel. At least now she had a telephone number for him, thanks to Greg. She also wanted to follow up on the Revuebar Rasputin story. The boring and unavoidable task of writing her weekly report was also something Anne had planned for today. She glanced at her watch, *time to get cracking.*

Still sipping her coffee, Anne left her cubicle to where her secretary was sitting.

"Frau Huth, could you please call our contact at T-Mobile to see if they can trace this number? The name on the card is Andreas Hetzel. I would like an address and a call log—that would be great." Anne knew that she was asking too much; Austrian privacy laws were so strict that she would be lucky to get an address for Hetzel. Even if anything came back, she suspected it would be the false address he had given Haffner. No harm in trying though.

Going back into her office, Anne dialed her Austrian police contact.

"*Grüss Gott.* Haffner hier."

"Rudolf? Anne Rossiter. I'm glad I caught you."

"Yes! I was about to call."

"Any news on Sidorov? Or Hetzel?"

"No, but we talked to the manager at Revuebar Rasputin. After some intensive questioning, he confirmed that the owner is in discussions with a Herr Hetzel regarding a sale. There will be a meeting tonight at the Rasputin. We will be there to bring him in for interrogation."

"Good. Meanwhile I'm checking a phone number. Probably fake though."

"We will get to the bottom of this. Hetzel gave the police a false address. That is already a crime."

"Surely, Rudolf, he should not be so hard to find."

"Tonight. We will get him tonight."

"Maybe that Sidorov character will be with him."

"Good point."

"Rudolf, I'd like to come. To the Revuebar."

"It is not really a place for ladies ..."

"I am the Interpol representative on the case."

"Yes, of course. If you insist. We will assemble at twenty-two o'clock outside. My men will cover all the entrances."

"Thanks."

Anne was frustrated, but felt that at least some progress was being made. All too slowly though. Too easy for the criminals to manipulate the situation and commit another murder or steal more nuclear material from Mayak or elsewhere.

*****

Frau Huth came into Anne's office. "Fräulein Rossiter, T-Mobile just called back."

"Yes?"

"The number for Herr Hetzel belongs to a SIM card that needs to be loaded up after several hours of use. It was bought at their kiosk on Kärtnerstrasse two weeks ago. For cash. No record of who bought it."

"Thank you." It was not the answer Anne had been hoping for; she knew that the task of finding Hetzel was not going to be easy. Perhaps tonight though, at the Revuebar. Or maybe Greg Martens knew more than he had told her. She would find a way to tease it out of him.

*****

Anne finished her report for the week—which was mainly about the Adam affair—by spelling out the next steps as she saw them. This also helped concentrate her mind; she had very few leads, so the focus had to be on probing more into Hetzel. There was also the blond, trying to track Fazkov's movements and finding that Sidorov figure.

Anne decided to give her report one quick read through before she had to leave for the Sacher to catch Greg's talk. Afterwards, she would have another chat with him. She made a few little changes and then sent it to the usual list of addressees, checked her email one last time and shut down the laptop.

84

Chapter 21

Greg slept late, went to the gym to work off his late night indulgence, and had two macchiatos and a croissant in the Sacher lounge. When he stepped outside, the sun was shining; he had ample time, so he took a longer route to Julia's through the gardens of the Belvedere Palace. The streets and parks were full of tourists, but also Viennese, out jogging or walking their dogs.

Barefoot and wearing grey sweat pants and an aquamarine tank top, hair loosely tied on top of her head, Julia looked fabulous, though a little sullen. Maybe she had a bad night after Hetzel pawed her, or just thinking of Adam ...

She invited Greg in to the bright, modern kitchen where she was fixing a caprese salad for lunch. They carried their plates, glasses and a bottle of a good Avignonesi Montepulciano into the one room that served as bedroom, dining room and salon, and settled into the deep, grey leather sofa. In front of them, on the glass coffee table, was the laptop.

As they were finishing lunch, Julia booted up and went into 'My Documents'. She scrolled through the folder names: Papers, CVs, Payments, Investments, Accounting, Travel, Letters, Parents' Health, and so on.

"Look under 'Papers'."

"Just a bunch of scientific works he downloaded. And here's one he's writing for *Foreign Affairs* on the security of Russian nuclear sites. That might be interesting reading."

"Go on. Try 'Letters'." Greg brought his face level beside Julia's.

"Nothing. Just one to T-Mobile Austria renewing his contract."

"Try 'Travel'."

"I know he made a reservation to go to Cleveland. I was there."

"Okay."

"Oh yes, here's Cleveland. No, this was last summer."

"What's that? The very last one."

"A confirmed booking to Chelyabinsk."

"For tomorrow! Via Moscow. The flight leaves at seven thirty in the morning," Greg read out loud over Julia's shoulder. "And a hotel booking. The Meridian Chelyabinsk."

"The rat! He lied to me. He told me he was going to Cleveland."

"Julia, he's dead!"

"He lied."

"No. He made plans to go to Chelyabinsk to try and catch the thieves. He must have made the booking after speaking to Fazkov. After he told Anne Rossiter. It all makes sense. He knew he'd have to go. The fewer people knew, the better."

"Well, he should have told me the truth."

"No. He would have only put you in danger. He was protecting you by telling you he was going to Cleveland. A good cover."

"I don't like it."

"I better tell the Interpol agent."

"Leave the police out of it. I am working here illegally."

"Look, Julia. Adam was murdered and probably Pfaff too. This is all becoming very dangerous," Greg said, echoing Anne's words to him.

Deep in thought, he poured Julia and himself another glass of wine. As he put the bottle down, his hand brushed against Julia's; the sensation of her skin touching his excited him and brought him back from his thoughts.

"Julia, I'm going to go to Chelyabinsk," he blurted out suddenly, "to try and find Adam's killers. The thieves."

"What? Are you mad?"

"No. Maybe. But I need to know what happened."

"But it's so dangerous!"

"Well, I've got to go. I have to find out."

"It is not that easy, Greg."

"I can go as a tourist. I've never been to Chelyabinsk. Or to Russia, for that matter. I speak some Russian, so I will get by."

"They won't let you near Mayak. It is still a very secret place." Julia burst into tears as she said this. Greg, taken aback, hesitated, but put his arm around her.

"It's okay. I know this is all overwhelming."

"No … no. It's not that."

"What then?"

"I didn't tell you last night. The reason I was so upset … was that the letter from my mother we picked up at my friend's …" She started sobbing again as she spoke.

"Julia, what is it?" Greg covered her hand with his.

"She wrote that she is sick. A tumor. In the brain. She was going for tests to see if it was cancerous. In fact, today is the day."

"I am so sorry. How terrible. How can I help?"

"If you go to Chelyabinsk, perhaps you could visit her. Check on her. I will give you the address."

"Of course. All the more reason to go."

"I want to go so much, but I can't. I won't be able to come back to Austria." She wiped the tears from her eyes.

"Don't worry."

"I can call my friend at the Embassy. She works for the Ambassador and can get a visa for you fast. And I will ask her also to get permission for you to go as far as Ozersk, where my mother lives. It won't get you into Mayak, but everyone who works there lives nearby in Ozersk. My friend will arrange it."

"Thank you. That's great."

Julia scribbled something.

"Here. This is my mother's address in Ozersk."

"I'll definitely go and see her."

"But first we need to get you the visa. Meet me in front of Adam's tomorrow at nine. The Russian consular section is just down the street. Bring your passport. Photos and money. Cash—I think it is one hundred twenty Euros. But better have a little more, just in case."

"Okay."

"I will call another friend at Aeroflot about a ticket. The travel agency is near your hotel. Here, I'll write down that address too and my friend's name. You can go by there later. If we go through my contacts, we may have a chance to arrange it all. It's very short notice and usually that doesn't work in Russia."

"Thanks, Julia."

"I can pick up the passport and bring it to the hotel tomorrow evening. It'll be on my way to work."

"You're an angel." Greg leaned over, wanting to give her just a peck on the cheek, but as his face drew nearer to hers, he suddenly had the urge to kiss her fully on the mouth. In the last second, Julia turned away.

"Here," Greg said, reaching into his pocket for the opera tickets. "I have these. Why don't you come to the opera with me this evening?"

"I'd love to, Greg, but I can't. I have to work. Adam got those for you and him to go. He told me. I'm glad you can use at least one. You can probably sell the other ticket at the door."

"Well, let's have dinner tomorrow then. Before you go to work. At seven. We can order something at the bar at the Sacher."

"I'll be there. With the passport."

Greg was glad to find a way to spend a little more time with Julia before he left for Russia.

Chapter 22

"Russia—the Soviet Union of my youth—was an evil state," Omi had said. "The oppressor of its own people and of all its client countries behind the Iron Curtain. Stalin was the worst dictator, a raging criminal who killed twenty million people directly or indirectly."

She loved to talk history. Her history. And Greg loved to listen to her recounting it.

"Hungary was under the Stalinist yoke from 1947 leading up to the 1956 Revolution, directly controlled from Moscow. The people were repressed, terrorized, made to spy on each other. It was very difficult to raise children. What do you say when your child is made to join the Young Pioneer movement, taken out on the streets to wave little red flags when Comrade Molotov visits from Moscow? When at school, they try to turn your daughter against you, get her to act as a stool pigeon? Let alone having to stand in line every day for even the most basic foodstuffs, bread and milk.

The discontent of the Hungarian people with their Communist masters finally boiled over in October of 1956, and we pushed the tanks and armies of the occupying forces out of Budapest for nine days. A democratic government of the people, by the people and for the people was formed under Imre Nagy, a more tolerant and liberal Communist leader, and there was great hope that American and other western forces would intervene to keep Hungary free and democratic.

But this was not to be. When Soviet planes started to bomb Budapest and the Red Army rolled back into Hungary with hundreds of tanks and thousands of well-armed soldiers, many people, seeking the freedom they knew would be denied them once again, packed their bags and fled across Hungary's western border. To Austria.

I too, insisted on going. Kálmán was more hesitant, more afraid. It was very dangerous, I knew, but I had had enough of oppression and terror, of misery and poverty. I was determined and when Kálmán pointed out that many would-be-escapees were being shot at the border or brought back and put in prison, I told him that I would rather we all died together trying to be free, then live under this régime of terror.

Kálmán knew I would not let him have any peace until we tried, so he relented.

I heard from friends—it was all just rumor and hearsay during the chaotic days of the Revolution—that some trains going west did not stop at the frontier. I persuaded Kálmán that we should get on one of those trains. So early one morning in December 1956—it was already late in the game and some stretches of the border were closed or more heavily patrolled—we took a train for Győr, where we had to wait for a small two-wagon local train. I wanted desperately to call my parents, but this would have delayed us and upset them very much. Also, we had learned that telephones were just not to be trusted.

We got on the local train and tried not to look conspicuous, but it seemed as if all the other passengers had the same thing in mind. After several hours of waiting, the engine gathered steam and we headed towards the border. We stopped in many villages and some people did get off, so there were fewer and fewer people in our wagon. Finally, after traveling for three or four hours—I don't remember exactly—the train stopped again and the engine driver came back and announced he was not able to plow through the frontier as he had promised. He had a family in Eastern Hungary and they would suffer reprisals. But, he told us, a good friend of his lived in this village and he would lead us across the border to Austria on foot. He gave us the friend's address and we followed the few remaining passengers from the two wagons to a ramshackle house. What else could we do?

The friend told us all to wait in the chicken coop in the back yard. It was muddy and cold, so it was difficult to find a place to sit and be comfortable. Once darkness had fallen, he came out from his hut and told us to follow him.

We marched side by side, I holding Klári's hand and Kálmán, little Péter's.

Just as we reached the outskirts of the village, out from behind houses on either side, in the darkness in front of and behind us, stepped several men with machine guns pointed at us. 'Hands up, or we shoot,' their leader said. He identified himself and his troop as the AVO, the dreaded secret police.

One man at the back of our group started to run; he was shot, left to bleed to death in the mud of the country road. A truck appeared from nowhere and we were told to climb in the back. As I clambered up with Kálmán's help, I saw the AVO leader hand our guide a wad of money. Payment for leading the poor, delusional suckers wanting to escape the socialist paradise of Hungary right into their hands. We and the other passengers on the train had fallen into a trap set by the secret police, starting with the train conductor.

As the truck sped away, I heard a lone voice strike up the plaintiff words of the Hungarian national anthem. We all joined in, with tears in our eyes.

The truck drove us through the night to Szombathely, a town near Hungary's border with Austria. Here, we were 'processed' and incarcerated—not in jail, because the prisons were already full with would-be escapees—but in the school gym. The next day, a soldier accompanied us to the station and told us to take a train back to Budapest and not to try anything foolish again. If we did, he told us, Kálmán would be executed in front of his family.

I was not ready to go back to Budapest though. We got off in Győr and went to my brother's place. His wife, Mária, told us about the sons of a former cleaning woman, who were successfully taking people across the border at Kopháza, another small border village. It was in the early hours of the morning that I finally let Kálmán go to sleep—but only once he had agreed to try to escape one more time through Kopháza.

We said our goodbyes the next morning and got on the train again, arriving in the village after dark. The two brothers lived up to their reputation. After feeding us and making sure we had enough warm clothes, they led us on foot over frozen fields and through dense and snowy forests to the edge of the cleared strip of land that was the border between Austria and Hungary. As flares intermittently lit up the frontier, they pointed out a safe path through the mine-studded field—'Run to that big stone, turn right fifty meters to that tree, then head for the little wooden bridge. Once you're across, you're in Austria.'

And that's what we did, Kálmán and I each tugging a child by the hand. I lost a shoe with some gold coins in it as I ran through the deep snow to beat the next flare, but we made it across the bridge and kept running, until from behind a haystack, two flashlights froze us in our tracks—and we heard '*Willkommen in Österreich*' in the singing accent of Burgenland. Even though they were in German, they were the most beautiful sounding words I had ever heard. We were led by two Austrian peasants into Deutschkreutz, where other refugees were already installed in the school gym. We were given warm soup and blankets to curl up with on the floor.

The children slept, but Kálmán and I went for a walk in the dark village, relishing our freedom. We walked to the eastern outskirts of Deutschkreutz, and under the stars and the periodic illumination of the flares, we looked back on the land we had called home for so many years and where we had suffered so much. With tears in our eyes, we said our good-byes and made our peace with leaving. From that moment on, we would only look forward to building a new life for ourselves and our children.

The very next day, I called Uncle Alfréd—a distant Viennese relation by marriage—and he sent his chauffeur to pick us up.

It was hard to believe but we had made it. We had nothing, except each other, but we were happy. And free."

Chapter 23

It was snowing again as Greg made his way down Argentinierstrasse toward Karlsplatz, the Ring and his hotel. He was now adept at saying "*Grüss Gott*" to the doorman, as he rushed through the etched glass doors of the Sacher.

Greg was standing at the bank of elevators, when he felt a tug on his right arm.

"Mr. Martens, this way. Quickly!" It was Crabbe. "You're late." He grabbed Greg by the arm and pulled him toward a corridor leading to the Marble Hall.

Greg looked at his watch. Four seventeen—he was supposed to be on stage speaking about the American novel this very moment. With everything that was happening, he had completely forgotten.

"We've already had to juggle several speakers. Mr. Martens, you must go on as soon as Mrs. Whipplestock finishes giving her comparative *tour d'horizon* of recent Pulitzer and Booker Prize winners."

Crabbe gently opened one wing of the French double doors and ushered Greg into the ornate *salle*, pointing him to an empty armchair in the front. Two of the other seats were filled with professorial types: one, tall and slender with an elongated head, and thick, black-framed glasses, the other, short and fat, with a balding pate. The tall one smiled and nodded at Greg as if he knew him, while the fat one dabbed his sweaty face with his handkerchief. Crabbe plunked himself down with a sigh of exasperation in one of the other empty chairs.

Mrs. Whipplestock finally relinquished the podium, by which time Greg had hurriedly assembled some thoughts on emerging trends in the American novel. He felt a sudden pang of guilt during Crabbe's flattering introduction of the other G. Martens, but soon got over it as he stood up and made his way over to the podium. Fortunately, he had given a similar lecture at the City College of New York six months earlier. But with all the turmoil Adam had brought into his life, he had trouble concentrating. In fact, for a moment, he lost his train of thought when he saw Anne enter the room, flash him a smile and stand in the back of the hall.

Greg got through the speech in record time and looked at his watch as Crabbe opened the floor to questions. There was a painful moment or two before finally a distinguished looking matron in the front row flashed a hand and cleared her throat.

"Frau von Hitzinger," Crabbe eagerly responded, "please ..."

"I have not read any of your books, Mr. Martens, I suspect they are too modern for me. But could you please tell us which writer has been the biggest influence on you?" She had an upper crust Austrian accent.

Greg hesitated, feigning deep thought. "Parker," he blurted out, "yes, Parker."

Crabbe gave him a puzzled look, scratched his head.

"Dorothy Parker? The poet and satirist? Yes, yes, I see." Crabbe was not quite satisfied though. "But I would have said your books are more influenced by ..."

"No, no. Robert Parker. A superb modern American author."

Greg could see many in the audience avidly taking notes. One man with horn-rimmed glasses in the front yelled out, "You don't mean Robert Parker, the wine critic? I didn't know he writes fiction."

"No, no, Parker, the crime novelist. I highly recommend him."

"Mr. Martens, perhaps you are joking," Crabbe was not prepared to let it go. "Is there anyone else who was a great influence? Like Hemingway or Fitzgerald?"

Greg was getting annoyed with Crabbe's self-importance, and even though he knew that financially he was at the weasel's mercy, he fought back.

"Have you ever read any Parker, Mr. Crabbe?"

"Well, I can't say I have."

"Then you don't know what you are talking about. Next question please."

Anne, standing in the back, was on the verge of laughter. Sensing that Greg could use some help, she shot her hand up.

"Yes, the lady in the back."

"Mr. Martens, thank you for that excellent overview," Anne said with an elfin grin. "Would you be prepared to share with us whether you are working on a new book?"

"But of course."

"May I ask what the title is?"

"Working title. *Twisted Reasons.*"

"Thank you." Anne flashed him another of her radiant smiles. "Not *Nuclear Heist?*"

"No."

An arm went up, over in the far back corner. Crabbe nodded to a large man, with a thick neck, flaming red hair and a freckled, but very white complexion. The man stood to ask his question.

"Mr. Martens, talking about twisted reasons, will you tell us what brought you here? Greg Martens, that is, and why are you impersonating Gareth Martens? How can you rationalize deceiving this serious Viennese literary audience?"

The question was greeted by a rustle among the conference participants as everyone craned their necks to see who had asked it. A huge, balding man in the front wearing a Tyrolean jacket several sizes too small, beer belly bulging over a belt pulled too tight, jumped up and wagged his finger at Greg, shouting, "What does he mean? You are not Gareth Martens?"

Above the din, Crabbe tried to gain control. "Please, please …"

Greg was too stunned to answer. Who was this guy with the bright red hair? He gave the man a penetrating look, glanced at his watch once more and decided it was time to leave.

"I'm very sorry, ladies and gentlemen, but I have an urgent matter to attend to. I will be pleased to answer any other questions by email. Mr. Crabbe will be kind enough to circulate my address in the conference notes. Thank you for your attention."

Leaving the chaos in the room and a speechless Crabbe behind, Greg bolted through the double doors and made his way toward the elevators as rapidly as he could.

Chapter 24

As soon as Greg flipped on the light switch, he saw that something was wrong. He remembered how he had left his belongings in his suitcase, which was still sitting open in the corner on the luggage rack. Messy, he had to admit, but his things were now in a different state of disorder. This was one of the qualities that had led to the break-up of his marriage; he always saw order in chaos. Laurie could never understand this and she certainly did not tolerate chaos.

Greg looked around the room. The suit he had brought for the conference (now superfluous) was hanging in the open closet, laundry thrown into a corner of the room, his briefcase with the first unsatisfactory notes for his next book, plus jottings on his grandparents, the wash kit in the bathroom, his ear plugs by the bedside, the crumpled letter from Hetzel ... Someone had gone through his things. And not just the chambermaid. This had been a meticulous search by a professional.

Fortunately, he knew there was nothing that would be of interest, nothing to steal, whether the searchers were Interpol, Austrian police, CIA, FSB, Russian mafia, terrorists or just plain burglars. The crumpled note maybe, with Hetzel's number and Julia's name and work place written on it, but that was still there on the night table. Anyone other than Hetzel would likely have been interested in the information on it.

Was it then Hetzel or someone linked to him who did the search? They did, after all, try to get him to leave Vienna.

Of course, the laptop! Yes, whoever it was must have been looking for Adam's laptop.

*****

A knock on the door. Since he had not requested room service, Greg's instinct was to remain silent and not open it. It may be the thugs who had searched his room, coming back.

Greg could not keep himself though, from looking through the peephole. Anne Rossiter. With the embarrassment of being found out and the shock of finding his room in disorder, he had forgotten that she was downstairs at the Conference.

Greg opened the door just as Anne was turning to walk back toward the elevators.

"Mr. Martens, I was sure you were here." Greg found Anne's British boarding school accent appealing. "I was concerned about you. Just about to get housekeeping to open up."

"How nice. But if you worry about me so much, you must call me Greg. It's about time. And do come in."

Greg opened the door wide to let Anne step inside.

"I liked your speech. And your answers. I remember seeing some Robert Parker crime novels on my brother's shelf. You certainly confounded them with that one though. Rather cheeky of you!" Anne said with a little laugh and a saucy look. "Too bad about …"

"By the way, Anne," Greg interrupted, not wanting to talk about the red-headed man's question, "I must thank you for not making more of a mess when you searched in here." Greg was still not sure it wasn't she who had gone through his things earlier in the day.

"Mr. … Greg. I did not search your room. I've not been in here before."

"Then who?"

"I don't know. Maybe the people who killed Adam Kallay. This is a dangerous affair. You should not be meddling in police work."

"He was my friend."

"The killers will know that. It's too dangerous for you here. For any friend of Adam. Now that you've finished your talk, you should go home to the U.S. Get out of Vienna. There are too many people here connected to the Russian mafia and terrorist groups. You are not safe." Even as she said it, Anne sensed that maybe this was not the right approach. She'd been too direct and needed to use more guile if she was going to persuade this man that he was in danger.

Greg had been on the verge of telling Anne that he and Julia had discovered Adam's plans to go to Chelyabinsk, but he didn't like her telling him he should go home.

"I am leaving. The day after tomorrow." Greg's tone was dismissive. He was telling the truth, but not the whole truth. He did not want Anne to know where he was going.

"Good. I'm glad," Anne said. But as she looked around, she knew she really did not want him to leave. She was starting to like this friend of Adam. "Did anything go missing? I'll come back later to take fingerprints. So please touch only what you need to."

Greg was about to show Anne out the door, but regretted being so curt to her. He had a sudden inspiration. "Are you doing anything tonight? I have two tickets to the opera. *Don Carlos*. At the Staatsoper. Would you like to come with me?"

"I'd love to," Anne was taken aback by the question, but did not hesitate with an answer. Even as she accepted, she remembered her intention to join Haffner and the Austrian police at the Revuebar. However, she so loved opera, had grown up with it in England, and never got the chance to go here in Vienna. And maybe she would be able to find out more from Greg about this case.

"The performance starts at seven. It's now five twenty. Does that give you enough time? I'll reserve for dinner somewhere after."

"Wonderful. I'd better get going then. And thank you!" There was no way back now.

Chapter 25

Greg was a few minutes early, but did not have to wait long on the steps of the opera house before Anne appeared. At the coat check, he helped Anne peel off her cape. What emerged from the cocoon was a ravishing woman dressed in a low-cut, simple black cocktail dress that sheathed the curves of her lithe body. A single string of pearls around the alabaster neck looped down toward a tantalizing cleavage, matching earrings highlighted by raven-black hair.

In their parterre row seven seats, they snuggled close, with just enough time to glance together at the English synopsis in the back of the program. Greg could not help letting his eyes stray down along the pearls before the lights dimmed and Ricardo Muti came into the pit amid enthusiastic applause. The performance was riveting: the singers were all first class, but most of all Netrebko, the Russian diva, the stage settings were like Brueghel paintings, Verdi's music soaring with brilliant tonality. Despite the fact that *Don Carlos* was his favorite opera, Greg did steal the odd sideways glance at Anne, finding it hard to believe that he, Greg Martens, was sitting in the celebrated Wiener Staatsoper with this stunning woman.

*****

It was not until they were finishing their dessert course at Meinl am Graben— he, a poppy seed chocolate volcano, she a variation on the classical Viennese *Kaiserschmarrn mit Zwetschkenröster*—that their conversation turned to

99

business.

"You know, I had no idea," Anne said, dipping a spoonful of the powder-sugared scrambled soufflé into a bowl of rich plum compote, "that your friend Adam kept such bad company."

"What do you mean?" Greg was distracted by desire as Anne licked the last drops of the delicious plum sauce from her spoon.

"No, I don't mean you," Anne laughed, innocently putting her hand on his. "I mean the two friends who found him and reported his death." She was fishing, but this was the professional side.

"You mean Hetzel? And that Russian?" Greg, above all, did not want her to move her hand away.

"Yes. We've started to investigate them. At least Hetzel. We have nothing on the Russian, Sergei Sidorov. A total blank."

"What about Hetzel?"

"A pretty nasty guy. He's buying the Revuebar Rasputin."

"What?"

"Why, we don't know. Maybe to launder some ill-gotten gains or as a front for another business. The Austrian police think for the sex trade. Trafficking women."

"That's where … Never mind." Greg caught himself just in time, realizing he had not told Anne about Julia.

"Don't tell me you've been there!" Anne's teasing look pierced right through him. As she said this, she remembered that she was supposed to be at the Revuebar that very moment with the police raid.

"Yes, last night." Greg didn't want to lie. "Hetzel had asked me to come. He introduced me to a Russian friend of Adam's."

"Sidorov?" Anne perked up.

"No, no. His name was Polyakov. Come to think of it, he was Sergei too." It was when he said this that he remembered the email from Polyakov saying that he would see Adam on the afternoon he died. "In fact, could they be one and the same?"

"Hmm. Maybe that's why I haven't been able to find anything on Sergei Sidorov. If Sidorov is an alias, that is. Do you remember what he looked like?"

Greg racked his brains to try and visualize the man. Short, stocky, muscular, balding, square jaw—were all the physical characteristics he could remember. Anne made note of them, intending to check out Sergei Polyakov tomorrow.

"How the hell did Adam get involved with these characters?" Greg asked.

"We're asking the same question. They were not in the picture until recently, as far as we know."

"Well, he talked about infiltrating the gang of thieves, didn't he? Could Hetzel and the Russian—or Russians—be part of it?"

"Yes, that is possible. We did discuss a plan to catch them the morning he died, but we were going to see what his friend Fazkov had to say. A bit puzzling though, that he would talk to me about his idea and then get killed that very day. He must have just gone ahead alone. Very dangerous."

"Adam had a penchant for wanting to do flashy things single-handedly. He loved being the hero."

"Unless he got into some kind of a jam and couldn't contact me," Anne continued to think out aloud. "Or perhaps he had already set his mind to do it before he talked to me."

"So you think they killed Adam because they somehow found out he was double crossing them?"

"That is certainly one scenario."

Greg finished the last sip of his 1966 Tokay Aszu Six Puttonyos and signaled the waiter to bring the bill. He felt guilty about hiding the fact that Adam had booked tickets to Chelyabinsk just before he was killed, the existence of Julia and his own impending trip. But he knew that if he did tell, Julia could be in trouble and Anne would prevent him from going. He was glad to have possibly helped her identify the Russian 'friend'.

"Well, we get the results of the DNA tests tomorrow. Late afternoon. That should be definitive proof that the body was Adam."

"How so?"

"We took samples from his apartment. You know, dead skin, the usual detritus," Anne said. "We're comparing them to tissue taken from the body before it was cremated."

"Good."

"And the Austrian police are hoping to pick Hetzel up tonight at the Revuebar. In fact, I was going with them until you tempted me away from my work with this delightful evening." She gave him a seductive look and added, "Thank you, Greg."

The waiter brought the bill over and Anne stood up as the *garçon*

101

maneuvered to pull the chair out from under her.

"Will you excuse me for a moment? Where are the restrooms please?"

The waiter led Anne off and Greg studied the check. But his mind was elsewhere. Despite what he had said about Adam's hero complex, it did not make sense to him that he would attempt to catch the thieves without support from Anne and Interpol. Or whomever. Too dangerous, too reckless even for Adam. Suicidal. Perhaps he did get into some trouble, could not contact her and then could no longer back out.

Greg put his Visa card down, not sure whether the bill would take him over the limit. He looked out the window, down the well-lit Graben, busy despite the hour, the glistening Christmas chandeliers still strung across the wide street creating a festive atmosphere, down the pedestrian way toward the Baroque statue of the Trinity, erected in the Middle Ages to thank God for the end of the plague. *What statue will the survivors erect, and to thank whom, after a nuclear terrorist calamity?* Greg wondered.

The waiter took the card and Greg's eyes followed him. He froze. Several tables away he thought he recognized a familiar balding head and square jaw nodding and talking to another dark-suited man. He racked his brain for a moment, but did not have to go far in the past to determine that the man resembled Polyakov. He wasn't absolutely sure it was he—but if it was, was it chance, or was it necessity that he was there? Was Polyakov watching him, or was Anne the target?

The waiter came back with the card at the same time Anne did. Greg signed quickly, stood up and said, "Shall we?" He touched her on the elbow as they headed towards the coat check and added, "I'll get the maitre d' to call a cab."

"No need to take me home," Anne said, but she wasn't sure that she wanted the evening to end.

"I insist. And I'd like to continue our discussion."

*****

It was when the cab turned off the Ring and onto Porzellangasse that Anne made up her mind.

"Would you like to come up for a nightcap?" She asked, sensing that she would not be refused. Anne knew as she posed the question that Greg would see through the words, but it had been well over a year since she had sex. And that had been a disastrous experience. Thinking of which always led her to memories of the horrid night at Adam's after the IAEA ball.

She really liked Greg, with his casual, somewhat standoffish, but endearing and intelligent approach. He had a sense of humor, but seemed to be serious about the right things. He was good looking and fit. And she could tell that he was attracted to her. There was also the added benefit that she would never have to see him again since he was going back to America. There would be no complications, like the last time with that colleague. A work justification to have him up also entered her mind: she still needed to pursue what he knew about Hetzel, Sidorov/Polyakov, and of course, that blond. Anne felt that she had nothing to lose.

*****

The first passionate kiss occurred just inside the door after Greg helped Anne pull the cape from her shoulders. He simply dropped the garment to the floor and continued into a hot embrace, finding her lips. They shed their clothes on the way to the bedroom, Anne leading Greg by the hand. By the time they reached the bed, Anne's legs were wrapped around his waist and Greg was inside her, very near to bursting point. Greg sat down on the edge of the bed with Anne on his lap, mouths, lips, tongues interlocked, both regaling themselves in the intoxicating sensation of flesh touching flesh.

To Greg's surprise, it was Anne who came first. But he was not far behind, coming just as her convulsions tapered off. They stayed like that, her moist breasts brushing his chest, her head on his shoulder, gasping for air. So that they could start again.

And they did. But this time, less desperately, more in harmony, their two selves undulating together. Again they came, Greg surprised that he could so soon after the first time. He had never experienced love making of this intensity, of this depth, before in his life. Not with Laurie, not with anybody.

Nor had Anne. And it had come to her so suddenly.

*****

They slept in each other's arms for a while and when they woke, started to make love again.

Greg, bending to kiss Anne's closed eyes, was suddenly shocked to feel the touch of a clammy hand on his shoulder. Turning around in the half-darkness of Anne's bedroom, he thought he recognized the interloper with his trademark smile and vivacious eyes.

"Adam?" Was his mind playing tricks or was it really him? Was his friend there in the room, looming over him in the darkness? Impossible!

Greg heard an infernal laugh emanate from the phantom's being. Or thought he did.

He twisted to grab hold of the apparition, but it was an awkward move since he was still inside Anne. Adam—if it was he—was already out of the bedroom and in the hall, as Greg rose to give chase. He looked out along the corridor, but by then, the specter was long gone.

*****

"What was that all about? Who was that? Should I call the police?" Anne, still in a post-coital trance, tried to rev up her professional self.

"I thought it was Adam. Am I going crazy?" Was he just being haunted by the experience with Laurie in college? "I felt him touch me." Greg continued, confused, trying to relive the scene. But the touch had been very, very light and he was no longer absolutely sure it was real.

"You're seeing ghosts." Anne, choosing not to believe Greg, pulled him back on top of her and they kissed hungrily.

"It must have just been a bad dream," Greg said, trying to convince himself.

"Adam's dead, Greg. You have to come to terms with it." Anne caressed Greg's head and rested it between her breasts.

*****

Anne woke when dawn started to creep in through the crack in the curtains, glanced at the clock by the bed and cuddled up to Greg. What a strange, wonderful feeling to wake up beside someone again.

While Anne was in the shower, Greg put his white shirt and suit back on, grabbed the glasses and empty wine bottle from the night before and made his way to the kitchen. He figured out how to start the Illy coffee machine and was already sipping a steaming cup when Anne came out of the bathroom.

"Am I right in thinking that you dreamt you saw Adam? In the room?" Anne asked as Greg handed her a mug of coffee.

"Yes. It was a pretty vivid dream. He once did that to me with Laurie, my

104

wife, way back when. Maybe that still haunts me."

"That's really weird."

"Yeah."

"I'm afraid I have a very busy day," Anne said, immediately regretting the words because they sounded like an excuse, "but call me. I'd love to meet up later." That did not sound very sincere either. *God, that's not how I want to leave it.*

Greg moved closer and kissed her again. "I will."

"But you're off tomorrow," Anne said playing with the button on his shirt.

"Yes. But we'll figure out something."

Anne turned away saying, "I've got to run. Just pull the door closed." She quickly put her coat on and left the apartment before Greg could see the tears in her eyes. Anne had thought she would be fine never to see him again.

It was only in the elevator that Anne remembered that she had wanted to ask Greg those questions about Hetzel, Sidorov/Polyakov and that blond, and remind him to be careful. But somehow, going back would spoil the magic of what they had had and she definitely wanted to keep that feeling alive in her mind and her body.

Greg stood there for a moment longer in Anne's kitchen, finishing his coffee. He did not want to let Anne go, but he was sure that this was not the last time he would see her.

Chapter 26

Although it was a bitterly cold February morning and Greg was physically exhausted after the wild but wonderful night with Anne, he decided to walk back to the Sacher. The bracing walk would steady the turmoil in both his brain and stomach.

What a day yesterday had been. First, the decision to take off to Russia to try and figure out Adam's murder and now—since his ghost-like apparition—the disturbing questions surrounding his death. Then there was the embarrassment of being outed as a phony in front of a Viennese literary audience, but there had also been two beautiful women, one of which had given him the best evening of his life.

What puzzled Greg most though was Adam. Had he come back from the dead? Had he been alive all this time or was it really just Greg's alcohol-soaked brain playing tricks with him?

The DNA test. That will prove he is dead—or possibly alive—once and for all.

*****

That episode with his ex-wife, the one he had mentioned to Anne. It did not fill him with pride, but it did symbolize how close Adam and he once had been. And how manipulative Adam could be with his friends. With everything. How self-centered. That was his nature and you had to love him in spite of it.

It happened back in college, in Dunster House, where he and Adam shared a suite, each with his own bedroom, a common living room and bathroom. Greg had been seeing Laurie for several months by then and they were keenly attracted to each other. Perhaps even in love, or so they thought then. Certainly, the sex was great. As this relationship developed, he confided his feelings and the details of the budding romance to his best friend. And, as men do, he bragged about the sex.

The event in question took place the day when both Laurie and he finished their first term exams and before they went home for spring break. Greg had taken Laurie to Chez Henri for dinner and had left a bottle of bubbly in the fridge to celebrate. They came home—both already a little tipsy—but Greg grabbed the champagne and two chilled flutes and took them into his bedroom while Laurie went to the bathroom. They were sleeping together fairly regularly by then in the queen-sized bed Greg had acquired from the previous inhabitant of the room. They had their routine, so he dimmed the light and put on a Beatles disc, poured two glasses, undressed and climbed between the sheets to wait for Laurie. She came in, closed the door, took her panties off and slid in beside him. He loved to feel her nakedness next to him; he caressed her and she him. She took him in her mouth, licked his penis with her tongue. This always brought him close to release. But soon he was inside her and their bodies moved in harmony.

Just as Greg was spent and ready to roll off Laurie, he felt a firm hand on his shoulder. There was Adam, grinning, naked and hard, climbing onto the bed beside him, gently pushing him aside. He heard Adam say, "My turn", as he pulled out of Laurie.

Why did he not object? He didn't, but instead somehow ceded her to his best friend. How drunk had he been? And Laurie? He had been a little excited by it. Laurie was, too. She started to protest, but clearly, was still aroused. Maybe even more than with him. Greg looked at the two entwined bodies beside him, heard them embrace, kiss, their moans increasingly intense until Laurie reached her climax and within seconds, Adam too. Almost at once, Adam rolled off to the other side and without a word, reached across the breathless Laurie, pulled Greg's face over to his and gave him a powerful, long and deep kiss on the mouth. Before Greg could react in any way, Adam jumped off the bed and left the room with a huge grin on his face.

Many times afterwards, Greg had revisited the confusion of that night.

Adam had never attempted to repeat the scene. It had not been mentioned again. Until now. Greg had tried to forget it, rationalize it as the times, youth, tipsiness ... He had shared everything else with his best friend, so why not the woman he loved?

Maybe that had been it, all the rottenness in the marriage stemmed from that one threesome. Maybe it was that event that had jinxed his life with Laurie.

Was that the hand of Adam, so nonchalantly controlling his friend's life? Was he at it again?

*****

If Adam really was alive, what was he doing in Anne's bedroom? *Was he playing me again or crying out for help? Or both?* So much the more reason to go to Chelyabinsk, to go after him, confront him with it, aid him in catching the thieves.

*****

And then he thought of Anne. He had spent the best night of his life with her. It was not just the delicious pleasure of lovemaking, but the joy of simply being with her. Catching sideways glimpses of her in the opera, returning her seductive looks as she licked the dessert from her spoon at Meinl, watching her compact, perfect nakedness recede toward the kitchen through the doorframe, feeling the delicate pressure of her fingers rest on his sternum. Was this love? He could not remember this searing intensity with Laurie.

But this could not work. He was leaving tomorrow. Her life was here with Interpol, his back in New York, where he had ...what? A career as a mediocre writer? Why couldn't it work?

*****

Was Adam alive and trying to catch the thieves by himself? In which case, he needed support. Maybe that's why the apparition ...

If he was not killed in the accident, did he feign his death with the help of Hetzel and that Russian? Maybe Adam had come up with the idea of faking his death as a ploy to convince the bad guys—if indeed Hetzel and the Russian were involved in the uranium heist—that he was with them and also give them the illusion of gaining time for them to carry it off.

But who was the body then?

Had Adam left other clues for him? Hetzel, leading him to Julia, Julia to the laptop, the reservations. Were these clues that he was alive and gone to unmask the thieves? Had he planned to bring his friend along as a back-up to catch the bad guys, if he needed help at all? Or was he imagining all this?

Adam had told Anne about the stolen nuclear material and discussed his idea for ensnaring the crooks with her in order to prepare her. Knowing that Greg was coming right around then, he had probably devised a plan that gave him a back-up without telegraphing it to the thieves and that would, at the same time, endanger as few people as possible.

Or was this just what he wanted to believe?

Had Adam also had a hand in engineering he and Anne getting together? The feigned death would be a stroke of genius! He had been sure that Anne, the policewoman, would want to meet anyone who came to the morgue and that his friend would do so. Adam had arranged their meeting so that Greg could bring her and Interpol along when he really needed help in catching the thieves. That would explain why he had just gone ahead with his plans without formalizing them with Anne—which, indeed, might have put him and her in greater danger. Adam knew he could rely on his old friend.

Although Greg could interpret much of what had happened during the last few days as clues left by Adam, were they really clues? Or just Greg's mind shaping reality? He was no longer sure.

*****

Greg was still chewing on these thoughts, as he turned left behind the opera and in through the swinging doors of the Sacher. He rushed through the lobby, hoping none of the patrons from the conference were there to recognize him. Up the elevators, into the room—which, he quickly ascertained, had not been searched again. He went straight to the telephone and dialed Anne's number, wanting to share his new insights with her. He was sure now that Adam was indeed alive but had gone underground and had a masterful plan to catch the crooks.

Anne did not pick up.

Greg ruffled the bed in exasperation to make it look like he had slept there, but afterwards, wondered why. For the chambermaid? He showered, shaved and dressed in black cords, a navy cashmere sweater and overcoat, and was out the door again within ten minutes.

Chapter 27

Turning onto the Ring, Greg thought of his grandmother. The love she had for his grandfather, then Kálmán and her two children. For him and his sister.

Whatever happened to his grandfather, the love of her life?

*****

"I did try to find out where he was taken.

The very next day after he was led away, I put on my best dress, summoned all my courage and went to the Andrássy út headquarters of the AVO in Pest to inquire.

Greg, this was an awful, notorious building in Budapest. Before the Communist secret police took it over, it had been the headquarters of the Gestapo in Hungary. Many people were tortured in its basement, many poor souls died there. Under both regimes. I had hoped—prayed—never to have to set foot in its dark halls.

I waited five hours before I was led into a small office by a stern looking woman. A ridiculous little jerk of a corporal in a blue uniform took down the details about your grandfather and told me to come back the next day. I did and waited many hours again, only to be told by the same slimy policeman that they knew nothing about my husband. They had no record of arresting him. No operatives had been sent to our address. It was as if your grandfather did not exist, his abduction had never happened. And, by the way, the corporal told me

I had better stop coming and wasting his time or else I would end up in the basement. The creep laughed at his own sick joke as I rushed out of his cubicle and the building, desperate to breathe the air outside.

I tried to get some information through my father, Apa, but despite his many contacts and several attempts, he was not able to find out anything either. The answer was always that they knew nothing; there was nothing in their files on my husband.

Many years later, after the Németh government in Hungary helped raise the Iron Curtain for good in 1989, allowing busloads of tourists from East Germany to escape along the Austro-Hungarian border, the people who had suffered under the Stalinist regimes throughout most of Eastern Europe were allowed access to secret police files. My dear Greg, I hoped that the time had come and I would be able to learn something of what had happened to your grandfather.

I hired a lawyer in the early nineties, when there was much hope that Hungary would confront its dark past. The son of Ilona Kovács, my best friend, back in Budapest, whose father had also disappeared. But nothing. Hungary refused to open its confidential police files and much incriminating evidence was destroyed by the ex-Communists who still controlled the organs of the state.

It was not until 2004 that limited access to secret police archives was permitted. I was already about to turn eighty, but I finally had hope that I would find out what had happened to my love. I needed to find peace before I died. Against my better judgment, I broke my vow never to go back to Hungary and booked a flight to Budapest, to look at the archives and to pay my respect at Apa's and Mama's grave. I owed it to them, since I never saw them again after Kálmán and I escaped, and took their grandchildren far away. They died from grief before Hungarians from the wrong background were allowed passports to visit the West.

The morning after I arrived, I took a short taxi ride from the Méridien—another prison that was used by the secret police, which has since been converted into a luxury hotel—to the former headquarters of the AVO. Now the building houses the Museum of Terror. Greg, you will probably go there when you go to Budapest to see, but I just cannot imagine why they made such a museum. There was enough terror in our lives without needing to have exhibitions of it.

Here they directed me to the archives.

They made me fill out a form to tell them whose files I wanted to see, my relationship to the person, his last known address and his personal identification number. It was very, very humiliating. I had to show my passport and I was ushered into a large room with high ceilings, where they told me to sit and wait. There were others at tables, some with stacks of files in front of them, some just staring at a single sheet beside a slim manila folder.

After twenty minutes of waiting, the clerk came back and told me the same story—that she was sorry, but there was nothing on my husband—any information must have been lost or destroyed, if ever there was anything.

There was, though, a thin file on me, the woman told me. 'Would I like to see that?' she asked, with a pointed look.

I did not grace her with an answer but just got up and stormed out of the building.

Still that morning, I took a taxi to the Németvölgyi cemetery and told the cab to wait while I found my grandparents' tomb, where Apa's and Mama's remains had been added. I laid some flowers and then went straight to the airport to catch a flight back to the U.S.

I regretted breaking my vow not to go back to the country of my youth.

One can never go back. Remember that, Greg."

Chapter 28

On his way through the Stadtpark, Greg wondered whether he should tell Julia about Adam's apparition. He decided not to, because he felt embarrassed about the circumstances. Also, it all sounded so surreal, so unbelievable, that she would doubt his sanity.

When he turned into Jaurèsgasse, Julia was already there in front of Adam's building, with her back towards him, shuffling from foot to foot for warmth. Greg slid his arm under hers and said, "Have you been waiting long?"

"No, but we better get going. There will be a line."

When they arrived at the Consular Section, down the road from the palatial building of the main Russian Embassy, there was indeed a long queue. But Julia went right up and talked to the security guard, who opened the heavy door for them. She led the way straight to a desk in the middle and asked for her friend. An obese *mamushka* with dyed red hair told them to sit down and wait. Julia picked up a form and told Greg to fill it out.

Twenty-five minutes later, a chestnut-haired, pleasant-looking woman came through a door on one side of the waiting room. She headed straight for Julia, greeted her and smiled at Greg, whom Julia introduced. They talked quickly, but Greg understood the gist of what was said. Julia pleaded with her as a special favor to get a visa immediately and also permission for her friend to go to Ozersk to take some medicine to her sick mother. She handed the woman the form and passport, a hundred and twenty Euros and two photos that

Greg had stopped to take in the booth in the Opernpassage the day before. The woman said something very rapidly to Julia and disappeared.

"Okay. My friend said she will try and have the visa and the permit ready for this afternoon. I'll come by and pick it up and bring it to you this evening."

*****

Outside, the wind was fierce and they pulled their coat collars up around their necks. As they exhaled, their breath condensed in the cold air.

"Julia, do you have time for a coffee? I haven't had breakfast yet. Then perhaps we could pick up the tickets. I wasn't able to yesterday."

"Sure. Let's go to the Café Schwarzenberg. That's near the travel agency."

Julia's friend at the agency representing Aeroflot had the ticket ready—to Chelyabinsk via Moscow, for the next day—so it wasn't long before they settled at a table. Greg ordered a macchiato, boiled egg and croissant, Julia a *mélange*. When he turned, Greg could see the statue of Prince Karl zu Schwarzenberg, the general who had twice beaten Napoleon. Down at the other end of the square was the monument to the unknown Soviet soldiers who had died during the Second World War to 'liberate' Austria from the Nazis— and who then subjugated a large part of it for ten years.

"How was the opera last night?" Julia asked, smiling at him over her coffee.

"Wonderful. Sorry you missed it." In fact, Greg was not sorry. Although he wondered for a moment how things would have turned out if Julia had been his date.

"How was work?" Greg wanted to change the subject.

"Funny you ask," Julia looked down into her lap. "In the intermission, the manager asked all the girls to gather in his office. He told us that the place is being sold to a consortium. Backed by Russian money, one of the girls told me after."

"It must be Hetzel and the gang. Anne, the Interpol agent, said as much."

"*Ja.* Maybe that's what he meant. Hetzel. About it not being long."

"You cannot go back there. The man is evil."

"I have to work, Greg."

"Julia, do not go back there. Anne told me they are investigating him. Hetzel will own the place. He'll think he can do anything. Julia, go to the police. Please."

"I can't go to the police. I'm working here illegally in a strip club. If anyone can go to the police it is Hetzel. And have me deported. But don't worry, they came last night, the police. They wanted Hetzel for questioning, but he wasn't there."

"Was Polyakov there?"

"No. I didn't see him."

Greg suddenly wanted to stay in Vienna to protect Julia, but that would mean not going after his friend. He regretted not telling Anne about her because then at least she could turn to Anne. It was all becoming more confusing, more dangerous with every turn.

Chapter 29

After leaving Greg, Anne walked rapidly to her office, picking up her almond croissant on the way. She had a lot to accomplish. Her first task, she knew, would be to see what she could find out about Polyakov. Working with Greg had helped her figure that one out.

She opened the search engine. Anne was sure that the Russian was a key to solving Adam's murder and the nuclear theft. She typed his name into the boxes and waited.

A number of entries for Sergei Polyakov appeared, of which she excitedly determined three to be relevant.

I've got you now, you bastard.

The first and most recent was from Interpol's own files, and while informative, it was not very extensive. Anne committed to memory what she read:

> Polyakov, Sergei—b. 1965, Omsk, Russia. Former General in Russian Army; commanded a tank division in both the First and Second Chechen Wars. Decorated with Hero of Russia award. Accused by Chechen diaspora of cruelty, summary executions, rape, etc. Resigned commission in Second Chechen War, possibly due to injury. Chechen rebels claim

Polyakov sold Russian weapons to them during the war. Suspected of continuing arms trading with access to weapons through contacts in Russian military. Founder and CEO of MILEXCO, logistics company registered in Cyprus, thought to be a cover. Current whereabouts unknown, but reports indicate still operating in the Middle East, Europe, Russia triangle. (See also entry for MILEXCO).

The second bio was downloaded from the files of the Russian secret service, the FSB, which Anne knew would have been carefully screened and doctored. In fact, it proved to be mostly historical and laudatory, but nevertheless interesting. Anne translated it to herself as follows:

General Sergei Polyakov, born December 18, 1965, in the city of Omsk. Brave officer who led Russian forces in the First and Second Chechen Wars, decorated by President Boris Yeltsin with coveted Hero of Russia award. Injured in February 2000. Retired from the services. Brother of Colonel Boris Polyakov, Deputy Director of FSB.

If Sergei is well connected, and no doubt still protected by his brother, Anne thought to herself, no wonder he is so adept at positioning himself in modern Russia.

The CIA's files were the most scathing and the most comprehensive. However, Anne was experienced enough to know that they too could not be fully trusted, as they often incorporated information that was merely hearsay and rumor.

Sergei Polyakov, Russian arms dealer. Born in Omsk, December 1965, Polyakov resigned from the military in 2000 after a purported injury. As one of the youngest generals in the Russian Army, he was in charge of tank divisions in both the Chechen Wars and was directly responsible for much of the destruction of Grozny. Polyakov had a reputation for extreme cruelty and carrying out many executions, and was accused of torture and rape by several victims. Although President Boris Yeltsin decorated Polyakov with the Hero of Russia medal during the First Chechen War, his sudden resignation prior to Vladimir Putin's inauguration as President may have been a result of suspicions that he was engaged in selling Russian weapons to the enemy. There is some evidence that he continues arms trading activities through MILEXCO, his Cyprus-based logistics company. His brother, Boris Polyakov, exercises considerable power as Colonel and Deputy Director of the FSB. The Polyakov twins are rumored to be the illegitimate grandchildren of Lavrenti Beria, who headed up the intelligence services of the Soviet Union under Stalin. Polyakov is dangerous and any approach should be carried out with great care and preparation.

So Anne now had a picture of what she was up against: a ruthless, professional arms dealer and former soldier, with strong connections in the murky waters of the Russian elite, among the *siloviki*.

*****

MILEXCO. Anne leaned back and waited while the laptop again contacted the central Interpol files to search for information on Polyakov's logistics company. Within seconds, the computer found what she wanted.

MILEXCO, company registered in July 2000 in Liberia. Activities listed as trading, transport and logistics. Beneficial ownership not declared in documents, but founder and chief executive is known to be one Sergei Polyakov, a former Russian General decorated in the Chechen Wars. Polyakov is reputed to have sold Russian arms to the Chechens during the war, and set up MILEXCO after his decommissioning. MILEXCO is the sole owner of Air Miliberia, which owns twelve Il-76 and three Antonov-124 second-hand transport planes, as well as a number of smaller aircraft. Two other Il-76s were grounded at Sharjah International Airport earlier this year and have not been allowed to fly, pending inquiries regarding the cargoes of military equipment, including Russian- and Chinese-manufactured surface-to-air missiles, tanks, machine guns, etc. in the hold. To date, no firm answers have been received and the aircraft remain parked, fully loaded, at Sharjah.

MILEXCO is thought to be active in illicit arms transactions, as well as the trading of drugs and blood diamonds. Suspected clients include North Korea, Iran and numerous rebel and terrorist groups, such as al Qaeda and its affiliates. As a fully integrated logistics-trading empire, MILEXCO has extensive reach. Its owner and executives are secretive and highly versatile individuals who leave very few traces. The FBI, DEA, CIA and Interpol are actively seeking to question Polyakov, however, he continues to elude arrest by largely staying in countries of the former Soviet Union, Central Europe, Africa, the Middle East and Latin America, He also frequently changes aliases. Polyakov has strong contacts in the upper echelons of the Russian government and the *siloviki*. His twin brother Boris is an active Colonel and Deputy Director of the FSB.

"Whew," Anne sighed, leaning back in her chair. She would have to move very carefully, but she was now more determined than ever to solve this case and put Polyakov behind bars. But she would also have to keep an eye on Greg Martens, who, it seems, did not know how dangerous and complicated the affair, he was naively trying to investigate on his own, really was.

*****

Right around the time Greg was sipping his macchiato with Julia, Anne left her office to cross the Danube to UNO City, where Adam had worked. She was seething at the thought that it had taken the IAEA this long to grant her access to Adam's office computer and papers. It wasn't just the IAEA's fault, it was bureaucracy heaped upon bureaucracy. She first had to make a written request through Interpol to the Austrian police, who then filed an application with the IAEA. This had taken three whole days. Never mind that in the interim, sufficient nuclear material might have gotten into the wrong hands to blow not just the IAEA, but all of Vienna sky high, and contaminate half of Europe with enough radioactivity to kill millions.

Once Anne arrived in Adam's office, his assistant, a short and square, but congenial Peruvian woman helped her log in on his desktop.

"Did Mr. Kallay have any travel plans?" Anne asked, as the secretary started the computer for her.

"Yes, I booked him tickets to Chelyabinsk for the week after next and I think he was actually planning to go see his parents this week. Until the terrible accident."

"Thank you. Yes, I know." So Russia. Chelyabinsk next week. Not this week. Hmm.

She was in the 'My Documents' folder, browsing through the sub-folders: Russia, China, India, Pakistan, North Korea, Iran ... There was a file on all the countries that had atomic bombs and all that ever wanted one. Files on terrorist organizations, from the Tamil Tigers to al Qaeda to the Sons of Jesus. Files on nuclear power stations. Reactor accidents. Chernobyl, Three Mile Island, Fukushima and so on. This was going to take her weeks to go through.

Anne clicked on the 'Russia' folder and scanned a file entitled 'NPFs'— Nuclear Production Facilities—until she came to Mayak. She glanced through the various documents, but did not find anything she didn't already know. Adam had documented the disappearance of the ten pounds of highly enriched uranium in an unfinished report. Nothing about the larger amount, although the Russian physicist's name and a question mark in brackets may have indicated that he was waiting for input from Fazkov. There was a running total of the HEU and plutonium catalogued so far in the Mayak warehouses. An organization chart for Mayak, headed up by a Dr. Irena Kolchakova. No trace of the plans he had formulated with Anne. Or of any other plans.

"Could I see his emails please?"

The secretary logged in to Adam's work email address. Anne quickly glanced down, recognizing some of the names. Kolchakova. Fazkov. They were the people she knew he was dealing with at Mayak. She opened the last one from the Russian physicist, intrigued partly because he had tried to call her the day of Adam's death. It gave the itinerary for his trip to Vienna. He was supposed to have arrived around 3:40 p.m. She glanced through Fazkov's previous emails, but there was nothing about the disappearance of larger amounts of HEU. If he and Adam had communicated about the second heist, it would have been by phone, which may have been tapped.

Nothing from, or to, Polyakov or Hetzel. Another Russian name she did not know cropped up several times though: Julia Saparova. Anne opened one short message, then another. Emails to arrange meetings. Julia Saparova was clearly Adam's girlfriend.

"Do you know a Julia Saparova?" Anne asked the Peruvian woman.

"Yes, let me see," the secretary mused. "I remember the name. Mr. Kallay gave me a résumé with that name on it, to send over to Human Resources."

"By any chance, do you have a copy?" Strange that Adam was trying to get her a job at the IAEA. Maybe as a secretary?

Anne was pleased to see an address and telephone number at the top and she quickly noted both. She glanced at the rest of the two pages. This woman had stunning credentials—a Ph.D. in nuclear physics—plus, judging from the picture, she was gorgeous.

Could this be the blond Greg has been seeing? She felt a tinge of jealousy.

"Thank you. I'm finished for today. But I'll be back, if I may."

Out in the corridor, Anne flipped out her mobile to call Lieutenant Haffner. As she did so, she noticed that Greg had tried to reach her. Earlier. She remembered that she had left the phone in her jacket pocket when she was doing all the research back in the office. And in her rush to get over here, had not checked it before. She was sorry to have missed talking to Greg. Anne hesitated a moment whether to call back or not, but decided that work came first. The battery was low and she had to make the call to Haffner.

"Rudolf, hello. I need you to get a search warrant for Karolinengasse 6, Apartment 12. Can you meet me there at eighteen o'clock? That should give you plenty of time, *nicht wahr?*" She had chosen 6:00 p.m. not just to give Austrian bureaucracy enough time to issue the warrant, but also because she wanted Ms. Saparova to be there so she could question her. Anne presumed that if she worked, six or shortly thereafter, would be a good time to find her at home.

*****

Anne was deep in thought as she made her way toward her car in the covered, but open-sided parking garage adjacent to the IAEA building at UNO City. When she was just five vehicles away from her Skoda, she took out her key to unlock the doors. It was then that she heard the rapidly approaching roar of a powerful engine behind her and, as she turned, saw a big black Mercedes with tinted windows speeding towards her. It took her a second to realize that the car was not going to stop and to remember that her Glock was in the glove compartment. Interpol agents are not allowed to carry arms into UN buildings without special permission.

Anne moved quickly and just managed to throw herself between two parked vehicles as the Mercedes screeched past. Her car was the next one over, so she crept towards it on all fours behind the neighboring van. The Mercedes was turning around and accelerating in her direction just as she climbed into the Skoda and scrambled to get the glove compartment open. As the Mercedes came level, a gun barrel out the window, she rolled out the front door and under the next vehicle. As her car was peppered with bullets, Anne fired a well-aimed shot into the back left tire of the Mercedes as it passed. The tire in tatters, the car careened at high speed into some parked vehicles. The windshield exploded and she guessed that the shooter in the passenger seat must not have been wearing a seatbelt. She waited another moment and the driver side door opened; a man waving a pistol stepped out unsteadily and looked around. He was easy prey for Anne's practiced marksmanship. She put one bullet into his right shoulder, making him drop the gun, and another into his left thigh. Anne saw the man collapse in agony as she jumped back into her car and drove out of the parking lot at high speed.

Shaken but back on the highway, Anne reviewed the episode in her mind and remembered that the license number of the Mercedes had been masked by snow. Driving across the Danube, she kept glancing in her rear-view mirror and out the side windows to see if anyone was pursuing her. Anne was still trembling when she got back to her office. Only then did she put the safety back on the trigger of the Glock. She called and left Haffner another message, this time about the attack.

Chapter 30

Greg spent his last afternoon in Vienna at the Kunsthistorisches museum, the spectacular art museum that showcases the permanent collection of the Habsburgs. He went through a special exhibition on the works of Arcimboldo, a sixteenth century painter, who for many years had been forgotten, but was rediscovered by the Surrealists. Greg liked the paintings, weird portraits structured from different natural items—fruits, vegetables, branches, animals and so on. The painter must have had a strange mind and a penchant for breaking away from normalcy, to play games on his friends. A bit like Adam.

After, Greg wandered through some of the permanent collection, stopping in front of the Brueghels, the lone Vermeer and the Rembrandts. He had always been partial to the late-Renaissance Dutch painters. The only distractions throughout were his several attempts to reach Anne, but each time he received the message saying that the subscriber could not be reached. This only made him worry more.

On his way back to the Sacher, on an impulse, he stopped in the Augustiner Kirche, the church attached to the Hofburg, where the Habsburg royals traditionally married. He remembered going there the last time he was in Vienna, with Laurie, one Sunday morning, to hear Haydn's *Nelson Mass*, the opus also known as 'the mass for troubled times'. Though he was an atheist, he loved liturgical music, especially the masses of Haydn and Mozart and the oratorios of Bach. Greg remembered the dissonance he had felt between the mass and the Canova side altar dedicated to Empress Maria Theresa's daughter, Maria Christine, to Virtue and to Love. Was it the similar contrasting emotions that he was now feeling—the troubled, foreboding concern for Adam and the euphoric yearning for Anne—that had attracted him here?

As he was standing before the altar, Greg noticed two men on the other side of the church. One tall and muscular, the other slightly shorter but still of strong build. They had been there in the room where the Vermeer was kept, he was sure. Greg had remarked that they were an odd pair to be going to a museum. He was being followed again, he was sure, and was surprised that the realization left him completely at ease.

Greg exited the church and crossed the street to walk in the opposite direction from his hotel, towards the Lipizzaner stables. He stopped under the arcade, along with the other tourists, to look at the majestic white horses in their stalls and waited for the two men to catch up. They, too, pretended to be interested in the famous stallions.

On an impulse, Greg eased his way over toward the men and before they could move to avoid him, asked, "*Bitte schön, wie komme ich zum Hotel Sacher?*" The two men looked at him as if he were a lunatic and without answering, moved off in the direction away from the Sacher. As he made his way back to the hotel, Greg could not help but chuckle to himself the entire way.

Chapter 31

The Lipizzaners brought back memories of Omi on the porch again. Late spring before he graduated, he was home with Laurie and they were talking about their plans to visit Europe. Omi had never liked Laurie and did not hold back when Greg asked her opinion. She thought her too self-centered to be a good wife for her grandson.

Omi was the one who first told him about the famous white horses.

*****

"You have to see them in Vienna, Greg, you must. The Habsburgs have bred these stallions since 1580 for their beauty and elegance, their capacity for dressage. Very few people know that three of the eight Lipizzaner dynasties are actually Hungarian bloodlines: *Maestoso, Tulipán* and *Incitato*.

I remember how thrilled I was when Uncle Alfréd—we called him uncle but really, he was the husband of my mother's cousin—took Kálmán, the children and me a performance in the Spanish Riding School at the Hofburg. As refugees fresh from our escape from behind the Iron Curtain, this was a treat beyond our wildest dreams.

But everything in Vienna was exciting for us then. Even though the city had emerged from Soviet oppression just one year before, what a contrast there was between the apparent wealth and bustle of Vienna to the drabness and misery of Stalinist Hungary!

Uncle Alfréd took the children up on the giant ferris wheel in the Prater and treated Kálmán and me to a night at the Wienerstaatsoper, to see a performance of Mozart's *Don Giovanni*. You must go there—take Laurie—to hear an opera. It is a beautiful experience.

Frédi bácsi—that's what we called Uncle Alfréd in Hungarian—bought the children toys and dolls like they had never seen before. I remember little Péter's joy when he got a Dinky toy Buick and sent it zooming all over the carpet, and Klári's happiness with her beautiful rag doll, Griselda. It was all so new to us.

We had our first Coca Cola in Vienna. I only took a sip, but spat it out immediately—it was disgustingly sweet and bitter at the same time. Give me rather a good Tokay white or a *Kékfrankos* red any day. The children of course loved it, although I laughed at your mother's funny face after her first gulp. I could not get enough of the fresh fruit—it was all so exotic to me—oranges, bananas, pineapples—and Kálmán, of the delicious coffees, strudels and Sachertortes.

But I did not want to stay in Vienna. It was too close to the country where we had suffered so much, not far away enough from the Soviet oppressor. We wanted to go to a land where we could raise our children in peace and freedom, where there was no terror, no constant fighting of some war. Away from troubled old Europe.

With the help of Uncle Alfréd, and the sponsorship of Kálmán's good friend, who had also left during the war and made it all the way to Cleveland, we managed to obtain the highly sought after papers to immigrate to the U.S. Greg, that is how Kálmán and I and your mother and uncle ended up in the city with the second largest Hungarian population after Budapest. Magyar blood coursed through almost 200,000 of its inhabitants.

And the grandson of Kálmán's friend is your friend Adam, who is often here at our house.

Fate has a way of marking our lives in funny ways."

Chapter 32

A short sleep and a shower later, after trying Anne a few more times, Greg went down to the Sacher bar a little after seven to wait for Julia. He ordered a half-liter of *Zweigelt* and read the *International New York Times*, glad to catch up on the news, especially the latest on the bombing of Grand Central Station. There was still nothing new on the perpetrators, although several editorials excoriated the security services for their failure to catch the terrorists.

One of these cited a letter to the editor of *The New York Times* from a Brother Peter, whom the author of the article surmised was the second-in-command of the Sons of Jesus. He concluded that unless the authorities acted quickly to eradicate this group, further attacks with much higher casualties were imminent.

Greg looked on the next page and found the letter by Brother Peter.

> Dear Editor:
>
> In reference to the recent articles in your paper on the episode at Grand Central Station, you will no doubt be pleased to note that the number of casualties and indeed the destruction could have been a lot worse. For one, the time chosen for the explosion was off-peak, therefore minimizing the count of victims. Moreover, it is not long before the

Sons of Jesus will get their hands on weapons of mass destruction, which will dramatically increase the degree of punishment meted out for the sins of American capitalist society.

We await the second coming of Jesus and look forward to the day when the righteous are rewarded and sinners are wiped off the face of the earth.

Glory be to God,

Brother Peter

*****

Greg sat there in shock. So now the terrorists are brazen enough to threaten further acts of wanton killing, including with use of weapons of mass destruction. Could they be the ones trying to get their hands on the Mayak HEU?

The barman had just disappeared to bring his second half liter of wine, when Greg heard a southern drawl from across the room say, "Well, if it ain't Greg Martens, the world famous author of smutty crime novels!" He looked up and recognized the fat man with red hair and freckles who had been the cause of his embarrassment at the conference yesterday.

"Don't you know me, Greg? You used to torment me at camp."

Greg looked again at the man, wracked his brains. And then the memory flooded back from a long-ago past.

"Billy Crawford." The man stood in front of his table, smiling and sticking his fat hand out for a handshake. When a stunned Greg did not respond, he sat down. "You and your friend Kallay made it hell for me."

The waiter brought the carafe and Billy reached over to the next table for an empty glass, pouring half the wine into it.

"Well, I'm so glad I figured you out. That was fun, watching you squirm yesterday." Billy took a sip of the wine, swirled it around his mouth and then sprayed it across into Greg's face. He stood up, towering over a surprised Greg, and said, "*Adios, amigo*. See you in the next life. Or maybe not. No, certainly not, you godless fiend." Billy quickly moved towards the swinging doors and disappeared into the darkness of the city.

Billy Crawford, from the Odd Fellows Youth Camp run by the Piarist Fathers in Prestonburg, Kentucky. That's whose card it was at Adam's. The local freak Adam and he had once caught brutally killing the camp's mascot rabbit in a sadistic act, after having watched it copulate with its mate. They had chased him down through the forest and beaten the holy living shit out of him. That was twenty-two years ago, when they were thirteen, and yet, the pervert just happened to show up in Vienna at this moment?

But that wasn't their first misadventure with the younger boy. Earlier that summer, Adam had caught Billy writing, "Greg masturbates. He will go to hell," on the outhouse wall with red paint. Adam was so angry, he enjoyed telling Greg later, that he had stuffed Billy's fat head as far as it would go into the shithole, down towards the stinking pit below. Later, the two of them cornered Billy and Adam held him while Greg landed several punches in his fat, soft belly. From then on, they had run-ins with him all summer, culminating in the rabbit incident. The two Piarist priests who ran the camp actually sent Greg and Adam home for that transgression, fearing reprisals by Billy's parents.

*****

Greg wiped his face with his napkin, sipping what was left of the wine. How did Billy Crawford come back into his life? Why now? And what was he doing in Vienna? That was definitely his card at Adam's, so they must have had some contact. But Adam had hated Billy even more than he did, so it would be strange for him to be involved with that jerk.

Might he have anything to do with Adam's disappearance? The question popped into Greg's mind. Not very likely. All very perplexing though. He needed to bring Anne in on this one.

Greg was troubled too by that fact that Julia did not come. It was after eight thirty. He tried her number, but got an Austrian voice saying something he thought meant 'not in service.' Exasperated, Greg remembered she was supposed to be at the Revuebar Rasputin at nine. That meant it was already too late for her to swing by and have dinner with him. Greg finished the last drops in the carafe, called the waiter over and paid his bill. He checked at the front desk for messages—nothing—and went up to his room to get his coat.

It was 9:20 p.m. when he headed over to the Revuebar, certain that he

130

would find Julia. The goon at the door told him that she had not arrived and that she was in real trouble because she was over half an hour late.

Now Greg was getting worried. All he needed was another death or disappearance. Especially if it were Julia. He was starting to feel protective towards her—*like an older brother*—now that Adam seemed to have deserted her.

In spite of all the wine, Greg was thinking clearly. He grabbed a taxi and gave the driver Julia's address. He rang her bell frantically and when there was no answer, started pressing other buttons. After the fifth go round, Julia's voice came through the speaker and she buzzed him in. Relieved, Greg bounded up the stairs, but as he approached Julia's landing, he could hear commotion coming from her apartment. The door was slightly ajar, so Greg let himself in.

"Greg! I'm so glad you're here." Julia rushed over and gave him a welcome hug and a peck. "Look what they're doing to my place!"

Then he saw Anne. *What's she doing here?* Greg was puzzled, but relieved to see her. He could not help blushing. Despite the five policemen rummaging through Julia's things.

"Well, hello again," Anne said. "I thought you were packing."

"I ..." Greg started to stammer, realizing he should have let Anne know about Julia "was worried about Julia ... Ms. Saparova."

"Perhaps you should be. She has no papers. My Austrian colleague wants to take her into custody. She's in Austria illegally and working as an exotic dancer, is that it? She faces deportation."

"Listen, Anne." He wanted to pull her aside, into the corridor, and explain, to share with her his new insights into Adam's disappearance.

"Plus, we'll want to question her because of her connection to Adam Kallay. We now have her computer and Kallay's laptop, so she cannot deny it. There are lots of emails between them which are—shall we say—quite revealing."

The Austrian police insisted on taking Julia with them, so they all went down at the same time. Greg took the stairs with three of the officers, wanting to think. He was angry with Anne for getting Julia arrested, but also at himself for not having told Anne about her. Perhaps that would have prevented all this.

Once outside on the poorly lit sidewalk, with the police van waiting with open doors, Julia wrapped her arms around Greg's neck and whispered in his ear, "Please help me. I've no one else. I cannot go back to Russia."

131

Greg blushed again as Julia was packed into the van, sure this time that Anne did not notice his change of complexion. They stood in strained silence on the sidewalk, staring after the receding police vehicle.

"Can I give you a ride to the hotel?" Anne asked with a smile.

Greg was still angry, but he needed to tell her the latest on Adam. He also had to pack and retrieve his passport. Surely, Anne would have remarked on it if they had found it in Julia's flat. So where was it? Was it still at the Russian Consular Office? He did not want to have to postpone his trip while he waited to get it back.

"Shouldn't you be focusing on Adam? Rather than trying to get an innocent girl deported?" Greg asked testily as Anne pulled away in her Skoda.

"Look, Greg. Ms. Saparova was Kallay's girlfriend. We accessed his computer at work, that's what led us here. Plus, she's an illegal Russian immigrant working in the sex trade, a mafia-linked business. She may very well be able to help us with Adam's disappearance."

"Anne ..."

"We got the results of the DNA test. The corpse was not Adam."

"Who was it?"

"We don't know."

"Then Adam ... Do you know where he is?"

"No. But that's why we want to question Ms. Saparova. She might know. And we have a search warrant for Hetzel and Polyakov."

"Then Adam is alive."

"Well, the corpse was not his."

"So, perhaps it was him the other night?"

"The vision of your friend," Anne said, smiling. "Maybe it was real, but very weird."

"No, Anne, seriously ... I've been thinking that if he did fake his death, it must have been an ingenious part of his attempt to catch the thieves. It makes them believe that Interpol thinks he is dead, which seemingly buys them time while you investigate his supposed death. It also brought us together as a back-up chain to help him if necessary. Without directly involving you and Interpol."

"Why so complicated? And why sneak into my apartment?"

"Well, that's the way Adam is."

The Skoda approached the Sacher. Greg hesitated whether to tell Anne about Adam's Chelyabinsk booking. He decided not to, since he wanted to get to Adam first. Having Anne and Interpol chase his friend down at this point could spoil Adam's carefully sculpted plan to catch the thieves and probably endanger his life, Greg thought. He would know when to bring Anne in. Adam would leave him a clue, he was sure.

The car stopped in front of the hotel.

"Anne, will you come up? My flight is early tomorrow, but I would love to have a nightcap."

"I would too." Anne's smile melted any residual anger Greg may have felt toward her. "But I have to go back to the office and see whether they have any news of Hetzel and that Polyakov. And to discuss where we go from here."

Damn her professionalism. "I'll call you when I'm home. In America. We'll arrange something soon," Greg said, turning towards her and pulling her to him. No, he would not yet divulge that Adam may have gone to Chelyabinsk and that he was going after him. But as they kissed, he remembered his intention to tell Anne about Billy.

"Anne, check this guy out," he said, pulling the card from his pocket. "An old acquaintance of Adam and me, who resurfaced just now. Out of the blue." Then he added, with a little laugh, "He was the guy at my talk who exposed me as a fraud. Maybe nothing, but who knows."

As he got out, he wondered whether he would see Anne again. He asked himself whether he would call, as he had promised. Yes, but only when all of this was over …

*****

Greg checked for messages at the desk and was surprised when the receptionist said: "*Ah ja*, Herr Martens, an envelope did arrive for you."

Greg tore it open as he hurried to the elevators and was relieved to see his passport, duly stamped with a Russian visa. Thank God the lovely Julia had come through, despite being carted away by the police.

Chapter 33

Julia sat across the table from Anne in the stark interrogation room of the police detention center. Anne noticed that the Russian girl was fidgety and could not keep her left leg still. Lieutenant Haffner was in the room and a junior policeman was recording the discussion.

"Look, Ms. Saparova, you're in a very difficult situation. Working in Austria without papers, you will be deported and send back to Russia. My Austrian colleague has just confirmed that your case is being prepared for submission to the immigration courts even as we speak."

"Adam was trying to help me get my work visa. I was only working to earn enough money to live. It is temporary."

"That's irrelevant. However, if you cooperate, I may be able to help you."

Anne took a sip of water and observed the Russian girl. Very pretty. Beautiful, in fact. No wonder Adam liked her. Greg too, it seemed. No wonder that she was recruited to be a stripper. But how? And by whom? Did Hetzel have anything to do with it?

"By the way, how did you get into what you're doing now? Exotic dancing." Anne continued.

"Adam said that he had a friend who could get me some temporary work without any papers. That is, if I did not mind performing. I didn't have too many choices."

"Hmm. Hetzel," Anne said more to herself than to Julia, but that line of questioning could be pursued later. More urgent to find out what Julia knew about Kallay's whereabouts.

The girl exuded intelligence. A high forehead to match the high cheek bones, vivacious blue eyes, fluency in English, German, Russian and God knows what else. And that Ph.D. in nuclear physics.

"Look, we know more than you think. For one, we don't think Mr. Kallay is dead. We also know you and he were close. We believe you know where he is."

"You think he is alive?"

"DNA tests. The corpse's DNA was not the same as Adam's."

"So he is not dead. Oh, that's great news!"

"He was not the victim in that hit and run accident. That's all we can say."

"Adam is a good man. He was trying to get me a job at the IAEA."

"In which area?"

"As a researcher. I have a degree in nuclear physics."

"Yes, I know. A doctorate. When was the last time you saw Kallay?"

"Four days ago."

"Did he say anything about going away? Did he do anything unusual, talk to anyone or act strangely in any way?"

"He did say he was leaving the next day. For America. His father was not well."

"Where in the U.S.A.?"

"Cleveland. But ..." Julia stopped herself just in time.

Anne, though, had not missed the hesitation. At least her story was the same as the Peruvian secretary's. "Look. Let's not play games. We can easily check whether he is with his parents. You're not in a good position, plus your friend Kallay may be in danger. Tell us what you know and you will help both yourself and him."

"What kind of danger?"

"He was helping us catch some uranium thieves. Now that he has disappeared, we don't know where he is. Although my hunch is he's in Russia."

"Greg and I ..." Julia hesitated, but decided it was no use holding back, "we think he's gone to Chelyabinsk."

"What makes you think so?"

"The e-ticket on his laptop."

"We have it now. We can certainly check that." *Why had Greg not told her about this?*

Anne turned and exchanged some words with Haffner, while Julia fidgeted in her seat.

"What do you know about Hetzel? And Polyakov? How friendly were they with Kallay? The police are looking for them."

"Ugh. Hetzel is not a nice man."

"Where did you meet him?"

"Where I work. At the Revuebar Rasputin. He tried to … pick me up."

"But you were Adam's friend."

"The first time Adam played along. He knew I would not go with Hetzel. I told you, I don't like the man."

"Did you see him again?"

"He came back several times. Two nights ago with some other friends. He came into the dressing room and started to … try and touch me. I threatened him with scissors and he went away."

"I'm sure then you will not be pleased to learn that Hetzel wants to buy the Rasputin. We suspect that he may want it as a front for the sex trade. To bring women here and sell them as sex slaves."

"Oh?" Julia looked up. Anne detected fear in her beautiful eyes.

"Did Hetzel have frequent contact with Kallay?"

"No, I think they were just … sort of friends."

"Did they talk about business? Anything to do with uranium? Nuclear material? Anything like that?"

"No."

"Did you ever meet Polyakov, with Hetzel and Adam? Or separately?"

"Yes, Adam introduced me to him once at the Rasputin. He came back several times after that, with Hetzel. He was there again two nights ago, but didn't say much."

Anne felt sorry for the Russian girl and went over to Haffner, who was listening to the conversation from the doorway. Julia could be of use. She was Russian and Adam seemed to be fond of her. She might be helpful in getting to Kallay, plus she knew Polyakov and Hetzel.

"Look, let me be frank with you," Anne said when she came back to the table. "I may be able to help you get your Austrian papers, but you need to help me. I want you to come with me to Chelyabinsk. To help find Kallay."

"But Greg has already gone after him," Julia blurted out.

"I thought he went back to the U.S.!" As she said this, the blood drained from Anne's face. "Are you sure?"

"Yes. Positive. I was there when he picked up his ticket. I also got him his visa."

"Why? Why would he go after Kallay?"

"He wanted to find out what happened to his friend."

Stupid, stupid Greg. Why had he not told her? It would have made everything so much easier. Now he was in danger too. What else was he keeping from her? Anne felt angry, exasperated, disappointed—and anxious — for Greg.

"Well, all the more reason for you to come." Anne looked at her watch. "It's too late to go today. We'll leave tomorrow. I'll let you know when to be ready."

"I'd like to come and help, also to see my mother. But I don't have papers … I want to be able to come back."

"Don't worry. I'll take care of that."

Anne got up and had another exchange with Haffner. "You may go now. Lieutenant Haffner will take you to your apartment. We'll post a guard outside and stay away from the Rasputin. In fact, don't go anywhere until you hear from me."

*****

Anne rushed to the washroom as Haffner led Julia to the elevator. Her world was in turmoil and she desperately needed to straighten things out.

Why had Greg not told her he was going to Chelyabinsk? Was that why he had acted so strangely?

And why had Adam set up this crazy disappearing act? Just after they had talked about catching the thieves. Was that a part of it? Why hadn't he told her that he was going? Maybe Greg was right, maybe it was all a carefully thought-out plan and Adam didn't have enough time to tell her. Or did he just think that it was easier to capture the sellers and buyers and get the HEU back if he was alone and on the inside?

And Greg. She thought she had established a relationship with him, but he had lied to her. He was following Adam. Why? To help him catch the thieves? Why hadn't he told her?

137

Chapter 34

Anne took the long way around the Ring back to the Interpol offices. She needed to reflect. So much had happened so quickly.

She was bothered that Greg had kept knowledge of Adam's booking from her. Greg had seemingly figured out that Adam had decided to catch the thieves on his own, but still felt the need to have support. A back-up chain as Greg had called it. He was probably right. Having Interpol operatives rush after him to Mayak would not have been a good idea. And also, both Adam and Greg must have been protecting her by leaving her on the outside. How stupidly macho, how exasperating!

That appearance the night before was a bit unsettling, though. Very weird. But from what Greg had said, quite in character. Adam was always playing games, wanting the upper hand. And he had done a similar thing before.

How did Adam get into her apartment?

Then it came to her: that night of the IAEA ball, when she had ended up at his place. Her key had gone missing and she assumed it had fallen out at his place. That embarrassing evening when she decided against pursuing something with him. A decision she regretted, until the other night with Greg.

*****

It happened two years ago, when she was new to Vienna and to the job. She had met Adam a few times since being assigned as his main Interpol contact.

He was to contact her in case there was anything amiss in his work to secure former Soviet nuclear material.

Adam had invited her to the IAEA ball in the Hofburg as a companion for his physicist friend, Fazkov, in town from Russia. Anne would have preferred to be Adam's partner, but she jumped at the chance for a blind date anyway—and not just because no one in Vienna had asked her out yet. She loved the idea of going to a ball at the majestic Hofburg, but there were also professional reasons. This Fazkov worked at Mayak, the most important of the sites where nuclear material from the former Soviet Union was being collected for long-term and supposedly secure warehousing. New in her job, Anne planned to learn as much as she could from him about Mayak and what went on there. The physicist could be a useful contact.

The evening started well. First, dinner at Appiano, an up-market Italian-Austrian restaurant just off Schottentor. Then Adam had insisted they take a horse-drawn carriage to the nearby entrance of the Hofburg—the former city residence of the Habsburgs—off Heldenplatz. Big, soft flakes glistened in the glow of the antique lamps that lit the way to the palace. Snuggled under thick furs in the carriage, on her way to the Imperial Palace for a ball, Anne was living out her childhood dream of being Cinderella.

The atmosphere in the Hofburg was magical. In each marbled *salle*, under gilded, chandeliered ceilings, a live band played. Spectacularly turned-out women of all ages danced or watched others strutting around in expensive gowns, hanging on the arms of their well-heeled beaux in white tie and tails. Anne, Adam and their dates strode from room to room, each more beautiful than the last, until they finally found their table in the ceremonial ballroom. This is where, at midnight, the waltz of the debutantes was going to take place. Adam's other guests, colleagues or acquaintances from the UN were already seated, sipping champagne.

Anne talked with Fazkov, asking as much as possible about Mayak and the program to secure nuclear material. She suggested they exchange phone numbers. But mostly, she enjoyed dancing with Adam. He was an impeccable dancer, equally smooth at the swooping turns of the waltz, twirling her around to a rock and roll tune or capturing the sultry mood of the tango. Especially during the latter, she felt an intense physical attraction for the handsome man holding her in his arms.

Adam's date, Ella, was a gorgeous, twenty-something blonde German model. She was also, as Anne had ascertained over dinner, neither especially bright, nor, as had become equally apparent, a proficient dancer, except when it came to shaking her shapely body to techno music. Adam seemed glad to be the centre of attention partnering Anne on the dance floor, and she was grateful for the ballroom lessons her parents had insisted she take.

Around one thirty in the morning, Adam proposed that the four of them go back to his apartment for a light post-ball meal, as was the Viennese tradition. At his request, his Serbian cleaning woman had prepared cabbage soup and a poppy seed strudel for the occasion—which was what his mother used to serve after the annual Hungarian Ball in Cleveland.

The animated conversation continued at Adam's, although Anne noticed that it was increasingly only between Adam and her. Fazkov had reached a state of inebriated incoherence and Ella, a level of boredom that just made her want to get Adam into bed. Soon enough, Fazkov excused himself to go to the bathroom and Ella slipped off to Adam's room. Adam was regaling Anne with stories of his college days. How he and his best friend, Greg Martens, with whom he had grown up in Cleveland, had been the mainstays of the Harvard fencing team. Adam laughingly even threatened to get his epée from his bedroom and show her a few swashbuckling moves. He was relaxed, self-deprecating, fascinating and, in her state of mild intoxication, Anne wanted to continue the evening, but knew that for professional reasons she should leave. She suggested he call her a cab.

"No need yet, Anne. Fazkov will pass out on the guest bed any moment. And Ella can wait." He moved closer to her on the couch, put his arm around her and whispered into her ear: "You are a beautiful woman, Anne." He pressed his lips against hers. Anne was shocked, but excited. She kissed back, gently biting Adam's tongue as it explored her mouth. At that moment, she cared nothing for how this might complicate her work. She wasn't thinking of that. She wasn't thinking of anything, only feeling the electric thrill of Adam's hands running along the curves of her body.

In a simple, fluid movement, he slid the string straps of Anne's evening dress off her shoulders and briefly pulled his head back to take an admiring look at her breasts. "Fabulous," Adam whispered as he caressed them, taking and giving pleasure. He pulled his face back once more and looked deep into Anne's eyes, mouthing the words: "Anne, come. Come to the bedroom, now."

He stood up, gently tugging at her to follow his lead.

"But … But … Ella. She's in there."

"Don't you worry," he answered, smiling at her. "Ella loves the taste of a beautiful woman. As do I."

At that precise moment, the magic of the evening evaporated, as if the clock had struck twelve and her gown had turned to rags. Anne returned to reality. She covered herself at once, stared at the floor and pulled the straps over her shoulders with one hand, tugging her dress back down then searching for her shoes under the couch with the other.

"I'm sorry. I mean … I'm not sorry. I have to go. Right now. Please call a taxi for me. Now."

"Come on, Anne."

"No, I am going. Thank you for the evening. We'll be in touch."

She stood up and scurried straight to the front closet to get her cape before Adam could react. He hesitated a moment, shrugged his shoulders and went to the phone on the desk to dial for a taxi.

"Be here in five. No hard feelings, Anne, okay?"

He was making it worse by the minute, but Anne was glad that he didn't try and impose some contrived romantic farewell on her. He could at least apologize, surely? But no.

They exchanged awkward, muttered goodbyes as she headed out of the apartment, slamming the door behind her with furious relief. When the ancient lift clanked to a halt in front of her, she sighed deeply and quickly got in.

Anne collapsed on the bench in the elevator and exhaled a harsh, whispered, "Stupid bastard."

"What an evening!" she muttered to herself as she stepped into the street. "And what a ridiculous end! How could I have been so moronic as to get into a compromising situation with my main contact at the IAEA? How utterly daft!"

Anne's confidence had been shaken. She had always prided herself on her restraint, her fundamental ability to gauge whatever situation she found herself in and to remain in control. Somehow or other, she'd have to put this sorry episode out of her mind. They had to work together and maintain a dignified, functional and professional connection. Anne resolved to keep a close eye on her own behavior and an even closer one on Adam's.

*****

In spite of this episode, their working relationship had always been positive

141

and she, in fact, had learned to respect the sometimes off-the-wall, yet correct way Adam had acted since then.

But she had lost her key that night, she remembered, and had to suffer the further indignation of waking the concierge at her building to let her into her apartment.

Chapter 35

Greg had never been to Chelyabinsk, or for that matter, the former Soviet Union. Up until the moment he looked it up on Google Earth in the Sacher's business center, he didn't even know where Chelyabinsk was. A thousand miles east of Moscow, one third of the way across Russia, just beyond the Ural Mountains, in the Asian part.

Greg wondered whether he was being rash in running after Adam and exposing himself to danger. This was something he had generally avoided in his life. But this time, instead of fear or foreboding, he relished the thought of adventure. His life as a divorced, mediocre author back in the States had become too boring.

The plane from Moscow was packed, but Greg had an aisle seat. As he reached up to put his carry-on in the overhead compartment, he was bumped by a tall, thin man with graying hair, who was folding his blazer to wedge into the bin opposite.

"Sorry," the man said in English as he slipped into the seat across the aisle. A Russian family on their way to find their places blocked his view, but after the commotion, Greg saw that the man had buckled his seat belt, loosened his thin black and white striped tie, undone the collar of his white shirt and settled into Solzhenitsyn's *One Day in the Life of Ivan Denisovich*.

Once the plane took off, Greg scanned the piece on Chelyabinsk in a dog-eared, grease-stained copy of the Aeroflot magazine in the seat pocket—it was in Russian. Although he understood the gist of the first few sentences, it was tough going, so he gave up. There were a few not very inviting pictures. A massive Soviet-era wedding cake of a building—the South Ural State University—in a gray, wintry scene, a modern shopping center, and rows and rows of shoddy apartment buildings. In a sidebar, the city's population for 2002 was given as 1,077,174. Rather dated, he thought to himself.

When the drinks service started, the man across the aisle finally put his book down on his tray table. As he poured first the gin and then the tonic, stirring the drink with a plastic swizzle stick, he looked across and addressed Greg:

"Hi. You're American, aren't you? My name is Charles Levinson."

Greg put down his glass of bright red drink that passed for wine in the Caucasus. "Hello. Greg Martens. Yes, I'm from New York. And you?" The name seemed familiar from somewhere.

"Not too many of us get out here. Is this your first time in this part of the world?"

"Yes. Never been to Russia before. And you?"

"Believe it or not, I come here often. I'm with the U.S. government."

"What brings you here, may I ask?"

"We're working on improving security at a nuclear facility nearby."

"Oh, which one? The friend I'm coming for is also somehow involved with one. He's with the IAEA."

"I'm up at Mayak."

"That's where he works too." Greg suddenly remembered where he had seen the name Levinson. Adam's email.

"You mean, Adam Kallay? He's the chief IAEA rep. They're doing an inventory of the nuclear material there and we're putting in security systems. We work closely together. He's in the office next to mine."

"It's a small world," Greg said as the trolley blocked further discourse. The dowdy-looking Aeroflot stewardess handed out what Greg ascertained, when he bit into the strange looking item, was a stale salami sandwich.

*****

The flickering lights below, as the flight approached the city, were a welcome sign of some form of civilization in the darkness of the vast Russian night. It was snowing when the plane finally touched down at Balandino Airport, forcing Greg to button his coat against the Arctic wind as he descended the roll-up stairs. The flakes came down fast and thick, clinging to his cheap winter coat. By the time he reached the Brezhnev-era terminal, he looked like he was wearing a white yarmulke and hockey shoulder pads. He had gone through passport formalities in Moscow, so once inside the dimly lit terminal, he headed straight for baggage claim. Greg felt sorry for himself, alone in this dismal place, with only a rusty facility for the language. Missing Anne.

"First impression is always bad. But you get used to it." Levinson, seeming to have read his mind, nudged towards him past two burly Russians.

Levinson's bag came first. "I've got a car to take me to my hotel. The Meridian Chelyabinsk. I'm sure you're there too—it's the only post-Soviet place here. I'd be happy to give you a lift."

"Yeah, that's where I'm booked. A ride would be great. Thanks," Greg said, finally retrieving his suitcase.

*****

On the way into town, sitting in the back of the 2002 Zil limo, Levinson told Greg that, for many years, Mayak—which meant 'lighthouse'—was considered to be the most contaminated place on the planet. Despite some half-hearted clean-up efforts by the Russian government, he noted, it still was. This had been affirmed a few years back by a Norwegian government study that concluded the contamination around the site was much worse than presumed. According to this report, the Mayak nuclear production facility spewed out more than twice as much radiation into the environment as Chernobyl and all the world's atmospheric bomb tests taken together. People living in the Chelyabinsk region were twice as likely to get leukemia as those living anywhere else in Russia. More than fifty per cent of the childbearing population in the area was sterile. The contamination continued and things hadn't gotten much better since then.

Levinson was a fount of knowledge and Greg was glad for it. At least he didn't have to say anything; he just listened eagerly as he stared ahead along the badly lit, slushy road bisecting frozen white fields that melded into the darkness. Greg was keen to find out as much as he could about where he was going. His newfound friend obliged him.

The Mayak atomic weapons complex—or Chelyabinsk-40 as it was known in its early days—was built in the late forties on orders from Stalin,

145

who became obsessed with developing a Soviet nuclear bomb after the U.S. flattened Hiroshima and Nagasaki with Little Boy and Fat Man. Stalin put Beria, his head of the secret police, in charge and construction of the new atomic city was started in November of 1945. More than 70,000 Gulag inmates from twelve camps were brought in at various times to build the complex. The work of constructing atomic reactors, radiochemical plants and laboratories to separate uranium isotopes, required better qualified workers than the other slave tasks for which gulag prisoners were used. The bulk of the convict laborers was thus made up of former Soviet prisoners of war and workers with mining and construction experience who were repatriated from German camps, as well as scientists and engineers rounded up from the occupied countries.

It was at Mayak that Russia developed its first atomic bomb. Levinson told him that, up until the end of the eighties, weapons-grade plutonium was produced there in five uranium-graphite reactors. During that period, there were at least four serious accidents at Mayak, as well as constant contamination through indiscriminate dumping into the lakes and rivers in and around the complex. And this was still going on, Levinson claimed.

The first serious failure at Chelyabinsk-40 happened in January 1949, in Unit A or Anotchka, the first plutonium production reactor to be built. The unforeseen corrosion of more than a thousand graphite-aluminum tubes containing some 40,000 uranium blocks turned into a catastrophe, as a result of a decision made by the higher ups to manually dismantle the rods, remove the uranium blocks and then separate the damaged from the undamaged. In the process, huge numbers of prisoners and scientists at Chelyabinsk-40 were exposed to lethal levels of concentrated radiation. The nature of this accident, and the reasons for it, remained secret until 1995. The number of victims will never be known, Levinson quietly said, but it is undoubtedly much higher than the number who died in the Chernobyl disaster.

The worst accident at Mayak or Chelyabinsk-40 occurred on September 29, 1957, when the cooling system of a radioactive waste containment unit malfunctioned and caused an explosion, spewing out fallout the equivalent of twenty Chernobyl nuclear disasters, according to some experts. Yet in the West, less was known about this catastrophe than about the explosion at the Ukrainian nuclear power plant. After all, Mayak was located in a little-known city in faraway Central Russia. U.S. intelligence did, however, have vague notions of a major disaster near Chelyabinsk and was eager to learn more about the goings-on at Mayak. In fact, the American pilot Gary Powers and his U2 plane were on a CIA surveillance flight over the site when he was shot down in May 1960. But until a 1992 Yeltsin decree, foreigners were not allowed to go anywhere in Chelyabinsk province, let alone near Mayak. The existence of Mayak and ten or so other secret nuclear cities was only finally acknowledged by the Russians in the nineties.

Levinson told Greg that Mayak was now one of the main focal points of the U.S. government's program to secure the former Soviet Union's nuclear stockpiles. Under the auspices of the U.S. Department of Energy, a semi-autonomous agency called the National Nuclear Security Administration had been created and given a huge budget. Levinson headed up the efforts of this agency to improve security and computerize the material accounting systems at Mayak. In this endeavor, he worked closely with his counterpart at the IAEA, Adam Kallay.

"So where do you know Adam from?" Levinson switched the focus to Greg as they turned on to a broad avenue.

"Oh, we go back a long way. We were roommates in college."

"At MIT? That's where I was too, but a few years ahead of Adam."

"No. Before. At Harvard."

"And what brings you here?"

The question was a good one, but he did not have a ready answer, so Greg was glad to see their car pulling up at the door of the modern Meridian Chelyabinsk. When he thought about it afterwards, he came to the conclusion that his presence in Central Russia would be very difficult to explain.

*****

Levinson and Greg checked in side by side.

"I'd be happy to give you a ride to Mayak tomorrow," Levinson said as he grabbed his bags. "I'm assuming that's where you're going if you're here to visit your friend. First thing in the morning, I have a few phone calls to make … By the way, do you have a pass to get into Mayak?"

"No. Just a permit to get to Ozersk. I promised to visit the sick mother of a friend."

"Well, that'll get you close. But I'll call ahead and maybe Adam can arrange one for you. It could be a problem though. Usually, this has to be done

147

well before. Major security checks."

"Thanks." Adam will find out that he has followed him, but he can't be too surprised. Wasn't that what he had wanted? If indeed he left all those clues.

"In any case, it's a couple of hours' drive, so let's leave by eight thirty if that works."

Greg thanked Levinson and followed him to the elevators. As he glanced around the lobby, he noticed several heavily made-up young women, tired and hard, but still pretty, standing around and smoking or lounging in the deep sofas. No doubt what they were up to.

And then Greg did a double take. Was that Hetzel in the corner, sitting in that big armchair, a cigar clamped between his thick lips? The profile was definitely his as he leaned forward to talk to two men, both enveloped in a cloud of cigarette smoke, one wearing a uniform. Greg could not tell rank from the quick glance, but from the number of stripes on the shoulder, a high-ranking officer. When he took a look at the other man, he thought he recognized the square jaw and balding head. Polyakov. *Jesus, what are these criminals doing here?* Greg suddenly felt out of his depth. He moved out of sight quickly, not wanting them to know he had followed Adam.

*****

Greg woke to a persistent, distant thudding inside his head. He blinked his bleary eyes open, but it was dark and the outside world was no different, except that the thumping became louder. After a few seconds, he realized it was someone knocking at the door. He lay there for a moment, trying to fathom whether it was important enough to maneuver his tired body out of bed and make his way to the door. But, he decided, this is a foreign country and it could be anything. Still naked, he lumbered over to the door and looked through the peephole. All his senses suddenly fired up enough for him to hear the muffled, drunken giggling of two of the girls he had noticed in the lobby last evening. He vaguely remembered dreaming about Anne, yes, and then Julia. And now this!

The knocking intensified as if the two girls knew he was there on the other side. But there was no way he was going to open up to these foolish creatures. He wasn't interested. He didn't want their diseases, didn't want to be photographed in compromising situations, didn't want their pimps coming after him. Get lost, he willed them, before going to the bathroom to urinate and

148

to fetch his earplugs. If only he had put them in last night, he wouldn't have been woken by these drunken whores.

As he lay back in bed, waiting for the knocking and giggling to stop, but still fretting, he suddenly felt sorry for the girls. They looked so young. No doubt they were doing their best to try and eke out a living. They were probably put up to it by abusive husbands or sadistic pimps—exposed to diseases, violence, perversions—but they had very little choice. Who was he to judge them?

Or had Hetzel paid them to do it? To compromise him or even have him killed? No, he couldn't have seen Greg checking in.

He was becoming paranoid.

Chapter 36

Greg could not fall asleep. He could not get the girls out of his mind. He thought of Omi, telling him, how as a young mother, she came close to being raped by some Russian soldiers right outside the house where she lived.

In the male Russian psyche, women were there to service men.

*****

"It happened in the early days of the Revolution, toward the end of October. Most of the fighting was taking place in Pest. Kálmán and I lived with the children in a residential area in Buda on Sashegy. But Russian soldiers were patrolling everywhere and strict curfews were enforced.

I was returning from a long trek to forage for food. We often had to walk to the villages on the outskirts of Buda for a loaf of bread, some milk, a few eggs, buying directly from the peasants. The shelves of the shops in the Twelfth District—*Közérts*, as they were known, meaning 'for the common good'—were empty and I would have to go farther and farther afield, even for the most basic items.

I was tired but pleased with the results of my expedition, loaded down as I was with two bags full of potatoes, onions, bread, eggs and fresh milk, having carried them for seven or eight miles. I was glad to be coming back to the one-bedroom apartment Kálmán and I called home in the villa formerly owned by my father. It was small but cozy. The children slept in the bedroom, we, in the combination living and dining room.

All of a sudden, from Korompai utca, a Russian Jeep careened around the corner, with several drunken soldiers singing and shouting, throwing empty *pálinka* bottles over the fence into the garden. There I was, just a few meters ahead of them, struggling with my bags, trying to get the gate open. Seeing easy prey, they slowed down.

The Jeep pulled up beside me and one soldier jumped out of the open back to grab my arm, while they all whistled and made rude gestures and what sounded like lewd remarks. The soldier tore at my jacket. I hit him in the head with a bag of groceries, dropping the other, while another Russian who had dismounted, came up behind me and grabbed for my breast and started tugging at and ripping my dress. I screamed as loud as I could, kicking and scratching with blind fury, but the one soldier had me in his grip and was forcing me to the ground.

Above my screams and the commotion, I heard the gate open and the deep voice of Bozsik néni, the Communist caretaker's wife, yell at the Russian soldiers. Then, with all her strength, she bashed them on the head and buttocks with her broom, shouting, 'Get lost you bastards! Leave the poor girl alone.'

Seeing this formidable opponent, and as other residents started opening windows and coming out, the driver revved up the engine, the soldiers jumped back in the Jeep, and they sped away. I, on my knees, clothes torn, scratched and bruised, broke out in tears of relief as Bozsik néni came over and helped me get on my feet.

'There my child, they have gone,' she comforted me. She helped me gather up whatever was left of the precious food—I was distraught that the milk had spilled and the eggs had broken. Bozsik néni insisted I come into her basement apartment to recover. She served me and herself a large *cseresznye pálinka*—a cherry brandy—that helped settle my nerves. She did not leave me alone until Kálmán returned that evening.

That night I cried myself to sleep in his gentle arms, bemoaning my fate and the state of my poor country. But I was thankful that the outcome had not been worse. That Bozsik néni had heard my screams and come to my rescue, and that at least we had been able to salvage the bread and the vegetables to feed my children.

With time, I was even able to laugh at the image of the huge bulk of the Communist Bozsik néni hacking away at the Russian soldiers with her broom."

Chapter 37

Anne was frustrated that her job required her to spend more time battling bureaucracy than fighting the underworld. Interpol was supposed to have easy, expedited access to Russian visas, but since the ex-KGB officials of the *siloviki* had gained power, matters had become a lot worse. After initiating the visa request through the usual channels, she used a good part of the next day anxiously looking into flight possibilities to Chelyabinsk and organizing a car rental at the airport. And, of course, trying to arrange access to Mayak through the contact group in the FSB, the intelligence agency Interpol worked with in Russia. Another frustrating task, with forms to fill in and numerous telephone calls that led nowhere.

Once all this was out of the way, she took out the business card Greg had given her when they parted. She missed him and wondered where he was, whether she would see him again.

Anne typed 'William Crawford' into the Interpol search engine and then asked Frau Huth to call the Imperial—the hotel and room number had been added in pen below the name on the card—to see if he was checked in there. She waited while the computer searched the files and spat out the results.

Nothing on the Interpol system. From the FBI though, data on two William Crawfords appeared. The first one, known as 'Bill' or 'Billy', was a serial rapist in Florida, safely behind bars for life in Jacksonville. The other was a repeat juvenile petty burglar in New York, currently out on probation.

Neither seemed relevant. And, of course, there was absolutely no reason why an acquaintance of Adam and Greg from long ago would have to be connected to what was going on in Vienna and Chelyabinsk, Anne told herself.

Frau Huth stood at the door.

"Fräulein Rossiter, the receptionist at the Imperial told me that a man called William Crawford checked out early this morning. He paid his bill with cash. They have no record of where he went next." Of course, with her luck, she should have expected this.

*****

As the day wore on, so did Anne's patience, and when it became obvious in the mid-afternoon that permits would not be forthcoming that day, she decided to go out to Laxenburg. This elegant sixteenth-century palace, located a twenty minutes' drive from the center of Vienna, was made available by the Austrian government to Interpol for use as its training facility. It was time for her second session of practice shooting that week and she needed to let off steam by firing a few rounds—if not at a Russian bureaucrat—then into a dummy target.

The results were good, but she was used to getting perfect, or near perfect, scores. Anne felt exuberant when she finished, so she decided that since her jogging gear was in the trunk of her car and it was a beautiful late-winter afternoon, she would go for a run in Laxenburg Park. She hesitated whether to strap on her Glock or not, but in the end, opted not to take it along —it would be very awkward to run with and just weigh her down.

Anne was at the farthest point out in the Park—where the wide gravel path wound its way through a forest of ancient deciduous trees—and just starting to head back, when she noticed that two men, roughly fifty feet in front, were coming straight at her. As she ran a few more steps towards them, she knew their looks meant trouble.

She turned around quickly and saw that two other men were rapidly running toward her from the other end of the path. They—whoever they were —were throwing more thugs at her each day. The two in front had pulled pistols from the pockets of their heavy jackets and the others were doing the same, so without hesitating, she veered off into the thick glade to the left and sprinted as fast as she could through the dense underbrush in the direction of the parking lot. Anne could hear the four heavy-set men crashing through the forest in pursuit, but she was far less encumbered, in top condition and confident that she could outrun them. After less than five minutes, she found the noise of breaking branches behind her receding, but she did not let up the pace.

Approaching the lot, Anne kept herself from view as she made her way to the Skoda and reached it without further incident. She vaguely considered that the car may have been booby-trapped, but calculated that her pursuers would have concentrated on trying to get at her in the park. She was relieved when the engine turned over smoothly and just as soon as she had the Glock cocked beside her on the passenger seat, Anne drove out of the car park and back onto the highway toward Vienna.

Chapter 38

Greg awoke late and had to rush to have a quick coffee and pastry for breakfast before checking out. Levinson was already in the lobby reading a paper and the Zil was waiting outside. With the two in the back seat, the car turned east onto slushy Lenin Avenue, past the ice-coated trees of a snow-covered park.

After some small talk, with Levinson asking Greg how he had slept and remarking how rough he looked this morning, the tall bureaucrat turned into a tour guide.

"That's Revolution Square, the city center just ahead," Levinson said as the car pulled into the left turn lane to head north. "And that's the Legislative Assembly for Chelyabinsk Province," he added, pointing to a monumental white and gray building on their right. Kirov Street was the main north-south thoroughfare and soon enough, a bridge took them over the Miass River. They passed another huge park—at least there seemed to be lots of green space, though all white now, Greg remarked—and then a string of soulless and decaying, concrete, Soviet-era apartment blocks lining both sides of the road. Reaching the outskirts, they passed an industrial zone and accessed the M5 highway, direction Ekaterinburg.

The highway passed by more factories and a quarry on the left. Beyond the pit, in the distance, Greg saw an airport.

"Is that where we came in last night?"

"No, that's Shagol, the military airbase. Balandino is somewhere off to the right."

Further along the M5, Greg was surprised to see bungalow-style houses with tiny gardens in neat, almost North-American style suburbs. The houses were much smaller though and seemed flimsier than in the States.

"This part of Russia has a growing middle class," Levinson explained. "The arms industries were good employers. There were more than a hundred and thirty thousand weapons specialists, mostly physicists, working in Mayak and its sister nuclear cities. Brainy people. In the new economy of the post-Communist world, many were able to translate strong scientific credentials into entrepreneurial success."

"Great!"

"Yes. It's a miniscule blessing compared to the suffering and abuse these people have endured, the lies they have been told, the conscious neglect of their health needs by the government."

The M5 came to an intersection that Greg deciphered as Dolgoderevensko, and they continued their trip north through a rich agricultural area dotted with small frozen lakes, snowy forests and slushy villages. The terrain here was flat, still the Siberian steppes, before the forested foothills of the Urals rose some fifty kilometers due west to demarcate Asia from Europe.

Greg was just settling deeper into the seat for a snooze, when Levinson asked the same question from the evening before.

"So you never told me what brings you to this God-forsaken place."

This time Greg was prepared. Overnight, he had come up with an appropriate lie, which had an element of truth to it.

"I don't think I told you, but I write for a living. Novels."

"I'm impressed."

"I've been thinking of writing a book about terrorists who get their hands on some nuclear material. When I told Adam, he loved the idea. And he thought that Mayak would be the ideal place for my terrorists to steal their uranium."

"He's right about that. Security is still minimal. Despite all our efforts." Levinson hesitated, before deciding to go on, glad to have a fellow countryman as a companion on the journey. A friend of Kallay's, so he could talk freely. "It'd be easy for a determined armed group to cut through the double barbed wire fence in the forest, get to one of the warehouses, overpower the guards and be out of there before anyone reacts to the alarm."

"Really?"

"The guards are not up to the job. They're the dregs of the conscripts, those rejected by the armed forces. But they still have to serve, so they join the Ministry of the Interior. Mayak is one of the worst places to be stationed. People know by now that there was a lot of contamination and cancer rates are very high. The guards are often drunk on cheap vodka. Or even anti-freeze."

"What about an inside job?" Greg wanted to steer the conversation in a direction that might help him understand what Adam was up against.

"Actually, that is the biggest danger in my view. Even with the systems we are installing, it's very possible. We can only step up the level of difficulty for any would-be thieves, not outright prevent it."

"What do you mean?"

"Well, for example, the new warehouse doors we're putting in require two keys to open and two codes to deactivate the alarm. At least two different guards, scientists or administrators are needed to get to the nuclear material and they would both have to be in on any plot."

"Not out of the question, I guess."

"But at least it ups the ante. The Soviet-era control systems relied on people watching and squealing on each other. So you'd have all those cultural factors to overcome if you were going to recruit insiders."

"I see."

"We're also installing video surveillance systems in the warehouses and modern radiation detectors at the gates leading from the facility."

"You mean there were none before?"

"Certainly not everywhere. But anyway, these detectors are almost completely useless, even where they are installed, because the guards more often than not turn them off. There's just so much radioactivity around that detectors are constantly being triggered. Set off by people's boots, clothes, briefcases, whatever. The guards get fed up reacting. It's easier to deactivate them."

"So what you're telling me is that it wouldn't be difficult to get some radioactive material out from Mayak."

"Definitely not impossible if you're an insider and know the system. And I've only talked about those storage facilities where we've set up modern r   itoring and accounting systems. Of the two hundred and twenty or so warehouses located in more than fifty sites, we've only worked on … Well, very few. Certainly less than half."

"Even at Mayak there are still storage sites we've not touched. And in those, there's not an accurate inventory of the amount and type of highly enriched uranium or plutonium."

"So they don't even know what's where …"

"Plus, in the old days, they liked to keep some of it off the books. In case of production shortfalls. So how would anyone notice if a bit of HEU or plutonium went missing?"

"Scary."

"That's why the work we and your friend are doing is so important. But as I said, even that will not prevent an insider group from stealing some nuclear material. There's no failsafe mechanism. We'll never be totally secure."

"Unbelievable!"

"Moreover, in this part of the world, stealing uranium is the quickest way to get rich. If you can pull it off."

The bleakness of Levinson's assessment matched the landscape whizzing by and they both lapsed into silence. After a couple of minutes, Levinson pulled out some papers from his briefcase, while Greg slouched lower in the seat and closed his eyes to try and get some rest. And to collect his thoughts before he met Adam.

Chapter 39

It was the thought of finally seeing Adam face-to-face that brought Greg back to consciousness half an hour later. He woke to the limo slowing down as it passed a small frozen lake on the right and then turn west off the main highway onto a narrower, but still paved road. There was another partly iced-up lake on the right and fields all around. The car slowed to a crawl as they approached the buildings of a village on the lakeshore.

"This is Bolshoy Kuyash," Levinson broke the silence as they passed a rusty Cyrillic sign. "The villagers from Metlino—we'll get there next—were first moved here in 1956 after the authorities discovered that the Techa River was badly contaminated. And when the big explosion happened in 1957, they had to be moved again, this time to Bolshoe Toskino. But that did not solve the problem as now, Bolshoe Toskino is also in a high radiation area."

"So who lives here?"

"The families of the people who didn't move. Or were not given the chance. In some villages, like Muslymovo on the Techa, only ethnic Russians were resettled. The Muslim Tatars and Bashkirs had to fend for themselves. Most who stayed now have cancer—of the skin, kidney, liver or lung—or another radiation-related illness. The children, the third generation, have it the worst. Very few people here and in the other villages around Mayak live beyond fifty. In fact, those old men you see out there are probably in their forties. Or even thirties. They age so quickly ..."

159

Greg looked out and saw the haggard, wizened faces of the people on the main street. Their tired eyes followed the Zil emptily, as if seeing, but not comprehending the mirage that zoomed by from another world. He wondered what it was like to live and die here. To have your family members taken by unknown illnesses. Not to know what was killing them. To have poison in the air you breathed, in the fish and vegetables you ate, the fields you worked, the dust of the road you trod on, the walls of the house you slept in. All around, inescapable. What was it like to raise children in a place you knew was cursed, with no possibility of leaving the godforsaken terrain?

In the middle of the village, the limo turned left and they headed southwest across the fine agricultural land of the Ural plains. Just then Levinson's cell phone rang.

"Hello, Adam. I was hoping you would call. Any luck?"

Some static and unintelligible words from the other end.

"Good. Good. We'll pick it up there!"

Adam. So he was definitely alive and in Mayak. It had not just been his imagination playing tricks. And he must have gotten clearance to get in. Greg had completely forgotten about the pass, so mesmerized had he been by the horrors Levinson recounted. Good! Adam now knew that his plan was working and that Greg had followed him. To this hell. But that's clearly what he wanted, why he had left him all the clues.

"Okay. We'll be there in half an hour." Levinson clicked his phone closed and put it away. "That was Kallay. He got you a permit for Mayak. Fortunately, he's good friends with the Director. He is meeting you inside the Ozersk checkpoint, at the Kurchatov statue. We'll drop you there."

"Thanks." Greg was relieved, though now that it was getting closer, he felt nervous and angry about seeing his old friend.

"What about now?" Greg asked as they entered the village of Metlino, with its prematurely aging men and women and pale, thin children. "Does the contamination still continue?"

"Dumping into the reservoirs and the Techa still continues. Accidents still happen."

"Surely, it's not as bad."

"The facts are difficult to get at. But I know some of what happened just a few years ago. Mayak dumped sixty million cubic meters of so-called 'industrial waste' into the Techa. And right inside the complex, radioactive

160

liquid waste leaked from a tank onto a mile-long stretch of road. Due to violations of safety rules, according to what was reported in the press."

"God, you're scaring me."

"You should be scared. Along most of the Techa's upper reaches, radiation levels still exceed the norm by dozens of times. And near several Mayak reservoirs, levels reach fifty to seventy-five times the normal background radiation. Where the contaminated water flows into one of these reservoirs, you can get a lethal dose in one hour."

"That's unbelievable."

The light changed as the Zil sped along the road, emerging from a heavily forested zone along the shore of a small lake.

"Wow! This is beautiful," Greg remarked, seeing the spotless, but snow-covered beach, and wanting to halt the flow of horrors Levinson was recounting.

"Yes, gorgeous. The locals swim here in the summer, but I certainly wouldn't. The water is contaminated. There are no fish in the lake."

The limousine slowed down and Greg saw that they were approaching some kind of a checkpoint.

"This is the first of a number of controls along the road to Mayak. There is one big one when we enter Ozersk—we will meet Adam just after that—and then the main one as you enter the complex itself. Adam said your pass would be here. You might be able to get through this checkpoint with the permit you got in Vienna, but certainly not into Mayak."

*****

The car pulled into the special lane as directed by barriers blocking the road. Seeing an armed guard approach, Levinson rolled down his window. He handed the soldier the passports and his Mayak card and explained that Greg's pass was waiting at this gate. The guard gave a gruff response and headed into the building with the papers. They sat there for at least fifteen or twenty minutes, Greg becoming more and more anxious, before the soldier returned and handed Levinson the passes, including one for Greg. He muttered something under his breath and waved them through.

"Adam does have clout to arrange a permit just like that, but keep this with you at all times. If you are caught without it inside Mayak, you will be arrested."

161

The forest gave way to houses on the left and the occasional vista of the lake to the right. They passed through the center of Metlino in no time at all and Greg again remarked on the tired, aged faces. These people had darker hair and complexions than the Russians Greg had seen. Must be of Turkic origin, he thought. Didn't Levinson say Tatars and Bashkirs?

Chapter 40

A memory of Omi came flooding back, of her sitting one beautiful autumn afternoon in her wicker rocking chair on the porch in Cleveland, telling him and Adam the story of Brother Julianus.

*****

"According to the '*Gestae*'—the chronicles of medieval Hungary—seven tribes of the Magyar nation left the original homeland east of the Urals and moved west, settling in the Carpathian Basin in the ninth century. The rest of the Magyars stayed behind.

At the beginning of the thirteenth century, King Béla IV, the wise and learned monarch of the Carpathian Hungarians, sent four monks to look for the legendary 'lost brothers' who had remained. After several years of traveling, they reached the region between the Volga River and the Ural Mountains, and found a large group of people with whom they could converse in the Magyar language. Because they estimated that there were several million inhabitants in this brother nation, they called the country '*Magna Hungaria*'—Greater Hungary.

According to the *Gestae*, only one monk survived the difficult journey home and he died soon after his arrival, without making a full report of what they had found. So Béla sent another group of four monks. One of these, Brother Julianus, reached the homeland of the Volga-Hungarians after a journey of more than two thousand miles, travelled by foot, horseback and boat. Once there, he lived with them for several weeks.

This large and powerful nation of Magyar speakers was engaged in pastoral and agricultural activities and trade with surrounding peoples in Central Asia. They had successfully repulsed a number of invasions by the Mongols to keep their independence. Julianus left *Magna Hungaria* on June 21, 1236 to return. Little did he know that he would be the last Hungarian ever to see the 'lost brothers' of the East.

King Béla invited these eastern Hungarians to migrate to the new homeland and form a powerful, united nation capable of resisting the threatening Mongol invasion. Julianus and three others set out again to deliver the King's message. But when they reached the southern Ukraine, they received news that the Mongol army had destroyed the once powerful *Magna Hungaria*, annihilating the entire nation, as was their custom with people who resisted them. Julianus returned to Hungary, accompanied by some Cumanian and Bashkir refugees, neighbors of the Volga-Hungarians, who gave a dramatic account of the last heroic struggle and destruction of these other Magyars. A few years later, western Hungary also fell to the Mongols under Khan Batu in 1241-2."

Greg and Adam had loved this story as children, often acting it out, taking turns on who would play Julianus, plotting his travels on a map.

Now Greg asked himself, could this god-forsaken, lethally contaminated land be the *Magna Hungaria* of the *Gestae*?

Were these Bashkirs the descendents of the Bashkirs who were the neighbors of the Magyars of *Magna Hungaria*?

On their way to being exterminated, not by the fierce Mongols, but by Russia's nuclear policies?

Chapter 41

They left Metlino, turning slightly south, through a rolling landscape of alternating fields, forests and lakes. Then the road curved around to the west and straightened out, cutting through the snowy dark woods on either side.

"The reservoir formed from the Techa that inundated many of the abandoned villages is right along here," Levinson continued his tale of horrors. "Just over there is Metlinsky pond, where a lot of dumping occurred during the first few years. And a little further south is Lake Karachay, which was the main radioactive waste reservoir for Mayak from about 1951 until a purpose-built storage facility was finally completed in 1953. This is where they focused their dumping after they realized what they'd done to the Techa. But even after 1953, lower-level radioactive waste continued to be thrown in there. A study done several years ago showed that the amount of Strontium 90 and Cesium 137—two radioactive by-products—in the lake was a hundred times as much as was released at Chernobyl."

"Incredible."

"It gets a lot worse. 1967 brought an unusually dry summer for Chelyabinsk Oblast. The lake dried up, exposing the radioactive sediments. A violent windstorm swept contaminated dust over a region the size of Maryland. The Russians revealed not so long ago that over 400,000 people were exposed to what is believed to be almost five million curies of radiation, the same amount as was released at Hiroshima."

"The human toll ..."

"Yes. Incredible, isn't it? Hundreds of thousands of people—possibly millions—dead or with cancers, radiation ailments, deformities, premature deaths. I could go on and on. Not to mention the loss of livelihood, forced resettlements, damage to the food chain and the destruction of the environment. The worst was the secrecy and the lack of accountability. The majority of those affected were not evacuated and when they sought medical treatment for their ills, they were not cared for properly and never told what the problem was. And, of course, we in the West never heard about any of this."

"I'm not sure I want to be here."

Greg stared out at the seemingly innocuous scenery that masked so much venom, so much damage. Levinson pointed to a sign as the Zil whizzed by. "See, that sign there says you are not allowed to stop along here for the next ten kilometers, until you get to Ozersk. The pollution is so bad, that if you get out and linger, you may be exposed to too much radiation. Imagine the people who live along here!"

Or don't any longer, Greg thought to himself, closing his eyes and trying to force his mind in a different direction. He did not want to think of the devastation of Mayak. Except, except what was he doing here? Why had he come after Adam? Why was he endangering his life and his health? Why did he leave Anne to come here?

Greg found himself starting to hate Adam for involving him in all this. For having pulled him out of his conventional, but secure life. *He's still my best friend. He needs my help.* He wondered though, what their meeting would be like and how they would react when they saw each other.

*****

The highway curved around to the right and just ahead was a low yellow building with a red roof, cars pulled up alongside. "The Ozersk checkpoint. Hopefully it won't take too long." Levinson glanced at his watch. "Adam should be at the Kurchatov statue already. It's not far from here."

The Zil pulled into an open lane and a guard came over. Levinson again handed the passes and passports over. While the one guard studied the documents, another soldier asked the driver to open the trunk. Papers given back, trunk closed up again, they were waved on in just a few minutes.

"Whew, I expected more questions. But I guess the orders came from on

166

high."

As the Zil drove away, on the other side of the checkpoint, Greg saw that there was a queue of at least twenty Trabants, Zigulis, Moskvichs and other cars from the Communist era, with the odd Ford or Fiat interspersed among them.

"They're leaving? Waiting to be searched?"

"Yeah. The security is supposed to be tighter going out, but it varies. And this is one of two main entry and exit points to Ozersk. If you wanted to smuggle some stuff out of Mayak, you would use one of the other gates."

The Zil drove through an industrial zone and then along the shore of a larger lake, finally pulling up on the side of the road opposite a park.

"There. That's the statue," Levinson said pointing to the snow-bedecked, bronze figure of a stern-looking, bearded man, standing feet apart on a block of rock, hands behind his back, located just a little way inside the park and up a wide cobblestone walkway. "That's where you're to meet Adam."

"Thanks a lot, Charles. For the drive and for all the info. You sure have scared the living daylights out of me!"

"Just don't stay long. I never stay at Mayak for more than a couple of days. Radiation accumulates and that's dangerous."

Chapter 42

Greg crossed the street and looked around. No sign of Adam.

After a moment of relishing the silent solitude of the snowy park, from somewhere ahead, he heard whistling. At first, low and deep, and then the sound morphed into a familiar tune, slightly off key. Greg recognized the Beatles' song, *Yellow Submarine*, that Adam had often whistled as he sat at his desk, bored with studying or on the way back from fencing practice, rushing to a tryst with his girlfriend-of-the-moment back in his room at Dunster House. Or for no other reason than to annoy his friend.

He felt his heartbeat quicken. Was it just the anticipation of seeing his friend after so many years or was it the radioactivity? So soon? Couldn't be, not yet. He was conscious of the condensation of his breath.

Greg moved forward gingerly, focusing the placement of his feet on the icy cobblestones.

"Hello, Greg! Old friend."

Adam appeared from behind the block of stone at the statue's feet, a mischievous smile on his lips. As he approached, Greg was struck by how much older his friend seemed than his idealized and oft-chewed-over memory of Adam. Hair prematurely silvery in strips, face flabbier, with black-blue bags under the eyes, frame stockier and less muscular than he remembered. But the classical attire was still the same. The lined, black Burberry trench coat with collar up, worn over the impeccable, bright colored Polo casuals peering through above and below.

"I am so glad you came. I was hoping you would." Adam reached his arms forward and moved to hug Greg. Greg let him, reluctantly at first, but after so many years of not seeing him, he could not resist the magnetism of his best friend.

"Adam, what the hell is happening?" Greg broke the silence as they disentangled.

"What do you mean?" Adam asked, impish grin widening. "It's so good to see you." He patted Greg's cheek with his right hand. Greg looked up at the stern visage of Kurchatov.

"When I arrived in Vienna and went to your place, I was told you were dead. Then I went to see your corpse in the morgue. When I got there, you had already been cremated."

Adam's response was a hearty laugh that ricocheted through the deserted park. A laugh that could only come from Adam's lungs.

"Pretty cool, don't you think?"

"Then you had Hetzel get in touch with me. And he led me to Julia. And she to the laptop."

"You were always good at following leads."

"And your feigned death—was that to make sure I met Anne?"

"Oh, Anne Rossiter? Isn't she a nice piece of ass?"

Greg felt his ire rise and his fingers curl into a fist. It took all the self-restraint he could muster to not smash it into Adam's face and break his nose. Instead, he posed the question he had wanted to ask since his arrival in Vienna.

"Adam, what the hell are you up to? Why all the games?"

"Hey man, ease off. That Anne ..." And maybe it was something in Greg's face that gave it away or simply that Adam's practiced clairvoyance could read Greg's emotions even after so many years, but Adam's voice changed, taking on a mocking tone as he continued, "Oh, Greg, you devil, you. You certainly swept her off her feet. I saw you and her in action. She fucks like a bunny, doesn't she?"

Livid, Greg moved forward, right fist in the air, ready to strike. Adam caught his arm and did not let up. "She has great tits, doesn't she? But you should try Julia. She's a real tasty bird! Or have you had her already?" Adam chortled as if to punctuate the taunting. "Oh, you dirty bugger, yes, you were just leaving her place after. I followed you."

Adam's incipient roar of a laugh turned into a gasp of pain as Greg jabbed his left fist with all his might low into his stomach. Greg was surprised —through the layers of clothing—to find how soft and flaccid Adam's midriff was. He took fleeting delight in determining that he was in better shape than his friend. Adam reeled backwards, almost falling between the giant Soviet scientist's legs, buckled over, coughing, and then knelt on the slushy ground, the wind knocked out of him.

"You filthy bastard," was all Greg could utter between his teeth. "Always making fun of me."

Adam coughed a few more times and then slowly got up, approached Greg, who was still trembling with rage, and put his right hand on Greg's shoulder.

"Peace, my friend." Adam raised his other hand, fingers in the hippie peace sign, and flashed his irresistible smile. "No need to take it out on me."

"Why the hell did you have me come to this godforsaken place? You left me all those clues in your little game, didn't you? I was to follow you here, wasn't I?"

"Well, Greg, if that's what you wanted to think, fine. But, come on, let's walk a bit. It'll do you good. Cool you down. I'll tell you everything," Adam said, putting his right arm around his friend. "No need to be angry."

*****

They walked in silence for a while, along the paths of the park, the bright sun and cold, crisp air calming Greg. He had forgotten how much his friend could annoy and anger him. He was also struck by how comfortably they had lapsed back into the stylized banter of their college days, with its *de rigueur* sexual allusions. Even though, this time, it had almost derailed him.

And why did he talk about Anne like that? Weren't they working together to catch the uranium thieves? Was it just his old, sexist self that couldn't resist?

"Look, Greg, I really wanted to see you. It's been too long." Adam turned around and took a few steps backwards. "When we first emailed about you coming to Vienna after Christmas, I was just happy that you were coming. It was a great idea. I wanted us to have some fun together, like in the old days. Go to Hungary, like we talked about many years ago. We're not getting any younger and if we don't do these things now, we never will."

Adam's words helped extinguish whatever anger was still smoldering.

170

"And then that conference on the American novel ..."

"But why all the clues to follow you here?"

"You know, Greg, if you wanted to come, I thought you could help me. Plus, it could be a great story for you to write about."

"You bastard! Is that it? Is that why you had me come?" Greg found himself getting angry again. "To glorify your heroic antics?"

"Now, now, Greg. Just cool it. I don't know what Anne told you," he said, giving Greg a mischievous look, "but we discovered that some nuclear material was stolen. We tracked it down and the thieves have now been caught. They're in custody in Georgia—Abkhazia to be exact—and I'm flying there this evening to retrieve it. I would like you to come."

"Is that what you want me to write about?" Greg couldn't help being sarcastic.

"Well, if you ask me, there is the nucleus of a great novel in this—you know—IAEA official helps Interpol nab uranium thieves. You could make me into a hero," Adam chuckled. "You could spruce it up with a little bit of sex with ..." Fortunately, Adam stopped there, because Greg would have lost it had he mentioned Anne's or Julia's name again. "And some violence. You know it's a great story. It could be a best seller, make you rich and famous."

"Adam, get serious."

"We could even turn it into a movie."

"Adam, there's a lot more at stake and you know it. This is no time to fuck around. Anne mentioned that a larger amount of highly enriched uranium was stolen just a few days ago—half a bomb's worth—and it hasn't been found yet. You were trying to trace it and that's when you disappeared. No, died. Apparently run down. Why? What the hell is going on? Tell me!"

"That's why I'm going to Abkhazia. To interrogate the men who were caught. It's quite likely that the same guys who stole the smaller amount also had something to do with the larger heist. We want to know who they are and how they are doing it. And of course, find the stolen HEU. I want you to come with me, in case I need your help."

Greg paused to reflect and when he did not respond, Adam added: "You may even lend me a hand in nabbing the thieves and become a hero yourself."

*****

They had circled back to the Kurchatov statue, which reminded Greg of his

171

promise to Julia.

"Adam, before I forget. Julia got a letter from her mother. She's really sick. Some kind of tumor that she was getting checked out. Yesterday. Julia asked me to go by and check on her."

"Do you have the address?"

"Yes, here," Greg said, pulling out a crumpled note from his pocket. "Maxim Gorkiy Street 27, Apartment 48. Julia did say it's near the park with that statue. That's why I remembered."

"It's close by." Adam glanced at his watch before continuing. "We can squeeze in a quick visit."

Chapter 43

Yelena Saparova lived alone in a four-storey apartment block not far from the park. Adam and Greg climbed the stairs and walked along the dark corridor till they found number forty-eight. Adam knocked on the flimsy, chipped door and after a long silence, they heard the shuffling of slippers on the other side. A latch was undone, the door opened a crack.

"Gospoja Saparova? We are friends of your daughter, Julia. Here from Vienna. My name is Adam Kallay. I have a friend with me," Adam said slowly in Russian.

At the mention of Julia's name, the gap widened another four inches and Greg saw a woman with white hair in a bun, wire glasses covering her wrinkled face. She must have been beautiful once, just like Julia.

"You American?" she countered in English, as Greg remembered Julia mentioning that her mother had studied foreign languages. "With Hungarian ancestors. Julia told me about you."

"Yes. And this is Greg Martens. He is also a friend of Julia."

Yelena sat them down on the narrow bed that served as a sofa and with tears welling in her eyes, asked after her daughter. She was pleased by Adam's assurances that she would soon have a job at the IAEA. But Greg did not want to deflate her by adding that she worked as a stripper and was in danger of being deported by the Austrian authorities.

While Yelena went behind the screen that partitioned off the tiny kitchen,

Greg looked around the small room. It served as living room, dining room, bedroom and kitchen, and was crowded with furniture, the walls covered with photographs, old and new. He went closer to look at these, starting with one that had pride of place in the center: a photo of Stalin and the bearded figure from the park, Kurchatov, with a number of other distinguished looking men.

"That is my father beside Kurchatov. He was great scientist. My husband, too," Yelena said, placing three chipped teacups, saucers and a plate of powdered teacakes on the small table in front of them. "Would you like pastry? I just put kettle on."

"Thank you. Yes, please, Julia told me about them," Greg said as he bit into one of the delicious almond cakes.

"You physicist, too, no, if you work at IAEA?" she asked Adam. She paused as she moved a plastic chair over from the table in the corner. "I have something to give you. My father left it. I get it."

Yelena shuffled back behind the divider and after a clatter of metal on stone, suggesting that something had fallen, she returned with a cracked porcelain teapot and a battered, rusty tin box. She struggled to open the old lid, then handed it to Adam, saying, "You try," as she picked up the pot to pour the black tea. Adam had no difficulty prying the top off the container, passing it back to her. Yelena sat back in the chair, and putting her glasses down beside her cup, leafed through its contents. After a few minutes of looking at some of the documents, muttering something to herself that Greg didn't understand, she pulled out a yellowed, folded sheaf of papers.

"This is it. I can tell from father's writing." Yelena waved the pages in front of her. "I found it with my mother's things. She lived with me until she died. She treasured it and told me the story."

"What story?" Greg asked.

"One day in 1949," Yelena recounted, "my father came home, shaking, very troubled, with this letter in his hand. He told my mother he could not go on with work, but he saw no way out. He cried in her arms for many hours before he told her what happened."

The old lady, overcome with emotion, took a sip of her tea.

"My father was given letter by young friend, person he knew from university before War. Prisoner in Soviet Union. They used convicts to do most dangerous work. Many foreigners. He tried protect friend but could no longer. He told my mother, friend was very smart Hungarian physicist, but his

174

knowledge not used by Kurchatov and other bosses. They are stupid, he said, because some of greatest physicists were Hungarian. Von Neumann, Szilárd, Teller ... and many more."

Gospoja Saparova paused and put her cup down.

"There was an accident a few days—maybe weeks—before. Then, too, he came home very pale and said that in rush to produce enough plutonium for bomb, they took many short-cuts. They endangered many lives. But there was no way to stop Kurchatov, Beria and. Stalin."

Yelena offered the teacakes around again. Greg was hungry, and did not resist.

"Prisoners were ordered inside reactor to save plutonium being produced and uranium from which it was being made. They were exposed to lots of radiation. Enough to kill them. Then not much known about radiation and prisoners were sent into reactor for many hours. After six days of such work, even before, they were good as dead, my father said."

"Unbelievable!" Greg muttered.

"The letter written by Hungarian friend who do this work for six days. He asked my father to get it to his wife. He knew he was dying, but ..." Yelena took a deep breath and then continued. "Anyway, you read later. In those days, Chelyabinsk-40 and nuclear cities were secret of state. Anyone telling, commit treason. Punishment death. My father took letter out many times, held it in his hands, looked at it, but never had courage to send it to friend's wife."

"They were bad times," Adam said taking another almond pastry.

"But here," the old lady handed the letter to Adam, "here is rest of story. My father wrote details of accident and what happened on back of friend's letter. And what friend wrote will finish story, but I cannot read it. Please, get it to the children of my father's friend or his children's children."

"Thank you," Adam said quietly. "We will try our best."

"What happened to your father?" Greg asked.

"He died in March 1968. Few months after terrible windstorm that spread radioactive dust from Lake Karachay across all Chelyabinsk Oblast and farther. As a good physicist and engineer, he was sent to Lake Karachay right after, to see what could be done to prevent this happening again. Of course, the ... sediments were all exposed then and very radioactive. He died of leukemia and cancer of ... of the ... pancreas very soon after."

"I am so sorry," Greg said, clearing his throat before continuing. "Julia told me that you had some tests just yesterday."

"Yes. For tumor in brain. Very large now. Cancer. Doctors say I have not even six months to live."

"Oh, no!"

"Please! Don't tell Julia. She makes new life in Austria. Good life. Thank you for helping her. You good man." Yelena took Adam's hands in hers and held them for a moment before continuing. "She should not come back here. Ever! Here is very bad."

*****

They walked back to the statue in silence. Adam's car was parked not far away.

"I'll show you Lake Karachay. I have to go there," Adam said as they reached the vehicle. "But first, let's read what we can. How good is your Russian? And your Hungarian?"

"My Russian is rusty. My Hungarian, like yours—non-existent. I guess we'll have to wait for the full story till we get back to civilization."

"But here, open it. At least we can see who the man was. He must have signed it. Look at the bottom of the last page," Adam said, handing Greg the letter. Greg opened the folded sheets, glanced at the first page, then at the second, and finally stared glassy-eyed for several moments at the third page.

"Well? Who was it?" Adam broke the silence.

"It can't be … It's not true." Greg fought the tears. "Adam, it was my grandfather. András Bányai."

Chapter 44

Adam, whose Russian was much better than Greg's, translated what Efim Pleshkov, Julia's grandfather, had written on the back of the letter.

"I am writing this to leave an account of the shameful proceedings at the Anotchka Reactor, or Unit A at Chelyabinsk-40 in early 1949, and the terrible end of the author of this letter, an honorable man, my friend and fellow physicist, and many others. I want posterity and especially his descendants to know the full story.

At Comrade Kurchatov's orders—which came from Stalin himself, since he signed every decision concerning the nuclear program personally—all one hundred and fifty tons of processed uranium we had at the time had been loaded into the reactor to produce plutonium for the first Soviet bomb. The uranium was in the form of small, cylindrical blocks, covered by thin aluminum casings. These were installed inside aluminum tubes with an external diameter of just over four centimeters and were about ten meters high and had graphite cladding. The graphite was to slow the neutrons during a chain reaction, but this happens only in dry conditions. The intent was to prevent overheating of the uranium blocks as a result of the chain reaction and the accumulation of the fission radionuclides by circulating water inside the tubes. There were 1,124 such tubes at Anotchka and altogether, they contained about 39,000 uranium blocks. During the chain reaction of uranium-235, the neutrons, which are slowed by the graphite, generate plutonium-239 as a by-product from the uranium-238. But it was not known then that at high temperatures and with such powerful neutron irradiation, aluminum would corrode and leak, allowing the graphite cladding to get wet. We only learned this after the reactor had been running for five months and on January 20, 1949, the reactor had to be shut down.

Stalin was informed and while there was a safe process to retrieve the plutonium and uranium, he, Beria and Kurchatov decided that a riskier, but quicker procedure was to be adopted. The program had fallen behind schedule and they needed to salvage all the uranium to have enough for the first bomb. Stalin, on Kurchatov's advice, ordered that the uranium blocks be extracted with special 'suckers' from the top of the tubes or if this didn't work, then the tubes should be pulled up with the blocks still inside, into the central operating hall of the reactor. After this, it was necessary to extract and sort by hand the undamaged blocks to see if they could still be used. The columns, which consisted of big graphite bricks, also had to be dismantled by hand and dried out for later re-use.

By this time, the uranium blocks were highly radioactive, equivalent to millions of curies. A large number of radionuclides had already accumulated, which made the blocks hot, with temperatures over a hundred degrees centigrade. Significant gamma radiation was being given off by the isotopes of cesium, iodine, barium and other elements.

Kurchatov was present at the site, supervising the work. Beria and Stalin received regular reports and were on top of all the decisions. It took thirty-nine days to extract all 39,000 uranium blocks—containing one hundred and fifty tons of radioactive uranium stuffing—from the reactor. Each block had to be examined visually.

Most of this work was done by prisoners from Chelyabinsk-

40, including my Hungarian friend, András Bányai, who gave me this letter. They were forced to work six-hour long shifts every day, but after five or six days of such work, their bodies had absorbed lethal doses of radiation. Their intestines, livers, kidneys and the rest of their organs had been damaged beyond repair.

But the worst was that these prisoners were not allowed to die in peace, in dignity. On the sixth day, after working inside the reactor, weak and dying of illness, they were herded onto trucks and driven away.

It was only much later, only this year that I figured out what happened to my friend and the other prisoners.

Lake Karachay.

After the terrible windstorm this summer that swept radioactive dust from the dried-out bottom of the Lake, I was sent there to find a way to prevent this happening again. Much of the sedimentation at the bottom had been blown away and in places, bare rock was exposed. To my horror, along both sides of the main spur that had been built into the Lake, I saw hundreds of skeletons, rotting shoes and the few less perishable items prisoners might have had on them. Some bones were broken and displaced and, on closer examination, I saw that several had bullets lodged in them. As I walked among the dead, I was sure that these were the remains of the missing prisoners, sure that my friend András was here.

It was clear that they had been made to walk out on the dam and were machine gunned down by the NKVD guards. The bodies fell into the polluted lake and those that didn't, were subsequently pushed or kicked in by the guards.

We poured truckload after truckload of cement into the lake to fix whatever radioactive sediments were still there. We poured it over the bones of those prisoners, binding them in concrete forever. The remains of my friend, András Bányai, are encased in cement at the bottom of what once was Lake Karachay.

Karachay is a terrible monument to these and other victims of Stalin and Beria and the Soviet atomic bomb effort. To my friend Bányai, the other workers who died at Chelyabinsk-40, and all the thousands, even millions who died because of the many accidents caused by haste and carelessness, by the disregard for human life and welfare of the Soviet nuclear program. They deserve that this letter be made public.

I only wish that I would have had the courage to send the letter to my friend's wife. And even more so, the courage to refuse to be part of Stalin's pursuit of the atomic bomb. But that would have been certain death for me, my wife and daughters.

Efim Pleshkov, December 14, 1967"

Chapter 45

Adam and Greg sat in silent shock, staring ahead blankly for several minutes after reading the letter.

"There you go, my friend," Adam said quietly, as he started the engine on his Ford Focus. "Now you know what happened to your grandfather. Wasn't that alone worth coming here for?"

"Yes."

"Here, you have it. It belongs to you. Take it to your grandmother."

"Thanks."

"But that's not all. Wait till you see what else I've arranged for you." Adam pulled away from the curb just in front of an oncoming Ziguli. "First, though, I want to show you around Mayak a bit. Very few foreigners get to come here, so you may as well see it. It is a marvel of Soviet engineering... and mis-engineering."

They drove along a broad, tree-lined avenue. Despite the cold, there were people on the sidewalks and in the parks, trying to catch the few moments of sun granted by the brutal Siberian winter.

"This is the city of Ozersk. It was built to house the workers for Stalin's nuclear program in the adjacent Chelyabinsk-40 production facility, now called Mayak. Ozersk has a population of around 90,000, 12,000 of whom work at Mayak. But already in 1948, a couple of years after they started construction on the first reactor, there were as many as 48,000 inhabitants, mostly prisoners and soldiers, all either building or working at the facility."

They came to an open space with a statue of Lenin placed in front of an arcaded yellow entrance to yet another park. Greg was struck by the extent of green space in this town. Was it to mask the terrible contamination?

"Lenin Square. Every Russian city still has at least one, if not several. Stalin Squares are fortunately rarer these days."

They passed through an industrial area, then the road turned left into some woods. Greg caught a glimpse of a large lake to the left.

"Lake Kyzyltash. This is the start of the Techa drainage system. But the pollution gets much worse downstream in the Koksharov and Metlinsky ponds and beyond."

"So I've learned. From Levinson."

After yet another sweeping turn, they came to a checkpoint.

"Get your pass out. This is the last guard post to get into Mayak. We shouldn't have any problems, though. They all know me. They see me often with the Director. Oh, I didn't tell you. We'll be meeting up with her later this afternoon."

"You mean the woman Fazkov thought was part of the heist? The insider?"

"Oh, so Anne told you."

The guard leaned down to look in the car, so Greg ended the conversation. The soldier gave a cursory glance at the passes and waved them through. Adam followed the main road to the right.

"I'm just going to do a quick turn through the complex," he said, glancing at his watch. "We're running out of time, but I do want you to get a feel for the extent of the activity that went on here under the Soviets. It still goes on, but in a different way."

"Thanks."

"Plutonium was produced here at five uranium-graphite reactors commissioned between 1948 and 1955. These were all shut down between 1987 and 1990. 'Anotchka' or Unit A—where the accident Pleshkov described took place—was the first one to produce the stuff. What's left of it is up ahead."

"That?"

"Yes. In the early years, irradiated fuel from the production reactors was reprocessed at the radiochemical plant, Unit B, which began operations sometime in December 1948. This is the one up front there and with several modernizations, it continued to operate until the early sixties. The reprocessing of irradiated fuel from the production reactors was continued at Unit BB, there, located next to B. In 1987, after two of the five production reactors were shut down, Plant BB was closed and weapons-grade plutonium production was supposedly stopped at Mayak."

"And was that it? As far as weapons-grade stuff?"

"Just let me finish. The plutonium product from the radiochemical facilities was transferred to the chemical and metallurgical plant, Unit V. That's down near Tatysh, about twenty kilometers to the southwest. It was built in 1948-49 to produce plutonium metal and to manufacture warhead components. A second line here was designed to manufacture HEU weapons components. We think that this plant still continues to process fissile materials and to fabricate weapons components, even though we are told that the plant has been blending down HEU from dismantled weapons since 1997. We're trying to gain access to this plant for verification."

"I thought Russia was cooperating with the IAEA—and us—in every way."

"The devil's in the details, as you know, but we do our best. Mayak also produces tritium and other isotopes such as plutonium-238, cobalt-60, carbon-14, irridium-192 and others, at those reactors over there, 'Ruslan' and 'Ludmila'."

"God, you're losing me."

"Never mind, the tour is almost done. This unit here, the RT-1 plant, reprocesses spent fuel from civilian, military and research reactors. It also serves as a storage site for thirty tons or so of reactor-grade plutonium. It's also involved in radioactive waste management, as well as research and pilot production of nuclear fuel. That's pretty well it. That's what Mayak is. Except ... but we'll get there."

"Wow, pretty huge-scale operation. And all fenced in, I see." As the road turned north, Greg made out the high barbed-wire fence through the trees.

"Yeah, that's the barrier around the complex. Double barbed-wire fence in a strip of cleared land, supposedly monitored. But there are no guard posts along it and no helicopters flying overhead. So you see, it would be very easy for someone to get in here—or to get out with some stuff."

"I see what you mean."

183

The road took them through more forests before coming to a T-junction. Here Adam turned right and within fifty meters, they came to another guard post.

"We will now exit the nuclear production facility of Mayak. So Greg, if you have any plutonium on you, please throw it out the window," Adam laughed at his own joke. "I don't want to be caught and sent to jail." He presented their passes, said something to the Russian and the car was waved through.

"Don't they check the trunk?"

"Naw. They know me well at this guard post. I pass through here several times each visit. In fact, much of my work is in that big building there, known as the Plutonium Palace."

"What do you mean?"

Off to the right was another high metal fence with barbed wire on top, beyond which, above the white-topped conifers, Greg could see a massive building with a snow-covered roof the size of a football field.

"That, my friend, is the infamous Plutonium Palace."

"It's huge!"

"Yeah, it's meant to be the ultimate storage facility for radioactive material. Walls of concrete, seven meters thick. The roof is eight meters of concrete and metal. Enough to withstand a conventional bomb attack. It was built by Bechtel and cost the U.S. taxpayer almost four hundred million dollars."

"You mean we paid for it?"

"Yep. It remained empty for four years. The Russians delayed its commissioning. They negotiated with us over the monitoring and communications systems. And transparency issues. How much oversight we'd have. It has taken forever and all the items are still not resolved."

"Wouldn't they want to get the radioactive stuff under lock and key quickly?"

"That's not how it works. They obfuscate and drag their heels whenever they can. But they've finally started to move some of the plutonium into the stainless steel canisters buried in the concrete floor. Maybe a sixth of the containers are at least partially filled now. But the warehouse's design capacity —fifty tons of plutonium and two hundred tons of HEU—will probably never be fully used. The Russians will only put stuff in here that they won't need for their own nuclear weapons. And slowly, since all these targets are very fluid."

"Don't they see it as being in their interest to have it all securely stored away?"

"It's not black and white. You know as well as I do, Greg, that the current regime is quite ambivalent about whether to disarm or rearm. They make the right noises, but they also want to re-establish Russia as a super-power. And there's control of the Arctic that's big for them. Although they haven't come out and said so, a modern nuclear arsenal could play a key role."

"But didn't we just leave the Mayak site? This is outside the complex."

"Yeah, technically you're right. The thinking was that it would be easier to tighten security in a more contained, purpose-built warehouse. The jury is still out on that. Then there is the issue of getting the stuff here, of course, and all the material within Mayak and elsewhere that's still loose."

They drove quickly by the huge building and into woodland again. Coming to a crossroads, Adam turned right on an un-traveled, unplowed and snow-covered road that seemed to lead into the heart of the dark forest.

"Where are we going now?" Greg asked.

"You'll see."

*****

After a while, they came to another junction, this time, with a still less used road. Greg was feeling the loneliness of the vast Siberian forest and wondering what he was doing there. Adam turned right.

"Down this way a bit," Adam said. "There!" They emerged from the forest and Greg saw a grey, brown and white wasteland spread out ahead of them, traversed by a raised single track from which several spurs took off in different directions. To Greg, it looked like a desolate moonscape.

"The infamous Lake Karachay. Or what's left of it. As you can see, much of it was filled with concrete after the big dust bowl spread radioactivity for many miles. Just as Pleshkov wrote in your grandfather's letter."

But Greg was not listening. He was close to tears as he thought of András Bányai, dying of radiation poisoning and forced to walk out along the dam up ahead, gunned down by machine-gun toting Soviet prison guards.

"Yes, Greg. This is where your grandfather was shot. I thought you would want to see it for yourself."

Adam drove out onto the raised road on top of the dam, right to where the

185

first spur took off to the left and stopped the car.

"Okay, Greg. We're going to get out here and go for a little walk," Adam said as he opened the door and started down the spur at a fast pace.

Greg followed without enthusiasm, thinking about the grandfather he never knew, about Omi and his mother. But when he looked down, on one side, he saw the rough concrete floor with patches of earth, ice, snow and water, and on the other, a murky liquid frozen along the edges. *I wouldn't like to fall in there.*

Which side is my grandfather on?

Greg's heart raced as he moved forward gingerly after Adam, focusing the placement of his feet on the less muddy, less icy patches. *What the hell are we doing here? Isn't this the worst of the worst, the most contaminated place on earth?*

When he looked up, there was no Adam. He was all alone in the middle of the most polluted lake in the world, in godforsaken Siberia. He looked around, wondering where his friend had disappeared to.

And then, the silence was interrupted suddenly by Adam's voice, from somewhere ahead along the spur. "No need to worry, my friend. A little exposure to radioactivity won't kill you." He reappeared, tugging what looked like an over-sized, heavy metal briefcase.

"What's that?" Greg asked.

Just then, he heard the purring of a motor to his right, way back where the road took off across the cemented-over lake. He turned and saw a black Zil pull up. Surely not Levinson?

"Well, speak of the devil! The friends we're going to Georgia with," Adam said in a low tone, seeing the surprise on Greg's face.

Two men wearing dark leather coats got out of the car and started walking quickly along the top of the dam in their direction. A woman emerged from the back seat and stood by the Zil, while another man got out the other side.

Adam did say that they were going to meet the Director. Was that she? Who were all the others?

Greg was getting more and more annoyed with Adam. The conversation under the statue came flooding back. Adam's comments about Anne and Julia, his glibness, his cageyness. All of it fuelled his anger.

But he was also angry with himself, Greg suddenly realized. This business of the letter and his grandfather had diverted him from his mission, the reason why he followed Adam to find out what he was up to and to help him.

If only Adam would let him, tell him how.

He did say he was going to Abkhazia to track the thieves and to recover the uranium. And Adam wanted him to come. Was that what this was all about?

"Let's go." Adam brought him back to reality. "We have to get back to the car."

"Adam ..."

"Come. I'll tell you everything on the way to the airport. I think you'll like the story." He punctuated this with a loud guffaw as he took off at a gallop towards the Ford.

Chapter 46

When Greg and Adam arrived at the car, the two leather-coated men were already there. Greg was surprised to see that both were brandishing pistols. Adam and one of them exchanged rapid words in Russian, then Greg heard Adam say *"Da"* as he put the briefcase in the trunk. Was the exchange about the briefcase, and if so, what was in it? Or was the discussion about him, who he was and what should be done with the unexpected interloper?

"Come on, my friend. Let's make ourselves comfortable in the back seat. We're going to Chelyabinsk and then you'll come with me to Abkhazia. One of these goons will drive us to the airport. Madame Directrice—whom you'll meet in a moment—and Hetzel—you know him from Vienna—will come in the other car."

Hetzel. That's who it was climbing out of the Zil! Greg knew he looked familiar. And hadn't he seen him in the hotel in Chelyabinsk too?

"What's he doing here?"

"I'll explain. Just get in and let's get going."

Greg did not like the tone in Adam's voice, but did as he was told. The older of the two armed men had started the engine and as soon as the doors were closed, he maneuvered the Ford expertly in a tight, three-point turn and drove slowly along the top of the rise in the direction of the other vehicle. They pulled up and stopped some ten or twelve meters away from it.

"Stay put for a second," Adam said, as he and the two men got out, and took a few steps toward the woman and Hetzel. The creep flashed his sleazy smile and waved at Greg from the other side of the Zil. A heated exchange in Russian followed, with the occasional glance and nod in his direction.

Greg, left alone for a moment, regained his composure. His mind clicked into high gear. What to do, what could he do? he asked himself. There was no way back. He had to go with Adam to Abkhazia. Maybe he could help capture the thieves. But what was Adam's plan? Did he have one at all? He seemed very chummy with all of them out there. He had to be. But what if they wanted to get rid of him and Adam couldn't convince them otherwise? No one would know.

Greg suddenly remembered his cell phone. He still had it on him, in his breast pocket. Holding it inside his coat and looking anxiously in the direction of those gathered outside, who were presumably discussing his fate, he ascertained that the battery was not dead and there was a signal, if ever so faint. *Yes!* He couldn't call, but he could definitely send a text message to Anne. He quickly scrolled down his list of contacts until he reached Anne and was just about to start typing a message, when the driver opened the front left door and took the keys from the ignition. To Greg's relief, after a quick glance, he slammed the door shut and went to flip open the trunk as the others joined him.

"Abkhazia"—it suddenly came to Greg that that was all he needed to say. Anne would put it together. She would know where that was and understand that was where he would be going. He wished that his thumb were more agile as he moved it feverishly over the mini keyboard, low down between his legs. He pressed the 'Send' key, then the power off button just as he heard the trunk close.

Adam opened his door.

"Greg, meet Irena. Irena Kolchakova, the Director of Mayak. Irena, this is my best friend, Greg Martens." The woman leaned down to look in and Greg saw that she was a stylish and pretty forty-something. She said a curt, hard Russian "*Dobruj djen*", and pulling her glove off, stretched her hand out for a handshake. Fortunately, Greg held the phone in his left hand, so he reached across with his right and took the proffered hand as Adam continued, chuckling, "Greg will write our story and we'll make it into a movie. You, Irena, will be a star."

With that, Adam slammed Greg's door, walked around the car and climbed in alongside him, as the driver started the engine and took off fast, too fast for the rough road they were on.

*****

Greg thought for a moment of telling Adam that he had text messaged Anne. But just as it was on the tip of his tongue, Adam announced, "She did not want you along, Irena. Nor did Hetzel and the other two. But I managed to convince them."

"What was the alternative?"

"Never mind." Adam turned away and looked out the window.

Greg wondered what the actual exchange had been. Had they debated killing him? Suddenly, he was afraid.

"So now will you tell me what the fuck's going on? I think I've pretty well figured it out, except for how we're going to nab these thieves."

"Well then, let's hear it, Sherlock!" Adam looked at him with a beaming, naughty smile. "And I'll correct you when you're wrong."

"Okay. Since you insist on playing games. You have the stolen uranium in the briefcase in the trunk." Greg started with a hunch that had crystallized that very moment.

"No. You're mistaken, my friend," Adam said, breaking into a hearty laugh. "Only half of it is in the briefcase in the back. The half Irena brought out a few days ago. The fifty or so pounds Fazkov discovered missing."

"The Director brought it out from Mayak? She stole the stuff?"

"It's easy for her. She knows when and where the detectors are down. And her car is not checked with the same rigor, if at all. No one would suspect her. The guards just wave her through. You saw how lax they were with me."

"God."

"She and Hetzel hid it back there, at the lake. They put it in a crevice in the dam just below the top. No one ever comes here and no one would think to climb down there."

"How did you find out?"

"She told me, you birdbrain. In bed. She and I have a thing going."

"I should've guessed."

"I offered to keep it off the books, for a share of the take. That's what we had agreed with Anne. The best way to infiltrate the gang."

"How much?"

190

But Adam kept going, pleased with himself. "And the other fifty pounds is in Irena's car. She brought it out earlier today on her way to inspect progress at the Plutonium Palace."

They arrived at the turn-off for the immense warehouse.

"So between the two cars, we are now carrying enough highly enriched uranium for a bomb?"

"Yeah. In two lots. You can safely carry fifty, sixty pounds. It doesn't give off much radioactivity. It's just a bit heavy. But if two lumps that big are brought close together—say within a few meters—it would be dangerous. Critical mass could be achieved. Uranium atoms do split randomly, throwing off neutrons, and one such event could spiral into a chain reaction and blow us all up."

"And we're now taking the stuff to Abkhazia, where the plan is to meet some terrorists who will pay a lot of money for it." Greg's mind raced ahead as he deciphered the plot more for himself than for his friend. "In fact, the alibi is that we are recovering a smaller amount and questioning the Chechens who were caught with it. This way it even becomes an officially sanctioned trip." Greg surprised himself with his ability to connect the dots. "Is that it?"

"Excellent. Your powers of deduction were always without par, Greg. You must admit, it is a pretty bloody brilliant plot."

"But Fazkov discovered the stolen uranium and told you, and you told Anne. And now you are here to try and retrieve it, no? All your antics were to try and cover your tracks."

"You might say."

"How do you plan to do it, Adam? Catch them, that is."

"I don't know what I'll do. I hope I can count on you Greg, when the time comes. Whichever way it goes."

Although Adam's words were reassuring, Greg was left thinking that his friend was not telling him everything. He must have a plan and that's why he had brought him along to help. But how could he, if Adam refused to tell him how he intended to catch the thieves?

Chapter 47

The same afternoon Adam was recovering the briefcase at Lake Karachay with Greg in tow, Anne's office received the call from the Russian Embassy that her passport was ready with an official one-month visa stamp. As she rushed out the door of her office to fetch it, Anne asked her secretary to book the next available flights for Julia and herself to Chelyabinsk. She would call the FSB again later to see where matters stood regarding entry to Mayak. There was nothing to stop her now from going after Greg and Adam.

Anne telephoned Julia to tell her they were leaving the next day, probably on an early flight. As she hung up, she noticed the new message indicator on the phone. A text message had arrived while she was on her call. From Greg. Her heart beat faster as she tried to speed up the action of her fingers to open the inbox, then the message. At first she was disappointed, then puzzled, when she saw that it was only one word: "Abkhazia".

As an Interpol agent, Anne had closely followed reports of Russia's brazen and illegal occupation of the two Georgian breakaway regions, Abkhazia and South Ossetia, a few years ago. She had read the press with interest, as well as the more comprehensive Interpol reports on the penetration of Russian forces deep into Georgia, the destruction of military and civilian infrastructure, the human casualties and the subsequent, tenuous ceasefire. Also, she was well aware that Russia had recognized these 'statelets' as independent nations and continued to maintain significant forces there, under the guise of peacekeeping. She knew that these rebel regions were now essentially part of Russia.

Did Greg's text message mean that he was in Abkhazia? Or on his way there? And if so, why? Was he with Adam or on his trail? The fact that he sent only a one-word message and did not call probably meant that he was being watched. Or maybe even in danger. So better not to phone just yet. Save that for when and if it became necessary.

Greg's directive was nevertheless clear. Abkhazia is where he was or was going to or being taken to. Either that or the missing HEU was there. Or both. Anne knew that she had to get there as quickly as possible.

But when she thought about it, it would be too dangerous for the exchange of HEU for money to take place in Abkhazia, given the fortified Russian presence. Unlikely that Chechen or Arab terrorists would be able to enter and leave easily. More likely to be in next-door Georgia, where instability continued to reign and where Russian forces still had no problem crossing the border. Terrorists would be able to move around without difficulty. From southern Georgia, it was relatively easy to make it through the mountains into Turkey on foot or on horseback or take a speedboat across the Black Sea to Romania.

But it was Abkhazia that Greg had pinpointed for the next act of this terrifying play, so that was where she would go, Russians or no Russians. Anne made a mental note to refresh and deepen her knowledge of what was happening in and around the 'statelet', as soon as she got back to the office.

Change in plans then. She and Julia would fly not to Chelyabinsk, but to Tbilisi, in Georgia. They would have to get into Abkhazia from there, as there were no flights from anywhere in the West to the breakaway state. It would be difficult to get across the mountains, especially in winter, but it was the only way. She would never be able to enter through Russia.

Luckily, Paul McClintock, the head CIA operative in Tbilisi, was a friend. They had trained and served on a number of missions together. She needed to get Paul to start working on this. Anne was almost at the Russian Embassy on Reisnerstrasse, but quickly dialed McClintock. He did not respond, so she left a message.

"Hi, Paul. Anne Rossiter. Am coming tomorrow with a Russian national, Julia Saparova. Need you to arrange entry and pick-up at airport. Will notify ETA, trip and passport details. Thanks."

193

That was at least a start. Paul would know that she was working on something serious and do everything he could to help. Fortunately, the CIA had a bit of clout in Georgia ... Unlike Interpol in Austria, Anne thought, smiling.

She next called her office to ask Frau Huth to book flights to Tbilisi, then a message to Julia. This, all on the corner of Reisnerstrasse and Jaurèsgasse, a few steps from where Adam's feigned accident had occurred. Seeing the site reminded her of Fazkov. "Have to check on him," she muttered to herself.

Two rough-looking men in jeans and black leather jackets jostled her, gave her an angry look and continued past the entrance to the visa section. She followed them, but turned up the stairs and in through the door. Anne quickly picked up her passport from the woman at reception and left the crowded consulate.

*****

Anne walked quickly, eager to get back to her office. She had a lot to do before she could leave for Georgia. Making her way through the Stadtpark, her sixth sense told her she was being followed. Opening her coat a bit to have easier access to the Glock if need be, she glanced back to see the same two men who had passed her by the Russian Embassy. She was sure they had also been part of the unsuccessful Laxenburg attack.

But she was equally certain that they would not try anything in the Park; too many people around. They just wanted to see what she was up to, no doubt. Actually, this seemed to be working out well, Anne smiled to herself. Whoever those men tailing her were, they would have to conclude that she was planning a trip to Russia. Why else would she be visiting the Consular Section of the Russian Embassy? They would not have any inkling of the sudden change in her plans. So much the better.

Abkhazia here I come!

*****

Frau Huth told her as soon as she got back that she and Julia were booked on an Austrian Airlines flight to Tbilisi that night at 10:25 p.m., so Anne knew she would have to work fast. She phoned Julia, this time getting her on the line, to tell her that she would pick her up in a taxi at eight thirty. Then Anne again called McClintock, who was delighted at the prospect of another mission with her. He confirmed that he would be at the airport at 3:50 a.m. when the plane arrived to meet them at the gate and ease their way through the controls. That was considerably earlier than his usual alarm, but it seemed he was prepared to do almost anything.

She also asked Paul to find out through his 'sources'—satellite-based listening and seeing devices, informers, the usual secret weapons of intelligence—where and when a plane from the Chelyabinsk area might be landing somewhere in Abkhazia. Or if there had been any kind of unusual ambient 'noise' out there that might help her investigation.

*****

"Anything on Fazkov?" Anne turned to the next task on her list.

"Yes, the DNA analysis arrived an hour ago."

Anne took the report and scanned through it. There was a clear match between the pattern from the mutilated corpse and that shown in the FSB report on Fazkov. So it was the Russian nuclear physicist who had been run over. By the arms dealers, no doubt. Fazkov must have known too much and had endangered their plans. He was the person who alerted Kallay to the disappearance of the HEU and there was Fazkov's missed call to her. It was still puzzling why he would try to get in touch directly with her, so many years after the IAEA ball.

But if he had come to Vienna to work with Kallay on the report and next steps, Fazkov was probably on his way to meet Adam at his apartment when he was run over. That was the only explanation Anne could think of.

And then a big question suddenly arose in her mind. If Greg was right and Adam had faked his death to go underground, surely he would not have been party to Fazkov's murder? Unless he did not know that Fazkov would be standing in for him as the corpse.

Never mind, she would have time to try to figure it all out later on the plane. Now she had to rush home and pack if she was going to make that flight.

Chapter 48

They were driving on a snow-covered road that sliced through the forest.

"Hetzel. What's he doing here?" Greg posed another question he wanted to ask Adam.

"That's another story. You'll love it," Adam said, brightening up again. "You know, he's one of those German Russians. There were many communities of Germans—going back centuries—that survived even during the worst times in Russia. Quite a number of these people, however, resettled in Germany in the early nineties, after the régime change. Hetzel grew up somewhere in Siberia—actually not far from here."

"Interesting."

"Well, you won't believe it. He's an old family friend of Irena. The Directrice. She put us together in Vienna."

"Umm," Greg grunted, wondering where all this was leading.

"They have a great little side business. No, it's not really a business … But it's doing good, in a way," Adam chuckled.

"What is it?" Greg was skeptical.

"Irena knows most of the families here in Ozersk. Just about everybody at Mayak works for her. People trust her. She grew up here and made a success of her life. But, you know, it's so polluted here. It's not a healthy place, especially for kids. So Irena and Hetzel try to help parents of teenagers—mostly young girls—find places for their children to work in the West. She tells the parents

196

that they must let them leave, because the radioactivity will kill them if they stay. Or—and that's why they focus on girls—lead to deformed births. Cancers and other illnesses. So Hetzel finds them a place."

"Hetzel? You gotta be kidding, Adam. Anne told me he is a flesh merchant! He brings these poor girls to the West as prostitutes. As sex slaves. Come on, Adam ..." Greg was ready to slam his fist in Adam's face, but restrained himself. "Open your eyes. Human trafficking. A nice little business, you say."

"Now, now, Greg. You're jumping to conclusions. They're getting the girls away from here."

It was the self-delusion, the willingness to minimize the evil, to paint it as something innocent, even something benevolent, that Greg found monstrous. This was not the Adam of old. But, he had always been able to close his eyes to something he did not like. This, though ... this was too much. Greg slouched lower in the seat and disappeared into his disgust.

*****

"So, Greg, what exactly did Anne Rossiter tell you?" Adam broke the silence of the afternoon as they turned onto another deserted road.

"I told you. That you and she, and your friend Fazkov, were trying to trace the HEU that disappeared from Mayak. She said it was the biggest heist yet. More than enough for half a bomb. And she thought there could be more taken soon."

"Well, that is all true. And yes, more can still be stolen."

"And then you made your disappearing act and it took everyone a while to figure out that, really, the corpse we had all thought was you, was in fact someone else."

"Haa. Haha," Adam chuckled. "Did they find out who?"

"No, but your friend Fazkov has also gone AWOL and hasn't turned up yet."

"You mean they think it was Fazkov?"

"Come on, Adam!" Greg was now furious. "Quit jerking me around. You must know."

And then it came to him in a flash. "Adam, you were the third man at the accident! In your stupid little game. And Fazkov the corpse."

Yes, the third man that was the key. Wasn't *The Third Man* Adam's favorite movie back in college? How could he not have seen it?

It was when he said this that the veil of any doubt was irrevocably lifted. Adam had no plan to catch the thieves; he had joined up with them. Adam was Harry Lime. And the horror of it all, the magnitude of the evil that had consumed his friend, finally dawned on Greg. Why did he not want to see it before? It was there all along. He had just refused to admit the facts. To preserve the sanctity of their friendship. Now, as he finally allowed himself to be convinced by the accumulating evidence, the love and trust he had nurtured and held onto for so long disintegrated. Greg broke out in a cold sweat.

"Are you okay my friend?"

"Yes, just tell me the fucking truth. I've had it with your games." Greg's face was white as the sheet of snow covering the fields. Even as he said this, he realized that his life was in danger. "I know the whole story, Adam. I'm not stupid."

"Greg. Cool it. You're jumping to conclusions again."

"But tell me, Adam. The truth. Are you really going to try to catch the thieves, or are you joining in this perfect little crime?"

"Well, Greg, if that's the way you put it—I haven't quite made up my mind yet. But it is pretty tempting isn't it?"

"Bloody hell." Even now he was continuing with his games.

They sat in silence for a moment, the tension palpable between them.

"I've got an idea. Why don't we both join them?" Adam asked, turning to Greg. "Then at least I wouldn't have to protect you. I could negotiate a couple million off the top for you. Just to keep quiet. And, in a few years, to write the story. About the heist. It needs to be made into a movie."

"A modern version of *The Third Man*, you mean?"

"Pretty good, no?"

Was his friend being serious?

"How much would you make?"

"Oh, we've negotiated fifty million. Split four ways."

Over twelve million for Adam. Is that what they had offered him to turn the other way?

"What would you do? There would be no place for you to hide."

"Don't be stupid Greg. I'll just go back to Vienna, to the IAEA. For a while, anyway. After all, we'll return with the smaller amount of HEU and there'll be no record of the disappearance of the two fifty-pound lots. My report will say that it was all a big mistake. A false alarm. I went underground to investigate, and there was no big heist. Bad record keeping at Mayak. Typical." *God, he has it all figured out, the bastard,* Greg thought. *And here I thought he had a plan to catch these criminals!*

"The only person who knew about it other than us was Fazkov and he's dead, as you just said. Killed in an unfortunate car accident. Of course, you ... you wouldn't tell would you?" Adam glared at him.

"What about Anne? You yourself told her. The two of you were working on catching the thieves." Greg, infuriated, ignored the implied threat.

"Yeah, I told her. Fazkov would have told her anyways, because they exchanged numbers some time ago. He said something in a garbled message on my phone that he would try and reach her since I was not answering. Not a problem though, because Anne will believe the story that it was all a mistake. My investigation will show that no HEU has gone missing from Mayak. Or, else, if she doesn't ..." But Adam did not continue the thought.

"I don't believe what I'm hearing. Are you really thinking of doing this?"

"The more I think about it, the more I'm convinced that there's absolutely no reason not to. I guess only you—if you don't want to do it with me—I'll have to figure out how to handle that."

So was his friend even thinking of sacrificing him, in his greed, his eagerness to pull off the perfect crime?

"Why, why?"

"It's very simple, Greg," Adam said, a cold, hard tone now in his voice. But then he hesitated, cleared his throat before continuing, as if trying to convince himself. "There are actually several reasons. First, there's the challenge of it, the perfect heist. The opportunity. It's just there, waiting to be taken. It's such an easy, but exciting game to play. '*Kinderspiel*', as coach Edo used to say. Just like my Tarzan stunt. Remember? No one ever caught me." Adam laughed again at his own cleverness, but Greg wondered whether he detected a tinge of nervousness in his voice.

"Secondly, the pure economics. It's the quickest way for me to get rich. A once-in-a-lifetime opportunity. A lot of cash, tax-free, in a bank account in Singapore. I'll never have to worry about money again. Nor will you. Just think about it, Greg, you won't have to churn out your stupid crime novels for your low-life readership. Ever again."

Greg sat in silence, shocked by what he was hearing. Had he changed this much? Or was it just that he had never really known him? Known what he was really like?

"And it is pretty well inevitable that this will happen, that some terrorists will get their hands on weapons of mass destruction to devastate a filthy, large city. I'm not the only one who has figured out how easy it is to make some HEU disappear from former nuclear cities in Russia. So why shouldn't I be the one who makes some dough out of it?"

"Have you thought of the consequences? Of what this could lead to?" Greg blurted out. "What if terrorists set off a bomb in New York with your stuff? Like al Qaeda or those Sons of Jesus for example? Or in London? Or anywhere? Think of the lives, the devastation. How can you do this?"

"Do I care?" They had just turned into Bolshoy Kuyash. "Do I give a damn about all these little people? Look at them, Greg, aren't they pitiful? Disgusting?"

Greg looked and saw the same haggard and sick, prematurely aged faces of the villagers he had seen on the way in with Levinson. He felt for them, all their suffering, their humanity. But his friend disdained them. And the rest of the world, it seemed.

"Survival of the fittest. Isn't that what we always believed in at Harvard? Or have you lost the faith? The survival of you and me. Our genes. Isn't that what matters, Greg? Survival and living well while we're here. We only have one turn on the merry-go-round and it better be a good one!" Adam's voice had a bitter bite to it as he continued. "In fact, that gets us to reason number three: there are too many of us in the world. Especially in those cesspools—the big cities—Beijing, Delhi, New York or London. They are no longer viable. Their environment is so polluted. They breed disease. They suck up resources. Someone has to take action!"

"You sound like that Voice of God. The one who had Grand Central Station blown up to punish New York for its sins and materialism."

"Well, in some ways he is right. It is the only way. I don't mind giving some Muslim fanatics or Jesus freaks the tools to blow up these megalopolises of contamination. Nature will regenerate in a few hundred or thousand years. The same as at Tunguska—remember, we discussed this in one of our geology courses—where the huge meteorite struck in 1908 and devastated the region. It's all lush vegetation there now. I've been there, seen it with my own eyes. The earth has a tremendous ability to heal itself, but only if we stop continually

200

infecting it. Things simply cannot go on as they are."

"Adam …" Greg tried to interrupt, but Adam had worked himself into a frenzy.

"How can I make you understand that this is my chance to shape the future of the world? And be paid for it!" Adam let out a low laugh, almost a gurgle. Positively Mephistophelian, Greg thought.

"You are sick."

"Is that your gratitude? Here I am offering you the chance to survive and have more than enough to live luxuriously for the rest of your life. Isn't that what it's all about, Greg?"

Greg did not answer. He could not. He looked out at the frozen lakes and snow-covered trees whizzing by, wondering how his friend had come to this. Was Adam just playing him or had he already decided? What was it that corrupted a man? Was it in his genes, had it been preordained that Adam would end like this? Was it the temptation—as he said, simply that the opportunity was there for the taking? The ease of it? A risk-reward calculation? Or was it the delusion of the self, that he was not doing anything wrong, but was in fact, doing good? Or, in Adam's case, all of these? It seemed there were layers upon layers, like an onion being peeled. Greg did not have an answer, but he felt betrayed by his friend.

What should he do? He was glad that he had the presence of mind to text Anne earlier. And that he had not told Adam. He was sure that she would deduce that Abkhazia was where the action would continue—in whatever form. He could just go along and maybe, at some point, be able to affect the outcome. But how, he did not know. Perhaps he could steal the briefcase—they would kill him though. Or should he kill Adam? What a thought! And how could he do that? Surely, Adam was armed. And in the end, what for? That would not save the world.

Chapter 49

Greg looked out the window at the deserted landscape as the meager afternoon light merged into the dusk of evening. The specks of snow that had started to fall just after they turned on to the motorway had given way to chunky, bite-sized crystals, and the road ahead was turning white with the accumulating flakes. Nevertheless, the chauffeur did not slow down. The world around Greg continued to hurl him forward, towards unknown danger.

Greg, however, was sullen and did not want to speak to anybody, let alone to the friend sitting beside him in the back seat of the Ford. He felt betrayed, used, by the one person to whom he had felt the closest.

Or had he been destined to feel disillusioned because he was not close to anybody, really? The friendship with Adam, even though it had gone into a dormant stage during the last few years, was still very important to him—probably the most significant relationship of his life. In retrospect, certainly more so than the one with Laurie—hitherto perhaps the only competitor. And now, to find it reduced to nothing—no, to a destructive, negative force—left him with an emptiness he had not thought possible.

There was no traffic, no sign of life, out on the Siberian taiga, other than the two cars speeding along the road. Greg imagined that this was what a nuclear winter would be like—few survivors, an empty, icy world, an all-encompassing hopelessness.

Adam exchanged a few words with the driver, who reluctantly eased up on the pedal and the Ford slowed to a more acceptable pace. It was time that he did, because visibility was poor, darkness was descending and the road was now completely covered. The wheels of the car plowed through the accumulated snow. The headlights of the Zil behind came closer and then maintained an even distance a hundred meters behind.

Adam's phone rang. He answered and spoke in Russian. Greg tried to pick out a few words. It was Irena at the other end. He thought she was telling Adam that they would not be able to fly till the next day.

Adam ended the conversation and, somewhat chagrined, confirmed Greg's understanding. "We may need to stay at Shagol for a while. That's the military airport. It seems flights are not being cleared for take-off and landing until this snowstorm passes. Let's hope by later this evening."

Greg kept quiet. He wondered if he should make an attempt to turn Adam back from the path he seemed to have chosen, to show him that there was a way to stop all this and be the superman he had always wanted to be. Yes, he owed it to his friend. Greg mustered his courage.

"Adam, we can stop this lunacy. You can still be a hero. Let's call Anne and tell her where the deal will take place. That you feigned your death to mislead the arms merchants, to convince them that you were one of them, and that you are now leading the thieves to the terrorists where both sides can be caught. She already thinks that you are trying to entrap them. Anne will get enough firepower together to arrest them all and recover the HEU. We'll just forget what you told me. We'll go on as before. I'll even write that story about the heroic IAEA official who risks his life to help nab the uranium thieves. We'll split the proceeds, make a movie, as you suggest. You can get rich that way."

Adam did not respond immediately and for a moment, Greg thought that he might have reached him.

But it was a naïve hope. In the receding daylight, Adam's face was twisted by evil as he let out a derisory laugh.

"You just don't get it, do you Greg? You've never outgrown your small-minded, middle-class, do-good morality." And Greg knew he had lost his friend for good.

"What is the point of all that moralistic stuff? Love thy neighbor and all that bunk." Adam continued and then deliberately halted to emphasize the fact that he considered the question rhetorical, unanswerable. "I know you stopped believing in all that God crap a long time ago. The Heaven and Hell bullshit. You're not as stupid as the rest of them. That is why I have always liked you. You have to admit that I would be foolish to pass up this opportunity to make a lot of easy money—and so would you. By the way, have you considered my proposal? If you agree to it, then we would have something to talk about."

Greg answered by not answering. He turned away again, sulking, and looked out the window at the desolate landscape streaming by. There was no way of getting through to the Adam he had known and loved. That Adam no longer existed.

*****

A few lights now penetrated the darkness on either side of the road and illuminated the white of the snow. They must be nearing Chelyabinsk, Greg thought. The driver slowed down and broke the silence to say they were arriving at Shagol. The indicator for a right hand turn came on and Greg peered out into the black and white void to see where they would be heading. He saw no road, no access. Just as he saw no way to get through to Adam.

The car turned and the beams of the Zil's headlights followed them onto a side road, barely distinguishable from the fields in the all-enveloping whiteness and blackness. Soon, the grinding wheels of the car took them to where Greg could see the dim lights of houses framing their path on either side. Must be a suburb of Chelyabinsk, he thought to himself.

What if, at this godforsaken air base, I managed to bring the two 'half bombs' in the briefcases close enough to each other to create critical mass and make the bomb go off? At least then I would spoil Adam's plans, his chance to make easy money. And, more importantly, prevent the destruction of New York or London or Rome.

But what of the people here, haven't they suffered enough? I would be the terrorist. No, better to try something later. For now, just go along with Adam. Perhaps even pretend to accept his offer of a couple of million. Otherwise will they get rid of me as soon as the car stops? To survive—is that, in the end, what matters most, as Adam says?

Suddenly, coming straight at them out of the darkness, just beyond a roundabout, the Ford's headlights illuminated a ghost-like object covered with snow, parked right in the middle of the road. As they drew closer, Greg saw the outlines of an airplane, suspended in mid-air, a giant white-headed egret, ready to swoop over them, devour them.

"That's the statue of the Ilyushin 28," Adam said. "Known as the Beagle. The most popular Soviet-era bomber. It carried their version of the atom bomb. No longer in use, except in North Korea. We're almost there."

"Adam, I've thought it over," Greg said in a quiet voice, almost a whisper. He tried to compose himself, to sound as convincing as possible. "I will accept your offer." He paused for a moment to let it sink in. "You're absolutely right, two million dollars is a lot of money. Set me up for life. And this perfect ...." Greg just couldn't bring himself to complete the phrase. "No one will ever know. I'll write your book. It would be silly to throw this chance away." Greg felt sick even as he said it.

"Very good," came the reply, with what seemed like a sigh of relief, followed by a chuckle. "I can sell that to the others, I think. I knew you'd come to your senses."

The road swept to the right, just in time to avoid the airplane, and then, after a grove of snow-covered trees, made a sharp right turn. The Zil, which had passed them after the Beagle, pulled up in front of a barricade across the road, beside a small, darkened guard hut.

"You know, we'll just tell everyone you're from the NNSA—the National Nuclear Security Agency in the U.S.," Adam said, interrupting the swishing of the windshield wipers. "That makes a lot of sense. We're an international team, chasing down the stolen HEU."

Perversely, Greg was glad that Adam had thought of this, an acceptable alias for him to be traveling with these renegade custodians of nuclear material. A rationale that would keep him alive, at least in the short term. But he couldn't help feeling that he was being sucked deeper and deeper into Adam's game.

After a ten-minute wait, a Jeep pulled up on the other side of the barricade and a lone soldier ran through the thickly falling snow to the front car. Greg saw the window on Irena's side roll down and the soldier launch into an impatient conversation with her. A few seconds later, the window closed, the soldier manually lifted the barricade and waved the cars through. He ran back to the Jeep, which turned around and made its way through the deep snow to the inner courtyard of what looked like deserted barracks.

The soldier climbed out of the Jeep again, directed the drivers where to park and indicated that they should all follow him to the nearest doorway.

"You stay near me, Greg," Adam said, as he opened the car door. He leaned back in to get the keys from the driver to open the trunk, grabbed the heavy briefcase and ran to the entry, Greg following close behind. The soldier finished struggling with the lock, pushed the door open and switched on a dull light that emanated from two bare bulbs in the ceiling of a corridor running the length of the building. They stomped the wet snow off their feet and filed in quickly. The place had not been heated for a while, but at least it was dry inside.

Out of the wet snow, in the small entranceway of the barracks, Irena and Adam talked to the soldier. Irena left with him, while Adam came back to Greg's side.

"There's no flight tonight, that's for sure," Adam said, and Greg could tell that he was not pleased. "We're now scheduled for 8:00 a.m. tomorrow. The Commandant has offered to put us up for the night here in the barracks. Irena will stay at his place. Come on, I've had it. Let's find a bed."

Greg followed Adam and the others into a big room off the corridor with some twenty bunk beds. He was happy to take off his wet clothes and collapse onto the narrow military cot. The turmoil in his mind, however, did not allow him to fall asleep, despite the long drive and the draining events of the day. The bed was hard and narrow and the sheets were like sandpaper, but he could not get his mind off Adam and what had become of him. He remembered another Adam, an Adam that he had loved as a friend, a partner in good and in mischief.

It wasn't until the early hours of the morning that his brain became less active, finally permitting him a light, fitful sleep.

Chapter 50

In spite of everything that had happened or not happened between them, Anne was eager to see Paul again. They had last met for a drink in Vienna, at the Bristol, when Paul was passing through three years ago. It ended up as an awkward rendezvous. Out of the blue, after several glasses of wine, he all but confessed his love and suggested that they should get married. All of this based only on the half year they had spent training together, a couple of short, banal joint investigations and a few fleeting meetings thereafter. Anne had always considered him a friend, never a lover, although they did have—unspectacular —sex once towards the end of the six months.

Not like with Greg. Their one night together had created fireworks in her body, mind and heart, and the memory of it still excited her. She missed him. It was Greg she wanted now, not Paul.

Anne's musings came to an end when the stewardess announced that the plane had started its descent and seatbelts had to be buckled. In the seat beside her, Julia stirred and started to grope around for her shoes.

Anne was excited by the prospect of what lay ahead. This was the part of the job she liked the most—the field missions, actively pursuing criminals and not just sitting behind the desk in Vienna. In fact, given the events of the last few days, Anne was quite glad to be leaving the former Imperial capital.

*****

Paul was waiting for them at the end of the covered ramp leading to the ultra-modern terminal. Anne recognized his prominent jaw, aquiline nose, raven black hair and huge, bear-like muscular frame towering over everyone else.

"Hi, Anne. Great to see you again!" Anne found Paul's mid-Western drawl—which would have identified him even in pitch dark—somewhat jarring. "It's been a while." Maybe it was also his expressions, the words he used.

She let him embrace her with his large arms and as she untangled herself, introduced Julia.

"Okay ladies, we gotta hurry. I've got the head of the airport's Immigration here to see us through the formalities. Give me your passports and follow me."

*****

Within fifteen minutes, Anne and Julia were climbing into Paul's brand new black Ford Expedition as his driver put their luggage in the back.

"First, we'll go by my place so you can clean up and change," Paul said, as they turned into the well-lit avenue named after former President George W. Bush. "It's on the way, but we'll have to be quick. We have a long drive into rough—and dangerous—country. That is, if you want to try to go all the way to Abkhazia. It may not be possible, but I'm willing to try. We'll no doubt be turned back by the Russians or the Abkhaz rebels. But we can talk about that later."

Anne had explained the broad outlines of the mission—that she was chasing down the sale of some nuclear material in Abkhazia—over her mobile when she finally talked to Paul from Vienna.

"So. What did you find out? Anything?"

"Actually, yes. Yesterday, there was a lot of noise about a special flight arriving at Gudauta from a military airfield somewhere near Chelyabinsk. Gudauta is one of the Russian bases that was supposed to have been closed when Georgia became independent, but the Russians continue to use it for their so-called peacekeepers. Now that Abkhazia is, for all practical purposes, a part of Russia, the base has become even more important for them. In fact, some of our sources claim that there's a major underground arms warehouse there. Never verified though."

"What about the flight?"

"It's odd that there'd be a flight from Chelyabinsk. Gudauta falls under the military command in Maykop. The plane was supposed to come in yesterday evening, but there was a big snowstorm up there and it couldn't take off. Now it's scheduled to arrive at ten or thereabouts. That's why we gotta hurry."

"That must be the plane bringing the HEU." Anne was thinking aloud. "Wonder if Kallay is on it. And Greg."

"Sorry?"

"No, no. Just ... that must be it."

"We also picked up some traffic, very murky, between somewhere in Turkey and the mountains northwest of here in the Kodori Gorge area. Maybe those are the guys who'll buy the stuff."

"The Kodori Gorge. Isn't that where there's still fighting between the Abkhaz rebels and Georgian forces?" Anne asked.

"Well, there was until recently. Till the Russians helped push the Georgians out. In fact, that's the way we'd have to go if we wanted to go to Gudauta. That way, there's at least a slim chance we might get through. There could be some Abkhaz rebels in the Gorge, though. Also, if the Russians are still manning the guard posts at the border there in the middle of winter, it's unlikely they'll let us through. Our relations with them are not good. The weather would have to co-operate too—roads in the winter are often impassable. Using the southern route, we'd never make it. No chance at all there. Major border patrols. Many checkpoints."

"Okay."

"Anyway, the gist of the radio traffic was about a meeting in Poti—so that's where I think the exchange will take place. Poti is the main port in Georgia. It's just south of the Abkhaz border. The Russians have supposedly withdrawn from there, but it's still chaotic. It'll not be difficult for your friends to get across from the Abkhaz side. It's also accessible for the buyers from Turkey or wherever. Overland or by water. Probably why it was chosen. I suggest we head for Poti, instead of Gudauta. It makes more sense."

"Is the route safer too?" Julia was finally waking up. "Than the one through that Gorge?"

"Safer than going into Abkhazia. But still not totally secure. We would pass through areas where there was fighting quite recently—especially close to South Ossetia. And ethnic cleansing. Order in Georgia has not been

209

reestablished everywhere. Russian troops still infiltrate the buffer zones, despite the fact that they were supposed to have withdrawn. The rebel militia is the most dangerous. We go through some rugged territory, where the authorities have very little control."

"It doesn't sound too good." Julia's fears had not been allayed.

"Don't worry, we'll be joined by Marines. A troop of well-armed combat soldiers in two fortified SUVs. And we have good drivers. Of course, you're welcome to stay behind if you'd like."

"No, I'm coming with you."

Anne was suddenly struck by the craziness of her work. She may well end up dead in the next few hours, killed by Abkhaz rebels, supposed Russian peacekeepers, Georgian soldiers, powerful arms dealers or Islamic terrorists. Or in a car accident on dangerous mountain roads in the dead of winter in a faraway republic.

Just then, the Ford turned off the highway and stopped in front of a gate set in a three-meter high wall with barbed wire on top. A soldier came out of the guard booth, looked in the vehicle, recognized Paul, and seeing the women, waved them through with a smile.

"Here we are. Our embassy compound. You ladies change quickly. I'll rally the honor guard."

Paul led the way into a simple, but neat, one-bedroom apartment on the third floor, and left them to clean up and change into warmer clothes. He went into the kitchen to make some coffee and call the Marines, who were on standby for the trip.

*****

Anne came out first, drying her wet hair with a towel, just as Paul hung up the phone. She felt refreshed after the shower and keen to get going.

"Thanks for organizing this, Paul. I'm glad we're doing a mission together again."

"Yeah. Maybe we'll have a little time to ourselves after it's done. I could show you Georgia. It's a beautiful country. You … you're as gorgeous as ever, Anne," Paul said, looking away. "Coffee?"

"Thanks," Anne answered, glad for the counter between them, taking the steaming mug.

"Here, I wanted to show you where we'll be going." Paul came over to her side, standing right next to her, to stretch a map out on the counter. Anne was happy to see Julia emerge from the room just then and join them.

A quick look at the map, with Paul tracing their route to the Black Sea, and he said, "Okay, ladies, we've gotta go." He went over to the front closet, pushed the hanging coats apart, and turned the combination lock on a large metal case on the back wall.

"Here, Anne, you may want this along." Paul handed Anne a sleek handgun. "It's a Glock 22. I know you've used the Glocks before."

"Would you like one too?" He asked Julia, as he put on a shoulder holster partly hiding a Springfield 1911. Seeing her hesitate, he took out a Taurus 22 from his mini-arsenal and held it out towards her. "You may find this useful. It's real easy to use. Just unlock and pull the trigger. The pistol is loaded and ready to fire. Here, take some extra ammo."

Julia cringed. She then looked over at Anne, made sure the lock was on and without a word, stuck the weapon in the inside pocket of her jacket.

Chapter 51

Greg woke to the ringing of Adam's insistent phone alarm in the identical hard cot next to his. His friend shook him by the shoulders and greeted him with a hearty "Good Morning" before strutting, in his plaid boxers, down to the communal bathroom.

The ringing reminded Greg that he had put his mobile under the pillow and just possibly might be able to get a message to Anne. He didn't know any more details to impart though, just that they were going to Abkhazia. In any case, now that he had convinced Adam that he was 'in' with them, it did not make sense to put his life at risk. But he did miss her—it would almost be worth it just to hear her voice. Greg managed to restrain himself, maneuvering his still-tired body out from under the scratchy gray blanket and into the showers.

There was only one showerhead free, next to the one dripping onto Hetzel's fat, ugly white body. Greg was repulsed by the hairless, translucent skin, the rolls of flab looking greasy in the water and the bad lighting, but had no choice. When Hetzel came up for air, blinked the soap out of his eyes and saw Greg, he reached over and patted him on the back, saying, "Glad you've joined us." Hetzel even managed a wink and a sleazy smile under the cascading water, as Greg buried his look of disgust in the lukewarm stream.

So now he was fully accepted as one of them, Greg reluctantly concluded. Even this white slave trader thought they were buddies. Was this his rite of passage, where all would be revealed? Or was it the ritualistic cleansing before the descent into Hell?

Would he—when the critical choices needed to be made—be like Adam and take the easy way, the road lined with millions of dollars, or would he be able to pull back and do what is right?

*****

After a stale roll and weak, chicory-tasting instant coffee in the sparse military canteen, they climbed back into the cars for the short ride to the terminal. The snow had stopped falling and it was a crisp and clear, sunny morning.

"Don't worry. It won't bite," Adam said with a grin, as he placed the metallic briefcase on the seat between them and saw Greg's nervous grimace. Greg wondered where the other half of the nuclear material was. Irena would probably be bringing it, but Adam and she had to be sure not to get too close.

"Lots of planes here," Greg said, more to himself than to Adam, to take his mind off the uranium. "Must be an important base," he continued as he quickly tried to estimate the number of aircraft he saw. There were at least forty fighters and maybe fifteen larger airplanes that he presumed were bombers.

"Yeah, it's the closest base to Mayak," Adam answered. "They would scramble fighters from here in the event of an attack. Terrorist, or otherwise."

What if the attack on Mayak is internal, Greg thought to himself. Then the entire facility would be blown sky high with contamination such as the world had never seen.

Once inside the terminal, Irena and the Commandant met the crew coming from the barracks. The officer announced how glad he was, indeed honored, to be able to assist this international team of nuclear safety specialists by making an airplane available for their grand task; it was ready and waiting on the tarmac. He wished them success in their all-important mission. To bring back the stolen nuclear material and the Chechen gangsters that the glorious Russian forces in Abkhazia have apprehended. The Commandant stressed that it was important for the new Russia not to be seen as the source of such dangerous substances. Russia had to show the world that it was able to disarm its nuclear weapons and store the radioactive material securely within its borders.

*****

213

The flight was uneventful; the two briefcases were kept well apart, at opposite ends of the airplane. Adam had one in the front seat beside him the entire time, across from Irena. Wanting to be with Adam, she had entrusted hers to Hetzel, who sat alone in the back. Greg was allowed to sit by himself somewhere in the middle and he was glad to close his eyes, to brood and think about Anne, the direction his life was taking, and what actions he could take when they landed.

He dozed briefly, but woke with a start to the figure of Hetzel looming over his seat.

"May I sit?" Hetzel sat down without waiting for an answer. "You know, Greg, we should be friends." Not on your life, Greg thought to himself, as he looked over at the creep. "You and I have a lot in common. We're both cultured, well educated, like the finer things in life. By the way, how did you enjoy the opera? *Don Carlos*, no?"

How did he know?

"Yes."

"Adam told me he got the tickets for the two of you. Glad you were able to use them." Did Hetzel know he had gone with Anne? Was he fishing? Greg had thought that Polyakov might have been at one of the other tables at Meinl. But were they followed the entire evening? He worried about Anne.

"We also both like beautiful women, Greg. Even though you did refuse my offer of a weekend with Ms. Saparova."

Greg kept silent, wanting to end the conversation.

"Now that I know you're one of us," Hetzel said, looking deeply into Greg's eyes, "I would be happy to ... shall we say ... introduce you to other gorgeous ladies. In Vienna or New York. Wherever. I have good contacts in most cities." The smile again, that horrible smile.

"No, thank you." Greg turned away, hoping the flesh merchant would get the message.

"Very well, but let me know if I can help. You have my card." Hetzel got up and started along the aisle toward his seat beside the briefcase.

*****

They flew across the Caucasus, with its rugged, snowy peaks. The visibility, after last night's snowstorm, was exhilarating. The morning sun was shining, etching the white and gray mountains against the azure blue sky and as they traversed to the other side, Greg could see the darker, deeper blue vastness of the Black Sea emerge down below.

Adam came back and sat down beside Greg.

"Greg, I'm so happy you've decided to be part of this. I would have been disappointed if you hadn't." He paused to let this sink in before continuing. "You know, I was always convinced that you and I would do something momentous together. We were destined for greatness. Now we'll go down in history for having changed the world. And you'll be the chronicler of it all. You will tell the masses."

Greg did not answer. He felt the more time he spent with Adam now, the more he was running the danger of being woven into the fabric of his evil deeds, his self-delusions, his twisted rationalizations.

"Soon we'll land in Gudauta," Adam continued, perhaps sensing Greg's discomfort at talking about his decision. "The Russian base in Abkhazia. From there, it's a little less than an hour by car to Sukhumi, the capital. That is where we'll collect the recovered stuff. Irena tells me it's a pretty town. It's where Stalin and Beria and those guys used to vacation."

"Good." Greg did not know what else to say.

Fortunately, the pilot came on the intercom to announce that they were starting their descent and all passengers had to take their seats and buckle their seatbelts. Greg looked out the window and watched as the airplane made its approach over the dark blue sea.

Chapter 52

It was a little after five and still dark when the convoy left, three armored SUVs, each holding four seasoned Marines, in front and back. They traveled fast, north out of Tbilisi and then west along a desolate riverbed, through rugged territory dotted with a few sleeping town. The driver of their Ford Expedition was also a Marine. Paul had been true to his word about arranging a mini-army for the trip into dangerous country.

As they approached Gori, night started to lift and Anne was struck by the setting of the city, the rugged beauty of the valley. Entering the town, the signs of battle were everywhere: bullet holes in buildings, burnt-out cars, twisted armor by the roadside.

"This is where Stalin was born." Paul turned around to explain to Anne and Julia in the back seat. "They revere him here as a hero, even now. Despite the repeated Russian attacks. They used to have the largest statue of the dictator anywhere in the world, right here in this square. It was only removed a few years ago, and although I'm not sure, I think it's been moved to the Stalin Museum in town," Paul said, as they passed through the main plaza, bathed in the rising golden sun.

Anne vaguely recollected that, according to some historians, the despot was responsible, either directly or indirectly, for the deaths of more than nineteen million people. How had Stalin been able to live with his conscience? How could he rationalize all his deeds? The torture, the deaths, the misery and starvation? The degradation and destruction of so many people for whose welfare, he, as their leader, had accountability. How could he say it was necessary for the good of the Soviet Union? The progress of mankind, the benefit of the downtrodden proletariat—wasn't that what Communism was supposed to have been about? And how could these people still worship him? Indeed, make toasts to 'our great comrade' at births and weddings. Human beings were sometimes difficult to understand.

And then there was the current leadership in Russia. Not averse to twisting truth, disseminating misinformation, bullying and destroying smaller neighbors, abetting ethnic cleansing, trampling on its citizens, stealing from the state, killing those who dared dissent. What had changed? Perhaps the degree was less intense, but had the fundamental mindset changed?

*****

The convoy passed through Gori quickly and out the other side. The road continued more or less along the riverbed and Anne dozed for a while, to catch up on much needed rest after the flight and the last few hectic days in Vienna. In her waking moments, she was glad for the presence of Julia and the Marine driver—it meant that Paul could not become intimate and the sparse conversation remained at a superficial level. Anne did bring Paul up to date on what she knew of the nuclear heist and Paul briefed her on the steps he had taken to organize help from the Georgian Special Forces in the coastal region. They agreed again that the exchange was likely to take place somewhere in Poti and the vehicles continued to head in that direction as rapidly as possible, given road conditions and the occasional, mostly military, traffic.

An hour or so after they passed the towns of Khashuri and Surami, Anne noticed that the landscape was changing. They had started to climb, first through snow-patched alpine meadows and then through dark, dense conifer forests. The road entered a tunnel, recently cut through the mountains. Anne felt a loneliness descend upon her—the loneliness of traveling through a war-torn land far from loved ones, of being in a subterranean, closed and dark world. She missed Greg.

The tunnel opened into a narrow gorge with formidable cliffs on either side, stumpy evergreens growing on the precarious precipice. As they climbed into the mountains of the Caucasus, white patches gave way to thick snow and ice that covered the asphalt, as well as the alpine vegetation and crags all

217

around. Anne was relieved, because it meant that they had to slow down. The insidious shaking she had been subjected to on the pockmarked section of highway gave way to occasional grinding as the ABS traction kicked in.

"This is not the Kodori Gorge, but it's still wild territory," Paul announced as they drove through a patch of fog—or was it a cloud? "At least until we get to Zestafoni. Then it flattens out a bit as we approach the coastal plains."

There was no traffic on this remote stretch in the early morning and the rays of the sun did not yet penetrate the depths of the rift where the road passed between two walls of rock. Only the headlights of the three SUVs sliced through the shadows and the mist. Massive icicles hung from the cliffs where falling water had frozen in the desolate cold.

Anne shivered in spite of the coziness in the Ford.

*****

It was when they rounded the next ice-covered spire of rock that the attack came. One blinding explosion followed the other, as first the vehicle in front and then the one in back turned into cyclones of fire and smoke. Scarcely a second later, the windshield of their transport shattered and Paul slumped forward; blood spewed out of his neck and covered his side window, the roof in scarlet Rorschach patterns. Another staccato of shots and the driver's head was annihilated. Julia screamed as she and Anne were spattered with his brains and blood.

Anne desperately tried to pry open the door of the van, but reconsidered, deciding that she would be an easy target for the snipers out there. She thought of using the gun Paul had given her, but knew that would only attract certain death. Julia was sobbing, so Anne instinctively put her arms around the younger woman and pulled her down low on the seat. She was momentarily comforted by the touch of Julia's face and the beating of her heart. *What will happen to us?*

After a brief lull, Anne spotted the men streaming out from under the cover of snow-capped rocks and approaching the remains of the convoy, Kalashnikovs waving menacingly. Two sleek Subaru SUVs appeared out of nowhere and came to a screeching halt alongside the destroyed Ford Expedition.

A heartbeat later, the door on Anne's side was pulled open and she felt the cold steel of a pistol against her temple.

"Well, well, well!" Anne was surprised by the English, though quickly noted the thick Russian accent. "Who do we have here?" The man reached across and roughly lifted Julia's chin.

Julia opened her eyes. "Polyakov! You? Here?" she said in Russian.

So this was the man she was hunting! Finally, Anne was face-to-face with the elusive arms dealer. But now, it seemed that she had become the hunted.

"And you … you, I take it, are the bitch who works for Interpol?" With one swift movement, Polyakov grabbed Anne's arm, twisted it and wrenched her from her seat, pushing her into the scarlet pool formed in the snow by Paul's blood, still dripping from the open Ford. Instantly, she was surrounded by four of his men, machine guns pointing at her head. Anne saw Julia fumble inside her coat, knew she was trying to get her gun. But so did Polyakov, out of the corner of his trained eye. He reached back into the vehicle, yanked Julia violently across the backseat and shoved her down beside Anne.

"Weapons, bitches, hand them over! Or do you want us to strip search you?" He put his left boot on Anne's behind, grinding her into the snow.

Anne slowly reached into her jacket and pulled out the pistol, throwing it in front of her, questioning her courage. Julia, too, took out hers and sobbing, laid it down by Anne's.

"Is that it, bitch? I don't believe you." Polyakov hauled Anne back to her feet. "Off with your jacket." When Anne hesitated, he forcibly tore her fleece off and left her standing in the cold wearing just her turtleneck and jeans. Although it was obvious that she could not have any weapon hidden in her tight clothes, he took great pleasure in patting her down all over and confiscated her cell phone before shoving her back on the ground.

"We could kill you here, throw you in the ditch and no one would find you until spring."

Polyakov moved over so that he straddled Julia. "You, you are a good stripper. And Russian. I thought you were Kallay's whore. How come now you work with this Interpol bitch?" He prodded her with his foot. "Eh, have you sold out?"

Julia was too scared to answer.

"Never mind, slut. I think my friend Hetzel will pay a lot of money for you."

Polyakov stepped over to where Anne was lying in the snow. "And you, bitch Interpol agent," using his feet and the Kalashnikov to turn her over, "I will find some use for you myself."

Polyakov exchanged a few words in Russian with his men and then turned back to the women who were still lying in the snow. Anne was shivering; her clothes were starting to soak through.

"Okay, bitches," Polyakov barked, heaving Julia up by the arm. "We move fast. Any funny stuff and you're dead. You, you whore, get in the front vehicle." He slapped Julia on the rear end and pointed forward with his gun.

Anne got up as fast as she could on her own and grabbed her fleece from the snow while she could, covering her wet front with it. "You, Interpol bitch, you come with me," Polyakov shouted with perverse pleasure, pushing her towards the second Subaru Forester. One of the men took out a jerry can from the back, poured gasoline on what remained of Paul's Ford Expedition and the two dead bodies, and threw a match on it.

Anne could see the desperate look on Julia's face through the window of the front SUV—the emotion matching her own state—but there was nothing she could do to comfort her. She clambered into the back seat of the second vehicle and Polyakov climbed in beside her. With a grinding of the snow tires, the two Subaru all-wheel drive vehicles pulled back on to the highway and took off at high speed. Anne cast one more look back, just as the Ford exploded in flames.

*****

Anne sat as close to the door as she could, with her seatbelt buckled and looked out the window at the bleak landscape. Still feeling devastated by the attack, freezing in her wet clothes and raw from the manhandling, she only subliminally listened to the conversation of her captors, peppered with self-satisfied laughter. Her Russian was good enough to understand that Polyakov was engaged in a heated exchange with his two men in the front about the success of the operation. They catered to his ego by praising the accuracy of his shooting; it was he who had fired the single bullet between the eyes that had killed Paul. This made Anne hate Polyakov even more.

"How did you know we would be coming along here?" When the men finally stopped boasting, Anne asked the question that had puzzled her ever since the attack. The ambush had indeed been well planned and executed. Not a random meeting on the road.

"Ha. I knew it wouldn't be long before you asked, if I left you alive. Why should I tell you?"

Anne did not answer. Polyakov had absolutely no reason to tell her, except out of stupid Russian male vanity.

"Your CIA colleague's driver was one of my men. He told us everything. When and where you would be coming."

"But you killed him."

"No use to us anymore. His boss is dead too."

Anne shuddered as she thought of Paul back there. She had involved him in this mess. Now he was dead. But she could be too. A good agent does not look back, she told herself.

She gazed out the window and saw they were descending from the highlands, the snow on the ground became intermittent and trees replaced the alpine scrub. The road twisted and turned, and looking down across the switchbacks, she caught sight of the terrified expression on Julia's face, peering through the window of the other vehicle.

"We go to meet your friend Kallay. And your girlfriend's future master." Polyakov let out a raucous laugh at the thought.

*****

The highway followed a riverbed and they reached a mid-sized town, Zestafoni, continuing as rapidly as possible out the other side. Anne nursed her bruises and frayed nerves, falling into a deep sleep. She woke sometime later to the warmth of sunshine bathing her face, and as she looked out, a radically different landscape. They were in lowlands, a river delta it seemed, with fertile soil. The vegetation was tropical. She opened her window and the fresh air revived her spirits. The climate too, it seemed, was not the same here as it was in the mountains or further inland: more benign, balmy, with a light breeze blowing.

A sign on the side of the road told Anne that they were approaching Poti —only five kilometers to go. So this is where Paul thought the sale might take place. *But what will I be able to do about it now, totally at the mercy of these well-armed monsters as I am?*

They passed another village and continued along a straight road lined with trees on either side. Anne caught sight of a huge dark body of water ahead —must be the Black Sea—and then they were in the town itself. She was struck by the sight of all the destruction, the wounds wreaked by the Russian forces when they mobilized against the port to punish Georgia and annihilate its meager naval forces. Very few houses remained untouched by the ravages of battle. Indeed, the signs of battle became more evident as they approached the harbor: buildings pockmarked by bullet holes, windows boarded up where glass once kept out the cold of the winter nights, the sullen, weathered, faces of people struggling to survive.

They proceeded to the harbor area, where there were some signs of activity. A few ships were being off- and- on-loaded, with enormous yellow cranes hoisting huge containers in the air and trucks and train wagons maneuvering to be next in line to receive them. It was a modern port, but had also suffered battle damage. Anne caught sight of a number of ailing naval vessels that had been pulled up for repairs.

Polyakov directed the driver with ease along the cracked roads separating administrative buildings and warehouses, until they came to a two-storey, bomb-damaged, derelict office building that rose beside a crumbling pier. Here, the Subaru stopped and pulled up alongside the other SUV that had arrived ahead of them. Anne caught sight of Julia's pale, frightened face. *This is where they will finish us off for sure. No question, this is the end.*

Chapter 53

Three ancient black Zils flanked by two Russian army Jeeps met them on the tarmac. As the plane taxied to a stop, Greg saw two men get out of the front car and a Russian officer from one of the Jeeps. He thought he recognized the shorter man in civilian clothes—square jaw, stocky build, balding head. This one was sporting a navy blue cashmere coat and a gray scarf, looking very stylish for this part of the world.

The thickset man greeted Hetzel and Irena with a triple kiss, then shook Adam's hand when introduced and Greg thought he heard him say "Polyakov". Hetzel presented him to Greg and this time he was sure he heard the name: Colonel Boris Polyakov. Greg thought to himself, is this the man I met in the Revuebar Rasputin? But that man's name was Sergei … Didn't Anne say he has a brother with the FSB?

There was some discussion among Irena, the Colonel and the other officer, after which Irena climbed into the front Zil with Colonel Polyakov, while Adam and Greg were directed to the middle car. A chagrined looking Hetzel made his way towards the last vehicle.

Adam pointed to the trunk and the driver went to open it. He placed the big metal briefcase gingerly in the coffer, then climbed in the back beside Greg and plopped another smaller, leather one in the middle. As soon as the doors closed, the Zils followed the front Jeep through the maze of Russian fighter planes and attack helicopters and away from the terminal, down a tree-lined road past a sports facility to a big, guarded gate.

"Lot of planes here, too," Greg remarked, "and choppers. Not as many as at Shagol, but still …"

"This is an old Soviet airbase," Adam explained. "The Ruskis should have left several years ago, but they never accepted Georgian independence, so they did not give it up. Now that they've more or less annexed Abkhazia, they're keeping it and in fact, expanding it. You know, they feel very threatened by Georgia's push to join NATO."

"Was that the other Polyakov you introduced me to back there? The brother?" Greg asked, thinking back to his conversation with Anne again. "Isn't he a senior official in the FSB?"

"Yes. He's one of the Deputy Directors. Very high up. But do you know Sergei?"

"Yes. I met him in Vienna."

"Oh, yes. Hetzel told me. You met at the Rasputin," Adam said, chuckling to himself.

And then Greg recalled where he might have seen this Polyakov: at the Hotel Meridian, in Chelyabinsk, as he was checking in. He was having a drink and a smoke with Hetzel and another man, an officer in the army. Or was that the other Polyakov?

The uniformed officer in the lead Jeep got out, ordered the guard to open the gate, and waved the Zils through. Leaving the airbase, they passed rapidly through the small town of Gudauta and came to the coastal road leading to Sukhumi.

Greg felt he had been transported to a different world, backwards in time. It reminded him of the pictures he had seen of Cuba under Castro. The tropical vegetation, tall palm trees crowned with huge fronds and slender cypresses reaching towards the sky. The few cars looked like they were from the fifties— rusty Ladas, Trabants and Moskvichs—all falling apart, barely chugging along. Everything seemed decrepit; even the people driving the mules that pulled the wooden carts they passed on the pothole-riddled highway. Along some stretches, on one side, the waves gently lapped the sandy cove, while on the other, grand but rundown villas, decorated with peeling pink and blue paint, that had served as vacation homes for the Soviet elite, hid behind palm trees like extinct reptiles from a lost world. It seemed ironic, Greg thought, that the nuclear age was at that very moment, passing through this sleepy land from a by-gone era. With the potency to destroy all its beauty in a flash.

*****

They reached an area where the hills, covered with lush, dense vegetation tumbled right down to the beach, mimicking the waterfalls that dropped from the ravines straight into the sea. Adam pointed to a stunning orange and ochre building, with turrets and silver domes rising like mushrooms high up on a hill, peeping through the veil of some magnificent cypresses. He asked the driver what it was.

"The monastery of Novy Afon. This region is full of caves and in the sixth century, a holy man, the Canon Simon, lived and died in one of them. The monastery was built in his honor. There are still fifty or so monks here."

Greg could not help but be struck by the beauty of this remote little sliver of land, a country that was trying to assert its independence. Hemmed in between mountain and sea, with the climate, beaches and vegetation of the Riviera on the one hand, and the untouched, rugged alpine ranges of the Caucasus on the other—no wonder the Georgians were so adamant about not giving it up. No wonder that the Russians were so quick to seize control. It must be a choice posting for the more than 3,000 Russian soldiers here now, Greg thought to himself—not like the contaminated work environment of those poor conscripts at Mayak.

Greg missed Anne and wished they were exploring this beautiful little 'statelet' together. He wondered whether she was able to decipher his one word text message and what she would be able to do about it. That would be difficult, he realized. It would be next to impossible for her to get into this breakaway part of Georgia or to trace where they and the nuclear material were at any moment. Or, for that matter, to take any action if she did manage to get in. The Russian military presence was very visible, with army vehicles constituting much of the traffic on the road. *I have to get another message to Anne somehow. But how, with Adam sitting right there?*

*****

Signs of settlement, of a bigger city, started to appear. The road crossed a broad river—the Gumitsa, according to the driver—alongside an old iron railway bridge.

"We're on the outskirts of Sukhumi," Adam said, as they passed derelict buildings riddled with bullet holes, gaping window sockets, bombed-away walls. The worst were the Stalinist-era apartment complexes, although many of them appeared to be still lived in.

"You know, this is where Lavrenti Beria was born," Adam said. "The head of the NKVD, Stalin's secret police. He was Georgian, like Stalin. In fact, he was Stalin's best friend. Partner in evil. Until the end, when Beria supposedly bested Stalin by killing him with rat poison."

Greg continued to look out the window, vaguely listening to what his friend was saying. Was that it—'partner in evil'—was that what he had become? Would he, like Beria, outdo his friend and kill him in the end? Would it have to come to that to stop Adam?

"Remember, Julia's grandfather wrote that Beria was the mastermind behind Mayak. He used the prisoners from the Gulags to build the secret atomic cities."

Yes, we can thank Beria for all this. Beria and Stalin.

"He was a real womanizer—some say a pedophile," Adam continued, in spite of Greg's silence. "Hetzel knows his story. In fact, he was telling me just the other day that the Polyakov twins are Beria's grandsons by the illegitimate daughter of one of his mistresses. Beria would have his men comb the streets to find good-looking girls for him. He would force them to be his whores for a while and then they'd disappear. Either to a Gulag or just plain dead. Their families would never hear of them again." Greg sensed that Adam felt some perverse pleasure in telling him this, but still did not favor him with a reaction.

The road approached the sea, again passing between rows of well situated, but war-wounded homes, and then came to a port with a few rusty, un-seaworthy hulks and two modern frigates sporting Russian flags. There was a sharp turn-off to the right, with a guarded wire-mesh fence immediately after the turn. The three cars pulled up, one behind the other, in front of the gate. Greg saw Colonel Polyakov get out and approach the guard post.

"This must be it," Adam said, "where the Chechen prisoners are kept. And the HEU. Greg, remember you're with the NNSA. The National Nuclear Security Administration."

"Of course."

"This is the new Russian naval base here. Shortly after recognizing Abkhazia, they made a big splash about turning the old cargo port in Sukhumi into a base for their Black Sea navy. They were going to clean out the ships they sank in previous wars and accommodate up to thirty war frigates. Apparently, they have a long way to go."

The Zils were let in through the gate and directed to the central building. Greg saw Irena get out, join the Colonel and come toward them.

They too alighted and the six of them—led by the Colonel—went into the main administration building. Polyakov walked up to the booth inside the entrance and said something to one of the soldiers sitting there. He came back and told them to wait while he went off with the other soldier.

*****

"Do you think we could use the washrooms?" Greg asked Adam after stomping his feet for a few minutes, needing to go, but also thinking this might be his only chance to try and contact Anne.

"Yeah, good idea. I'll ask." Adam went up to the window and spoke to the soldier in the booth. He pointed down a whitewashed hallway towards a door at the end.

"Go ahead. You go first," Adam said.

Greg entered the small cubicle and closed the door. The facilities were very primitive and after he finished, he turned on the tap and quickly found his cell phone. It took an eternity for the mobile to rev up and Greg hoped that the running water masked the silly start-up music. He knew that, with Adam outside, he could not talk at all, but thought at least another text message might be possible. To his dismay, though, once the phone was up and running, it would not pick up a signal. He quickly pressed the off button and put the mobile back in his pocket, turned off the tap and came out to where Adam was waiting impatiently.

Greg was dejected. He felt alone and considered what he might do next. It seemed that he was the only one who had any chance of stopping the sale of uranium that could cause a nuclear holocaust. Anne was nowhere. And without her, there was no prospect of armed intervention.

What could he do, alone?

Chapter 54

It was not long before Colonel Polyakov came back with the soldier and two officers whom he introduced to the others, including Greg. One of them, a Major Semprenov, told them to follow and they were led down one flight of stairs, along another whitewashed corridor and then through a locked metal door and down a narrower stairway. In this lower cellar, there was no daylight and the way along the damp, dirt-floored hallway was illuminated by naked light bulbs hanging from the ceiling on frayed wires. They came to another metal door, which opened into a windowless room with bare stone walls and a hard dirt floor. There was a table in the center with three unmatched chairs on one side, two on the other, and a bench along the wall. Semprenov went over to the middle of the three seats, gestured to Polyakov to take it, to Irena to sit on his right and he took the one on the left. Greg sat down on the bench beside Adam and was not pleased when Hetzel squeezed in next to him.

Within moments, the door opened and two haggard looking men with dark features and scraggly beards, wrists handcuffed behind their backs, were brought in and shoved roughly onto the chairs across from the triumvirate. On their faces and in their demeanor, they wore the emotional and physical scars of harsh imprisonment and torture.

Colonel Polyakov exchanged a few words with Irena, then turned to the prisoners. "Names?"

The Chechens did not answer. Some shouting from Polyakov.

The Colonel looked at the papers he had been passed by the other officer and turned to Irena.

"No matter. We have already identified them. Shall we get to the point?"

He addressed the two men again.

"You are criminal vermin. You were caught smuggling five kilos of highly enriched uranium across the border from Karachay-Cherkessia. The punishment for such terrorist activity is death."

The two sat stone-faced, staring straight ahead, seeing nothing.

"The only hope you have is if you tell us who gave it to you. Otherwise you die." To accentuate the point, Polyakov unbuttoned his jacket and took out his pistol from its shoulder holster, cocked it and placed it on the table.

"You first," the Colonel pointed to the older of the two Chechens, shouting, "you, stand up and tell us."

The man did not budge. Polyakov yelled at the two soldiers standing in the background.

"Pull him to his feet."

They dragged him up. The man wobbled but held his ground.

"Okay, you shit. Last chance." The Colonel pointed his pistol at the heart of the Chechen and turned to Irena, saying, "You have to be tough with these insects."

Greg blanched and saw that Irena, too, was shaken.

"Don't want to answer? Then …" Colonel Polyakov fired two quick shots in rapid succession at the Chechen. A red spot appeared first on his forehead and then on his chest. Greg saw the defiance in the eyes replaced by the blankness of death as the two stunned soldiers allowed the prisoner to slump to the ground.

A moment's silence and Polyakov turned to the second Chechen. He was only a teenager, Greg observed. The poor boy was shaking, on the verge of tears.

"Okay, now it's your turn. Tell me how you got the nuclear material. Or do you want to die a dog's death too?"

Greg saw the fear in the young man's eyes.

"Stand up and answer!" The Colonel pointed the gun at his heart.

The young man tried to get up and fell back on the chair. He had a confused look, as if something had snapped in him when his partner was shot. The officer shouted at the two soldiers, who jerked the prisoner to his feet. The

229

boy glanced again at his fellow Chechen, sprawled on the dirt floor, dead.

"We … we …"

"Speak up man!"

"We … we were told by one of Ruslan's friends." Greg surmised that Ruslan was the older Chechen. "He told us we could make some money if we met a doctor in Teberda and took a briefcase for him to Sukhumi. Across the mountains. Please, we did not know what was in the bag. Please … that is all I know."

"What was the doctor's name?"

"Please … I do not know."

"How did you recognize him?"

"In a tea room. We met in a tea room."

"I did not ask where. I asked, how did you recognize him?"

"He had dark glasses."

"What did he look like?"

"I don't remember … "

"Was he tall?"

"Yes. That big." He nodded with his chin at the soldier standing beside him.

"Fat?"

"Yes, sort of …"

"Hair?"

"Brown. Like that." The boy pointed with his chin to Greg.

"Well, I doubt that he was American." Polyakov let out a raucous laugh.

"No … "

"Was he Chechen vermin? Or Russian?"

"Russian. Not Chechen. No, not from Caucasus."

"Well, at least now we know he was Russian," the Colonel said sarcastically, turning to Irena.

"And whom were you supposed to deliver the HEU to?"

"Sorry … the what?"

"The briefcase, vermin."

"A man in Sukhumi. But we were captured, so I don't know."

"His name?"

"I … I don't remember."

"You better try harder." Polyakov picked up the pistol.

"We were told he was called Khalid. But that's all."

"Khalid what?"

"I don't know. Please, I don't know!"

"How were you to make contact?"

"I don't know. I think Ruslan had a number to call. But I don't know …" the boy answered between sobs.

Semprenov leaned over and whispered something to Polyakov.

"Anything else?" Polyakov shouted at the boy.

"No …"

"Take him away."

The two guards grabbed the young man under his arms and all three swiveled around. As they moved towards the door, the Colonel fired two shots at the back and head of the Chechen, just as he had with his older friend. The body jerked and slumped between the soldiers, and only then did the telltale red marks appear through the shirt and hair. The guards just let the young man fall to the floor next to his compatriot.

*****

"These rats deserve to die," the Colonel said as he turned to Irena, placing his pistol back in its holster. "Well, there you have it. That was all we could get out of them. Major Semprenov and his men tried before, but had no more success."

"Thank … thank you," Irena stuttered, still shaken by the summary executions she had just witnessed.

"Were you able to figure anything out?"

"No. No. Not immediately. I will have to ask some questions back at Mayak. Then hopefully I will be able to make some connections. But thank you, Colonel Polyakov, you have been very helpful. I appreciate you doing the questioning. And you too, Major Semprenov, thank you for letting us be part of this interrogation. And for your earlier efforts." Greg did not want to think about what those might have been.

"But of course, we are all on the same side. We all want to stop these terrorists."

'All on the same side'. What a lying, hypocritical, criminal lot of thieves and murderers, Greg thought to himself, angry and disgusted. Some were clearly conspiring to let nuclear material get into the hands of terrorists. And engaging in torture and execution of people they considered their inferiors, supposed enemies they used as tools to pursue their criminal purposes. Greg could not help think that the Chechens had been set up—they were the mules to transport the bait across the border. Set up by Irena—and it would seem, Adam—so they would have a great excuse to get enough HEU for a bomb into the hands of terrorists. And how convenient that now the Chechens, a crucial part of any evidence, had been vaporized. Just like Fazkov.

Greg wondered whether Colonel Polyakov was in on the plot. Probably, since his brother clearly was.

"Now, Major Semprenov, if we can just get the briefcase with the HEU so we can take it back to where it belongs," Irena, having regained her composure, said in a beguiling voice.

"Of course, of course," the officer answered, standing up from the chair. "That is upstairs under lock and key in my office. Shall we?"

Semprenov led the way, stepping over the older of the two Chechens. Irena and Polyakov followed, as did the rest of them, Greg casting a pitying look at the dead teenager.

*****

Up in his office on the second floor, Major Semprenov went straight to a big metal safe, dialed the combination and waited for the lock to click open.

"I put the briefcase in here to safeguard it. I hope it did not give off too much radioactivity."

"Don't worry," Adam answered, "highly enriched uranium in this form is not dangerous. Plus, it's not enough for a bomb, so I don't know why terrorists would want it."

"Maybe they are gathering smaller amounts from everywhere to make one big bomb," Semprenov said.

"That could take forever. It would be much easier to steal a large enough quantity from say, Mayak. HEU that is ready to use." Polyakov looked at Irena, smiling. "Don't you agree Irena?"

"Not if I can help it," Irena replied with a little laugh.

"There," the Major said, producing a smaller version of the metal briefcases still in the Zils from the bottom shelf of the safe and handing it to Irena. "In any case, I am happy to be rid of this."

"And I'm very glad to get it back. Thank you, Major."

Chapter 55

Greg only felt disgust at the perversion of justice, the insane executions he had just witnessed. He thought of Omi telling how his step-grandfather was repeatedly taken in for questioning by the AVO.

*****

"My dear Kálmán was hauled in at least once a year—if not more often—by the AVO. Greg, you don't know—I don't even know—how much he suffered.

Friday. Yes, it was always on a Friday. At night. Just like when your grandfather was taken away.

Always after a long day's work at the factory, after finishing the meager evening meal of salami and bread, after kissing the children good-night, just as he finally settled in to spend a few peaceful moments with me before collapsing in bed.

A knock on the door. The black leather-coated thugs. It was always the same two. One, the leader, a big guy, cigarette hanging from thick lips, sporting a moustache. The other, a small weasel of a man, with shifty eyes and pock-marked face. Sometimes a third thug and even a fourth accompanied them.

They would take him down to Andrássy út 60. For questioning.

And it was always the same. Hours later, at three or four in the morning, after I had bitten my nails until my fingers bled and cried till I had no more tears, a feeble knock on the door. There, leaning against the wall, face bruised and bleeding, glasses broken and clothes torn, arm twisted out of place as if broken, would stand Kálmán, spitting teeth and blood onto the white tile of the hallway.

I would undress him gently, dab his wounds with cotton batten and alcohol, bandage them. I would make him sip some tea and then put him to bed, letting him sleep well into the next day.

When he would finally wake in the afternoon, moaning from the pain and the bad memories, and I had sent the children out to play, we would talk. The story never varied. The AVO wanted Kálmán to tell them everything he heard from my father, the doctor, the Director of the tuberculosis institutes. They wanted him to spy on his father-in-law.

He refused. He told them we only talked about everyday, mundane things. That Apa never talked about his profession, about his patients, about what they might have told him.

Which was true.

He did not tell them lies to stop the beatings.

Kálmán had moral courage; he knew what was right and what was wrong. Even though the reward for making the right choice was to be beaten to a pulp. And to be told that your children would never get past grade school, that they would be marked for life as offspring of traitors."

Not like these amoral beasts Greg was traveling with, who looked forward to profiting at the expense of hundreds, thousands of lives.

Chapter 56

They quickly passed through the city center, where the somber Communist blocks were replaced by stately old villas painted pink and yellow and blue. In this Riviera climate, lush palm and cypress trees surrounded the houses, although it was the middle of winter. But even these older mansions—once the dachas of the Politburo and others among the exalted in classless, Communist society—had not escaped the bruises of battle.

"Why don't you buy one of these palaces with your share of the money? You could fix it up very cheap." Adam asked, chuckling at his own attempt at humor.

Greg, still traumatized by the executions he had just witnessed, did not respond.

The main road, leaving town, followed the curving beach of the bay and then, after crossing the second of two small rivers, turned inland. They traveled fast despite the bad road. There was very little traffic, other than the odd mule-pulled Abkhaz cart or Russian military vehicle.

They passed the village of Kvermo-Gilpish and turned off the highway that led through Gali to the main checkpoint at the border with the rest of Georgia. They were heading towards a smaller border post used by local traffic only. This route led through battered villages, forests and swampy wetlands. The road was narrow, in parts barely passable.

All of a sudden, there was a strange muffled ringing coming from inside the briefcase Adam had placed on the middle seat.

"Finally," Adam said, opening the briefcase. "The radiophone—there is no cell phone reception here in Abkhazia."

"Hello. Polyakov, is that you?"

"Yes. We're here at Ops 1," Greg overheard the scratchy voice on the other end. "Everything is secure and ready. Where are you?" It was Sergei, not the Colonel.

"We're on the way to Poti. Left Sukhumi about thirty minutes ago. Mission accomplished. No problem." So Poti was where the transaction would take place.

"You will arrive in about an hour. I will contact Khalid and tell him to be here in an hour and a half."

"Good." Khalid—that was the name the Chechen teenager had also given. Greg surmised he must be the terrorist buyer. Where would he be coming from?

"I have checked out the Russian commander on the Abkhaz side responsible for the border post where you will cross. Lieutenant Kuznetsov. He served under me in Chechnya. I called to tell him that an important mission with high-ranking IAEA and Russian officials is coming through in pursuit of Chechen terrorists who crossed into Georgia with stolen nuclear material."

"Great," Adam said beside him.

Well, well, they were using that story again.

"Kuznetsov will go with you to the Georgian side and make sure they let you through. You may have to figure out something for your American friend. Or else get rid of him." Adam looked at Greg. It was obvious that Greg had heard. He tried to remain calm as he strained to listen to the rest of what the Russian had to say.

"No Georgian border guard would want to be responsible for allowing nuclear terrorists to get away. They are members of IAEA, no?"

The radiophone crackled as Kallay said, "Excellent, Sergei. Excellent."

*****

Definitely not excellent, Greg thought to himself, as Adam put the radio receiver back in the briefcase and closed it with a thud.

"You heard, Greg. We're coming to the border and may be stopped by the Georgians. They're sensitive to incursions from this side, especially now that the Russians control Abkhazia."

Greg's mind was racing; what should he do? At the border, should he try to alert the Georgians to the real mission? Is this the last chance? Or was there hope for a better opportunity later? And how could he let Anne know that Polyakov was already there in Poti, where the sale was going to take place?

"Polyakov is good. Very good. We'll say we're chasing Chechen terrorists who were trafficking stolen nuclear material. The Georgians can't refuse to let us through. He's right. The risk is too high for any simple border guard to take on. Besides, this is not really an international frontier between two countries. Just a made-up one between two parts of the same country. If we have problems, we shoot our way through."

*****

The cars came to a T-junction and ahead, behind a ramshackle house and some fields, Greg could see a broad river. The Zil in front pulled up, they behind it.

"Enguri," Greg heard the driver say. "The Enguri River. This is the cease-fire line between Abkhazia and Georgia. On the other side is Anaklia. That is already Georgia proper."

Irena started back toward their car. Adam got out and met her halfway. Greg also climbed out to stretch his legs and saw that she had lit a cigarette and the two were having a heated discussion in Russian. He could make out the names Polyakov and Kuznetsov here and there.

A few minutes later, a Russian Jeep approached from the east and pulled up on the other side of the road. A smartly dressed officer jumped out, crossed to where Irena and Adam were standing and shook their hands. The discussion continued and then Greg saw Adam pointing to him and to Hetzel, who was still in the other car. The soldier—who Greg surmised was Kuznetsov—nodded, jumped back in the jeep and had the driver turn it around to face the same direction as the Zils.

"Okay. That's the Lieutenant who heads up the Russian contingent in Pirveli-Otobaja near here. We'll follow him a couple of kilometers to a small bridge and he'll lead us across. It's just for local traffic. Not an official crossing. But it'll cut a good forty minutes off our time and it's not well guarded. Kuznetsov will deal with the border guards. We'll need to give him our passports."

The road meandered through fields and villages, roughly following the river. It did not take long until—in the next small settlement, where a single-lane wooden bridge crossed the Enguri—Kuznetsov's vehicle pulled off the road and parked on the grass beside another Jeep. Greg saw two soldiers inside, one with eyes closed, head resting against the door, obviously sleeping. His partner woke him quickly and the two got out to salute the officer, smoothing out their uniforms as they approached him.

After a short exchange, the soldiers grabbed their Kalashnikovs and started on foot across the bridge. Kuznetsov went over and talked to the drivers of the Zils, collected the passports and jumped in his Jeep. His driver followed the soldiers and once they were across, the first Zil squeezed onto the narrow bridge. When that one was across, it was their turn. The soldiers walked beside Kuznetsov's Jeep around a turn in the road to the Georgian border control—a hut with a single barrier across the lane.

A man, unshaven and dressed in a soiled crew-neck sweater and torn jeans, appeared. Kuznetsov got out, and with the soldiers at his side, approached the Georgian. There was an extended exchange and Kuznetsov gave the man the passports, looking at his watch impatiently. The Russian officer lit a cigarette, while the border guard took the documents inside the hut. In less than ten minutes, the passports were back in their hands.

"Phew, that wasn't hard,"Adam exclaimed. "We have the rest of the day to chase down the thieves and recover the uranium. We're supposed to come back through before dark. Remember, you're now formally an official of the NNSA."

So that was it. There went his chance to alert the Georgians that the Zils were carrying a hundred pounds of HEU to be sold to terrorists on Georgian territory. He should have done something, he told himself. But what? Even if he had been able to make himself understood and convince the Georgian, what could the two of them have done against three armed soldiers—plus the drivers and Adam, who all carried guns? Hetzel and Irena probably did too. No, it was not the right time.

Was he just rationalizing his cowardice? Or worse still, was he lethargic because of the big pay-off offered by Adam? He had to stop this somehow.

*****

The road crossed what looked like a canal, then snaked through forest and marshland. The driver said something in Russian that Greg missed, but Adam translated: "Kolkheti National Park. Ancient wetlands. Peat bogs. Heaven if you're a birdwatcher."

They crossed another large river before changing direction to go west along the south bank. Soon, Greg saw the sea and the cars turned south following the stunning beach, with rich swampland on the other side. What were they doing transporting one of the most dangerous explosive, radioactive substances known to science through this pristine land, Greg wondered.

And then another river to cross. Followed by small, dingy-looking houses and stark Communist-era apartment buildings, indicating that they were approaching a larger town.

"Poti," the driver said.

It was not long before they turned off the main road and within minutes, Greg could see the moored ships, the large yellow cranes and dilapidated warehouses of Georgia's main port. The buildings were still in rough shape from the war. Indeed, some were in such bad condition that they had been abandoned. Greg was surprised when the Zil convoy pulled up in front of one such derelict structure and parked alongside the two Subaru Foresters already there.

"It seems we have arrived," Adam said. "This is where we meet our friends. The buyers."

Chapter 57

Polyakov climbed out of the car and sauntered over to Anne's side, opening the door with one hand and brandishing her Glock in the other.

"Okay, bitch, let's go. Any funny stuff and you both die."

The others got out of the cars too, and Anne yelled to ask Julia if she was all right. Polyakov rammed the pistol into her right kidney screaming, "Shut up, cunt," at her. Julia, too, was shoved along at the end of a Kalashnikov by one of Polyakov's men. Others in the entourage carried briefcases as well as their weapons, still another, a coil of nylon rope.

One of the thugs led the way up the outside stairs to a rickety wooden gangway that seemed to encircle the entire building. The rest of the group, including Julia and Anne, followed, clambering over rubble. The men knew where they were going; they had obviously been here before. Several of them walked in opposite directions on the walkway, guns ready, looking through windows and kicking doors open, making sure the building was not compromised. When they gave the all-clear signal, Polyakov led the way into a large room, empty but for a few chairs and a table, broken glass and detritus on the floor.

"You two in here." Polyakov pushed Anne through a doorway that led to a side office, signaling to Julia's guard and the man with the rope to follow. The room was furnished with a table and a chair. A window and a door led to the gangway on the water side. Through the broken pane, Anne caught a glimpse of a boat moored alongside the pier.

"Okay, bitch. Spread your legs," Polyakov said, shoving Anne onto the table face up. While the other guard held her shoulders down, he took the rope and tied her ankles firmly to two of the table legs, then roughly pulled her arms back and up above her head and secured her wrists tightly to the remaining two table legs. Anne was spread-eagled, stretched to the limit and hurting on the hard tabletop. Polyakov grabbed her crotch with his left hand, squeezed it hard and said, "I'll deal with you later."

Then he sauntered over to where Julia was standing at gunpoint against the wall. "Here, you whore, you sit here," Polyakov barked, pushing Julia onto the rickety chair. With the remaining rope, he tied a knot on one of the chair legs and then wrapped it around and around her until it was all used up. Julia squealed and tears came to her eyes as the arms dealer pulled tight and fastened the end to the chair back.

"Okay, bitches. I'll be back. Any funny stuff and you're dead meat."

Polyakov left through the open door. Anne, in her pain and discomfort, could hear him say something and the men laugh. She panicked: what was going to happen to them? Was there no way to escape? She tried to move her limbs but they were tied tightly; there was no give. She looked over at Julia, who was equally immobile, trussed up on the chair.

Anne's ears caught the whirring of a laptop starting up in the other room, distracting her from their plight. She heard what sounded like a radio and then dialing—must be a radiotelephone. The volume was so loud that Anne could hear the ringing clearly.

"Hello. Polyakov, is that you?" Anne could distinguish Kallay's suave voice through the static.

"Yes. We are here at Ops 1. Everything is secure and ready. Where are you?"

Kallay and Polyakov are in it together! Adam, how could you...? She hated these men, these criminals. The conversation droned on, but Anne only caught a few words until the very end. She heard a "Great" from the Kallay side and then Polyakov push his chair back and raised his voice.

"Kuznetsov will go with you to the Georgian side and make sure they let you in. You may have to figure something out for your American friend or else get rid of him. No Georgian border guard wants to be responsible for allowing nuclear terrorists to get away. They are members of IAEA, no?"

241

The radiophone crackled but Anne heard Kallay say at the other end: "Excellent, Sergei. Excellent."

*****

No, damn it, Anne thought to herself. That border is the only obstacle that could avert a nuclear disaster. She had to do something. And fast.

"American friend." That must be Greg. Thank God, he was alive. And coming there. They must be in Abkhazia, about to cross into Georgia.

"… Or get rid of him …"—*oh, please no.*

She tried to listen as Polyakov made another call, then gave a few orders to his men. She heard him push his chair back and slam something shut. Fear gripped her as his voice sounded closer and footsteps approached. And then she felt his presence enter the room and close the door firmly.

"Okay, bitches, now the fun begins. Which one shall it be?"

Out of the corner of her eye, Anne saw him approach Julia, waving a huge knife. He sat on her lap, knife in her face, free hand caressing her breasts. Then the hand grabbed Julia's disheveled hair while he forced his lips onto hers.

"You, you whoring bitch, you're lucky today," Polyakov said, pulling Julia's head back until her neck almost snapped. "Russian soldiers don't rape Russian women. Even though you fuck Americans. But you watch real good to see how Russian men do it." He laughed and patted Julia's cheek with the flat of the blade as he stood up from her lap.

Anne sensed in an instant what was in store for her and after another momentary bout of panic, knew there was nothing she could do. She had to try to relax, clear her mind. Above all she must survive, get through it alive.

Polyakov came over to the table, put one hand on her left breast and stroked her throat with the knife.

"Okay, Interpol bitch. You're the lucky one. You'll never forget this fuck."

Polyakov reached into Anne's jeans with his free hand and pulled her turtleneck over her head. He slashed her bra at the sternum, ripped it out from under her and threw it aside. He cut the rope tying her right wrist, and roughly pulled the turtleneck all the way off that arm and over her head, so that it dangled from her left wrist. Anne's upper body was now naked and Polyakov gave her left nipple a hard squeeze that sent shivers through her body. He then undid her jeans and yanked them down as far as they would go. The brute disappeared under the table for a moment, pulled her boots and socks off, and

242

sliced the rope tying her ankles so that she was only secured firmly by her left wrist and his iron grip. He shoved her fully up on the table so that her head hung over the end, finished pulling the jeans off and cast them aside, all as Anne was just starting to sense the newfound freedom of her limbs. She tried to kick him and roll off the table but Polyakov grabbed her by the panties, twisted them tight and used the knife to cut them off her. He lifted his right hand, holding the weapon high in the air and with a loud grunt stuck it violently in the table just to the left of Anne's head, so that she could hear the twang of the blade quivering right next to her ear.

The Russian straddled her, pinning her with his legs and one arm. With his free hand, he fondled her breasts and suckled and bit her nipples so hard that Anne came close to crying out in pain. He then hastily unzipped his trousers and spread himself on top of Anne, forced her open with first one, two and then three fingers, and when he was hard, entered her.

Anne felt like she was being pierced by cold steel, a sword sawing through her insides. *Oh God, please make it fast, make him finish.* She tried to take herself elsewhere but the only thought that came into her mind was, "What will I tell Greg?" Even though she had been trained to expect this possibility, trained to try and remove herself from her body, she had never, never imagined how terrible rape was. It was her spirit that was sawn in two, the will to live destroyed.

And then it was over, as suddenly as it had begun. Polyakov was finished, spent. The sawing, the violent rocking movement, the raucous breathing stopped. Anne felt like she was in a tunnel, outside reality. In the distance, she could hear sobs, Julia weeping. And the crackling of the radiotelephone, somewhere in the other room. She felt the weight removed, contact ended.

Anne heard Polyakov pull up his zipper and light a cigarette. She felt the life-giving air in front of her face extinguished once again as he grabbed her chin and turned her face toward him, breathing vile cigarette smoke at her. She closed her eyes, not wanting to look at this monster.

"Okay, Interpol bitch. That was the first thing you had to do to stay alive. Consider yourself fortunate." He took another drag before he continued. "The next is that you will work for me when you go back to your job in Vienna. I could use someone inside Interpol. If you refuse or if you ever betray me, you, your parents, your stupid American lover and that bitch over there will all die. Understood?"

243

Anne did not answer. She was trying to hold back the tears surging within her. How did he know about Greg and her?

"Now pull yourself together, bitch. Get dressed quickly, or I will let the others have a go." Polyakov took a last drag on his cigarette butt and the next moment Anne felt searing pain as he extinguished it by pressing it into her left breast. Her scream drowned out his sadistic laugh and Julia's sobbing. The animal glanced at his watch, then sauntered over to Julia, melting into mocking laughter when he saw the fear in her face. He adjusted his pants ostentatiously and pushed the chair with her on it violently over on its side. Still laughing, he left the room, leaving the door wide open.

*****

Anne was sore all over, feeling used, dirty. She desperately wanted to wash every drop of sweat, every bit of Polyakov from her body, from inside her, but there was no basin, no bathroom. She curled up, facing away from Julia and wept.

After a timeless period in the fetal position, Anne's training started to kick in—*I've got to move, I've got to stop these bastards.* Her neck ached, her breast was still pulsing with pain, but she slowly raised her head to peruse her battered body. In addition to the burn, there was a trickle of blood on the inside of the other breast and just below her navel where the Russian had scratched her with his knife. Her nipples hurt, there were the brute's teeth marks, and internally, she felt soreness, but knew that that, too, would heal. There was the wounding of her spirit, the emotional scarring—would that ever go away?

"Oh God, poor Anne," she heard Julia sob.

Still lying naked on the table, Anne shivered: she was cold, drained of all emotion. Slowly, mechanically, she reached across with her left hand to pull down the turtleneck. As she leaned over to untie her right arm, the blood rushed to her head and she almost passed out. She struggled with the knot, but the challenge helped her focus on what needed to be done, not the horror that had just happened to her. *Got to free myself, then Julia, get dressed, before they come back in the room. The door, wasn't there another door too? Maybe they could get out ...* She looked up, searched the office and seeing the exit to the gangway, redoubled her efforts to free her fettered arm.

And then, in the other room, she heard Polyakov say something to one of the guards. Footsteps approached, just as the knot gave way. Anne was overwhelmed by fear: *Oh, no, not again, please, not again.* She hurriedly looked for her panties, remembered that they had been shredded, picked up her jeans from the floor and clumsily tried to pull them over her aching body. Just in time, but she couldn't quite close them, as a pistol-waving thug entered. He came straight to her, grabbed her by the just freed-up arm, pulled her back into his body, with his left arm squeezing her breasts, and roughly shoved the pistol-holding right hand down into her unzipped jeans, entering her with his last two fingers. He smacked his lips lewdly and said something like "Very nice" in Russian, then forced Anne back on the table, this time face down. He pulled her two wrists together and tied them to a table leg, so tightly that Anne could feel her fingers go numb. Then he grabbed Anne's flailing right leg and secured the bare ankle to one of the other three table legs—but not before she managed to land a couple of solid kicks on his chest, resulting in a vicious smack across the back. He finally overpowered her and tied her remaining ankle to another table leg, so that she ended up facedown with legs spread wide apart. Picking up his pistol, he whacked her on the rear end with it, barked "I will fuck you later" and left the room.

Anne could not hold back the tears—the tears of pain, of humiliation, of helplessness. *Oh Greg, where are you?*

Chapter 58

Greg followed Adam and Irena up the rubble-covered open stairway and along the wooden walkway that ran right around the building. He heard the Russians in the big room well before they got to it and was surprised by the activity. As Adam opened the door, Greg caught sight of Polyakov, hunched over a laptop on the table in the middle of the room. Two men with Kalashnikovs in their hands and huge knives at the hip were by the windows—one, on the water side, the other, looking out over the parking lot. By the door they entered, there was another Russian and still two others guarded the small doors leading to rooms on either side.

"Good that you've arrived," Polyakov welcomed Irena, Adam and Hetzel with hugs and kisses on two cheeks. "Khalid and the others will be here soon. Everything is set up. The banks are standing by. They know we will be calling and have all the information."

"Excellent," Irena said. "We have the two cases." She nodded to Hetzel to put the briefcase he was carrying on the corner of the table.

"I'll keep this over here," Adam said, as he gently put the other container on the floor where he and Greg were standing near the door behind Polyakov, adding, "For obvious reasons."

Greg perked his ears to the sound of a powerful motorboat docking just outside. He tried to see out the window, but was too far and the view was partially blocked by the rusty hull of a ship moored alongside the building.

"That must be them." Adam, too, had heard.

"Good," said Polyakov. "We're ready to begin."

*****

A tall, muscular man with a dark complexion and short-cropped beard appeared in the doorway, Uzi in hand. He was followed by three well-armed Middle Eastern compatriots. Last through the door was a large man with flaming red hair and a very pale face dotted with lots of freckles, whom Greg instantly recognized as Billy Crawford. He was dressed in camouflage combat gear and army boots, and carried a machine gun.

"Hello, Khalid," Polyakov greeted the leader in English, "long time no see."

"Yes, it has been. Time to do another deal. High time."

"And this must be Brother Peter, no? Pleased to meet you."

Billy Crawford … Brother Peter. Yes, the Sons of Jesus, that must be it. Now allied with al Qaeda—the shocking realization surged in Greg's brain. They were buying the uranium together and had a common, terrible purpose in mind.

"Howdy all." Billy waved his free hand. "Hello, Adam. And if it ain't my favorite writer of smutty crime trash, Greg Martens," he added, pointing his machine gun at Greg. "I didn't know you were in on this." But how did he know Adam was? Did they … of course, that was it! The card. They had met up in Vienna.

"I assume all these men—and lady—are trustworthy?" bowing to Irena, Khalid asked Polyakov.

"Yes," came Polyakov's reply, but Greg thought he saw the Russian throw a fleeting glance towards him.

"Can we see it? The uranium." Khalid asked.

"Of course. Half—twenty-four kilos of bomb-ready HEU—in this briefcase," Polyakov said, placing his hand on the metal case on the table. "The slightly bigger half—twenty-six—is over there," and he pointed to the one sitting between Adam and Greg.

Khalid opened the briefcase on the table and studied the contents. Billy joined him and said, "Beautiful, ain't it?" Khalid went over to where Adam and Greg were standing, gave them a quick glance as he squatted to open that container, and again was satisfied by what he saw: a softball-sized hemisphere, with a slight bulge on the flat side, sitting in a gray metal casing.

"Ali," Khalid called to one of his colleagues, "come and weigh this one."

The summoned man came over, put his weapon and knapsack down and took a portable scale from the bag. He then put some gloves on and gingerly picked up the lump of nuclear material, placing it on the scale.

"Very good," Ali yelled to Khalid.

"All ninety per cent?" Billy asked, turning to Polyakov. "You guarantee it?"

"Yes. Or more." It was Irena who answered.

"You can trust her," Polyakov said. "She's the Director of Mayak, where it comes from. If you like it, we can supply more."

"Excellent. That's what we want to hear."

"Shall we start? I have the banks standing by. I will dial your two first so you can give the instructions for the transfers. They already have the accounts. Twenty-five, or one half, from you, Khalid, in mine, the other half from Brother Peter, in Adam Kallay's, as agreed. Distributions to others will be made from there."

"Fine."

Polyakov pushed one button and the radiotelephone speed dialed. He handed the receiver to the Arab.

"Hello. Khalid al Basr here."

A pause.

"Code is XJ8209PYG. Mother's maiden name: Hamadan. Confirm that transfer to go ahead as per pre-authorized instructions."

And then, apparently, a question from the other end.

"Vortex," came Khalid's answer. Must be another random check, Greg thought.

"Thank you." He pushed the button to hang up. "Done."

"Now you." Polyakov passed the receiver to Billy. After a few moments, Billy, who had strolled over to the window on the far side, mumbled something in the phone and then came back with a satisfied look on his face. "That was easy," was all he said as he handed the receiver back to Polyakov.

"I will now dial my bank." The radiotelephone again made a scratching, scraping noise.

"Polyakov here. Did the transfer come through?"

A question from the banker.

"Yes, sorry. Galkova. 9054JPT."

A moment's wait. Activity on the other end.

"The full twenty-five? Thank you. Good-bye." And he hung up.

"Good. Now, yours?" Polyakov turned to Adam.

"Hello? Adam Kallay on the line. Yes, it has been a long time. Are you well, Mrs. Kim?"

A short wait for the answer.

"Yes. I'm just wondering if the transfer of a major sum has arrived in my account. Yes, yes. But of course." Adam held the receiver away from his mouth and said, "She's just checking."

Another pause.

"Oh, yes, of course. It's Wagner." And then Adam mumbled a string of numbers in the receiver that even Greg could not hear.

"That's right. Thank you. Fantastic! Good-bye, Mrs. Kim. Hope to speak to you soon."

"So, you have the money. We will take the uranium and get on our way. Great to do business with you, as always. Until the next time. Praise be to Allah. Good-bye." Khalid moved toward the table to shake Polyakov's hand.

Irena, who was standing beside the table, reached forward to close the slightly ajar metal briefcase on the table. At that instant, Greg heard a loud bang, a shattering of glass and saw, to his horror, that her entire head had been shot away. Blood and brains splattered all over, even spraying him where he stood several meters distant by the wall. The dark red fluid was everywhere, flowing down the grooves on the light grey metal briefcase, onto the table and dripping to the floor. Kolchakova's headless body crumpled, blood still gushing from where the neck had held the head a few seconds earlier.

The Russians, other than Polyakov, rushed to the parking lot side, from where the shot had come. There was a tense moment while Khalid aimed his Uzi at Polyakov, but the Russian raised his hands and nodded at the remains of Irena's body on the floor.

"No, no! It was not us," he shouted, pointing outside, as they heard running up the stairs and along the corridor.

Out of the corner of his eye, Greg noticed Adam pick up the briefcase from the floor and slowly edge towards the door behind where Polyakov had been sitting. In the same instant, he saw Hetzel try the door on the far side wall and heard the yell, "This way!" Billy closed the bloody briefcase on the table and grabbed it in his free hand, running after Hetzel and waving his machine gun around with the other.

Meanwhile, wild shooting continued out and through the windows. Ali, the terrorist with the rucksack, dropped his automatic and tumbled to the floor, blood streaming from his chest. One of the Russians by the window went down, one side of his face obliterated. Polyakov simply kicked him aside and moved into his position.

As he heard a female voice he thought he recognized as Julia's in the next room shout a surprised "Adam!", it suddenly dawned on Greg what his friend was up to. He grabbed Ali's pistol and bolted after him, while the combatants were firing their guns all around. He saw Billy look back from the door, searching for the other case. Or was it for him? But the Son of Jesus' attention was momentarily distracted by a commando who ran past the window on the water side of the building, allowing Greg to plunge through the small door after Adam.

*****

The terrible shock of what greeted him there was, as he described it later, possibly the worst experience of his life. Anne, the woman he now thought he loved, face down, spread-eagled on the table, disheveled, ravaged, underclothes shredded, so that it was not difficult to figure out what had happened. Julia, trussed up in a chair and pushed over into the rubble on the floor. Meanwhile, Adam, his erstwhile friend, was disappearing through the far door with half a bomb's worth of highly enriched uranium in a briefcase.

For a second he stood there in shock, then rushed over to Anne.

"Anne, what have they done to you?"

"Polyakov …, " she barely whispered between the uncontrollable sobs.

"Oh, God," he said, stroking her back with one hand and starting to untie the rope holding her wrists with the other.

"Greg. Adam … You have to go after Adam."

"No, Anne, I must get you out of here."

"Go after Adam. You have to. We cannot let him get away. Otherwise this will all have been for nothing." She had to dig really deep to find the willpower to say this. Her whole being wanted Greg to hold her and comfort her. "Go."

He kissed her neck even as she said this and concentrated on setting her hands free. Greg did not want to leave Anne, now that he had found her.

Especially not in that state and with all the shooting going on. But she was right. He could not let his rogue friend get away with half the uranium and half the money. And the fate of the world in his hands.

Once Anne's hands were free, he went over to Julia and with one more glimpse back at his love, he deftly undid the knot securing Julia to the chair. Greg told the Russian girl to take care of Anne before going through the door and onto the walkway. Looking right and then left, he caught sight of Adam about fifty feet in front up on the railing. When Adam turned, their eyes locked briefly. With his free hand, Adam started to reach into his inside pocket, but thought better of it. He hesitated for a moment, like a condemned man before stepping off the end of a gangplank, then with a flourish, threw the briefcase across to the deck of the rusty old boat and launched himself into space after it.

Chapter 59

Greg rolled on the deck as he completed his leap. He felt pain in his left hip when he got up, but nothing was broken. He looked for the pistol and seeing that it was still in his left hand, took off in the direction Adam had disappeared.

The boat was old—it must have been taken out of commission well before the last Abkhaz-Georgian war. The painted surfaces in most places had deteriorated to rust or rotting wood. Although Greg did not know a lot about ships, he thought this must have been a large fishing boat.

Greg came to a door through which he thought Adam had entered. He found himself in a corridor leading aft and at the end, a small doorway opening to what had been the crew's quarters. No doubt Adam had a gun—that was what he was reaching for on the railing. Greg ducked through the entrance and hid behind one of the rusting metal bunk beds. He tried to look through the frames, but could see nothing in the poorly lit room.

"Adam, I know you're in here. Come out so we can talk. You cannot get away with the uranium. Give it up."

Greg listened for any sign of life.

Nothing.

He moved gingerly, past the first bed frame, the second, then the third, looking to both sides each time.

Nothing.

Then he spotted it. Right at the end of the room, beyond which was only the metal hull of the boat.

An open hatch in the floor.

A putrid waft of rotting fish struck him in the face as he approached and looked down. Amazing, that the smell lingered after so many years.

Climbing carefully down the ladder into the hold, Greg peered through the darkness for any sign of Adam. All he heard was the scurrying of rats on the metal floor. His own feet were firmly on the bottom now, while bats or birds flew wildly back and forth across the chamber, disturbed by the intruder. As his eyes grew accustomed to the twilight created by the few portholes high up on either side, he ascertained that there was nowhere to take cover in the hold. It was empty and there was nothing to hide behind. If Adam was there, he could have shot him several times over. Greg moved forward slowly.

"Adam! Come out, now. Let's talk. You cannot get away." His voice reverberated in the darkness.

At the far end, he saw another metal door and headed for it. It gave way easily, creaking on the hinges, almost falling away in his hands. He stepped across the threshold into what was once the boat's engine room and peered beyond the skeleton of the rusty machinery, stripped away for spare parts, in the direction of the scratching of little rodent feet on metal.

"Adam, I have to speak to you. Come out. It's no use."

Greg was startled by the sudden movement of a shadow, as Adam stepped out halfway from behind the remnants of the ancient engine.

"Here I am, Greg. Do you want to cut a deal? Is that it?" The phantom asked.

He had not changed. Why would he?

"Adam, you will not get away. Give yourself up. Hand the briefcase over."

"Greg, we can split the twenty-five million in my bank account and still sell this stuff. Fifty-fifty."

"This is the end, Adam. There is no deal."

And then the darkness was shattered by the sound of a shot that echoed like a drum roll across the metal-walled engine room. Greg felt pain sear through his left shoulder, even as he heard his friend scramble in the other direction. He threw himself after Adam and caught a glimpse of him as he started to climb a metal ladder behind the engine remains. A ladder leading to the world above, the world of light and air.

Greg fired Ali's pistol, the deafening noise danced from wall to wall, and he saw Adam slump to the floor, grabbing the bottom rung as he went down. Adam made another feeble attempt at climbing, but could not pull himself up.

Greg stood completely still until well after the echoes of the shot and the hectic scraping of rats running amok died away and all was silent. Then, the faint and familiar music of a slightly discordant, weakly whistled rendering of *Yellow Submarine* brought Greg back to the moment. He started to step slowly forward. It was as if that tune was a magnet, pulling him back in time to the Adam he had known and loved.

"Adam," Greg said as he moved ahead, carefully, not knowing whether his friend still had his pistol, whether he was capable of aiming and shooting.

"Adam," Greg repeated as he saw him sprawled in his own blood, still clutching the briefcase, no gun in his hand. The bravest of the rats were starting to reappear at the edges of the shadows, only to be scared away again by Adam's groans. Greg bent down over him and felt the warmth of his fading breath as Adam turned his face toward his best friend. Adam tried to speak, but the only thing that came out of his lips was a hoarse "Stupid bastard ..."

Greg did not know whether Adam had meant that for himself or for Greg, or perhaps for both of them. For the choices they had made to get to this point. But in the end, it did not matter.

Adam began to groan and whimper again. Greg felt pity at first, but then, revulsion and anger overwhelmed him. Revulsion, at the moral decrepitude of his former friend. Fury, that Adam had, all his life, played with him like a toy. And everyone else too. That he had involved him in this monstrous affair. Thinking that he would just go along with him.

A cough spewing more blood onto the metallic floor and then an infernal chortle from the depths of Adam's being broke the silence, startling Greg and echoing through the engine room for what seemed an eternity. When it died away, Greg reached down and unwound Adam's stiffening fingers from around the handle of the briefcase, pushed the body aside and started up the ladder. From the top, he looked back down at his friend, lifeless, sprawled in his own blood, pecked at by rodents.

He would never forget the look on Adam's face.

*****

Greg rapidly climbed up the ladder, despite the shoulder wound and the heavy briefcase that made this difficult. Opening the hatch up top, he was relieved to breathe oxygen, to be able to see the sun again.

His mind, too, was starting to focus on the world above. Anne—what had happened to her? Thank God, she was alive. What had they done to her? And Julia? He needed to find them. Greg picked up speed as he searched for the best way to get back on land.

Who were these commandos, who had come to the rescue? Irena was dead, but did Polyakov and Hetzel get away? And Billy? Did he have the other briefcase?

Greg's shoulder ached where he had been grazed and there were patches of blood drying on his sleeve, but it seemed that the bleeding had slowed. He found a place where, if he climbed up on the boat's railing, he thought he would be able to jump to shore even in his wounded and exhausted state. He threw the briefcase across and then launched himself into the air.

Chapter 60

The blood took a while to flow back into Julia's fingers as she worked to untie the rope around Anne's ankles. Although she was sore all over, she was more worried about the Interpol agent, who was now lying motionless on her stomach, still moaning and sobbing.

When the troublesome knot finally gave way and Julia unwound the rope, she saw the raw red marks around Anne's ankles and wrists where she had struggled against the tight rope and the bodily abuse. She moved up and sat on the table, gently cradling Anne's head on her lap, stroking her face as she said, "Anne, it's going to be okay. Greg will soon be back. I know you have been through a terrible ordeal, but we have to get out of here." Julia helped Anne sit up, then stand and rearrange her clothes. Anne leaned against her, again breaking into violent sobs. They were still holding each other when the door on the water side was violently kicked in and suddenly, the small room was teeming with armed men yelling something first in a language they didn't understand, then in Russian and lastly in English. It all sounded like "Hands up! Don't move!" With several machine guns pointing at her, Julia raised her hands and a stunned Anne slowly did likewise.

"Who are you?" Lowering his gun, the soldier in command asked—surprised at seeing two beautiful, disheveled women huddled together in front of him, "What happened here?"

"This is Anne Rossiter, Interpol, and I am Julia Saparova, a Russian citizen working with her ..." Julia said hesitantly.

It was when she heard her name and 'Interpol' that Anne finally managed to gather enough strength to force the horrors she had just experienced temporarily into the background and switch back to the present. "We're in pursuit of criminals from Russia who are selling highly enriched uranium to terrorists," she said. "You don't know how glad we are that you've come."

Anne saw that it took the commander of the unit a moment or two to be convinced by her words, but eventually, he came over to her, and seeing the shredded underwear and the fragments of rope on the floor, adopted a gentler tone.

"What has been going on here? Are you ladies okay? I am Lieutenant Rakasvili of the Georgian Special Forces. The CIA notified us that there would be a sale of nuclear material somewhere in Poti. That's why we're here."

Anne tried to place his accent: definitely southeast—Virginia or the Carolinas. He must be one of those Georgians who left and then came back. Trained by the U.S. armed forces.

"Next door. That's where they were, the arms dealers and terrorists. The sale was taking place there." She shuddered involuntarily as she said this and nodded towards the main room. They all started to move in that direction, Rakasvili first through the door, finger on the trigger of his machine gun.

"Not pretty," Rakasvili said, surveying the carnage. "But good work. We did good to get so many."

Anne was stunned by what she saw—a headless woman, blood still trickling from the stump of a neck, pieces of hairy skull all over the floor. Two Middle Eastern men—a smaller one with a rucksack, another whose chest had been partially blown away—as well as two Russians or Abkhaz who must have come with Adam and Greg, sprawled on the floor in pools of blood. She was glad and repulsed at the same time to see the Russian who had tied her up and threatened her lying there, but angry that Polyakov seemed to have escaped.

"This is where they were doing the deal," Anne said. "But an American got away with some of the uranium through the door in the other room. He was armed. One of our men went after him. You better send some of your soldiers to help."

"The others must have escaped through there," Rakasvili said, pointing to the small open door on the opposite wall. He yelled something in Georgian and two of his men rushed through the doorway, while the other pair pushed back into the room they had just left.

"I want to take possession of the laptop and the radio telephone," Anne said, seeing the abandoned hardware on the table. "They could yield information that might help us trace these criminals." She made her way over towards the table, suddenly realizing when she stepped on a shard of glass from the shattered windows that she was still barefoot.

"Who are these people?" Rakasvili asked, frowning as he leaned down over Ali.

"I didn't meet them, but that one must be a terrorist. And she must be the Director of Mayak. One of the Russian nuclear facilities. There were indications that she was involved."

Rakasvili leaned over the remains and tried to search in the corpse's side pockets for identification. But he didn't get very far since everything was soaked through with blood.

"We'll leave this to the forensic experts," he said, withdrawing his hand with a frown.

"Greg!" Anne suddenly heard Julia shout with joy and looked up to see him silhouetted in the main entrance to the room. She was too overwhelmed to utter a syllable, but simply ran barefoot through blood, glass and rubble to him. Greg put the briefcase down and opened his arms to hold her close. As she leaned into him, she gave way to a torrent of tears.

"It's all right, Anne." She heard Greg's words from afar. "We're safe now. We'll get those bastards!"

*****

"Anne, are you all right?"

"Yes. Now that you're here. We'll talk about it later," she said, looking into Greg's eyes.

Rakasvili's radio crackled and there was an exchange, presumably in Georgian. "Greg, this is Lieutenant Rakasvili of the Georgian Special Forces unit. We owe our lives to him and his men. He sent some of them after you."

"Thank you, Lieutenant."

"It took us a while to find the place."

"You and how many?" Greg asked.

"I had four in my unit. But we also had four sharpshooters outside. They're the ones who killed most of these guys."

258

"What happened with Adam?" Anne asked, looking up at Greg.

"He's dead. Here's the uranium." Greg put the briefcase on the table.

"How?"

"Did Crawford get away with the other half?" Greg asked, as he surveyed the room. He was not ready to tell her that he had killed his friend. The horror of it all was just starting to dawn on him.

"Who's Crawford?" And then she remembered the name on the card. "What was he doing here?"

"I'll explain later. Did he get away?"

"Yes, it seems he did. The terrorists had a speedboat tied up alongside and got to it in time. Was he one of them? Lieutenant Rakasvili has alerted the CIA and the Georgian Air Force, but it'll take a while to get a search party out there. They'll be long gone."

The jarring noise from the radio again—stops and starts, voices.

"And Polyakov? Hetzel?" Greg glanced at Julia, knowing her feelings toward the flesh merchant, and saw that Anne came close to tears when he mentioned the Russian's name.

"That creep Hetzel was here?" Julia asked.

"It seems they got away," Anne replied in a muted voice.

"Your guys didn't get the terrorists in the boat I understand," Greg said, looking at Rakashvili. "What about the Russians?"

"No. The ones in the boat got away. We don't know about the Russians for sure. Two cars are still out there. A Zil and a Ford. Abandoned. My commandant will be here shortly and a medic to look at your wound, sir." Rakasvili pointed to the graze on Greg's arm—he had completely forgotten about it. "And the ladies, of course."

They all moved out onto the railed wooden walkway overlooking the parking lot, to get away from the carnage, to breathe the fresh sea air, to relish the late afternoon sunshine. A convoy of two Jeeps and a covered army truck drove up and stopped right underneath them. Rakasvili's radio crackled again and he said, "That's Major Goradze. Let's go downstairs."

The Major confirmed that his forces had not been able to stop the Russian convoy, that two Subaru SUVs had left the harbor area, and soon after, had been joined by two Russian-armed Jeeps. The four vehicles were now speeding north towards the Abkhaz border. At this point, it would require a significant force to try to stop them and without the approval of the President, he was not willing to take on the Russian military.

*****

The Georgian army medic was a corporal who had studied medicine at the University of Vermont. He recounted with enthusiasm his experiences of skiing at Stowe and boating on Lake Champlain as he cleaned Greg's bullet wound with alcohol after treating Anne and Julia's physical wounds.

"Ow, that stings!"

"Don't worry, I'm here." Anne held Greg's hand firmly.

"I just have to put the bandage on."

"You know … Polyakov." Greg wanted to take his mind off the pain in his shoulder. "Amazing that in no time at all he has the Russian army giving him cover."

"Incredible, yes." Anne fought back her memories of the attack.

"Do you think it's just that he has good contacts? His mafia? Or do you think some of the Russian leadership is on his side? His brother surely must have known. Certainly, from the way he handled the interrogation of those Chechens. But what about the politicos, were they in on it?"

"I hadn't thought about it, Greg. The Russian authorities seem to have looked the other way, if nothing else."

"That's what I was thinking. In some respects, it may nicely fit with their foreign policy. To allow some nuclear materials to get into the wrong hands. I can just see some people in the Kremlin—some of the *siloviki*—I hate to say it, be glad if terrorists detonated a nuclear bomb in New York or London. You know, if we can't bury them ourselves, let's just help others do the job—even their own fanatic groups, like those Sons of Jesus who blew up Grand Central Station—then just sit back and watch as they are buried."

"What a horrible thought!"

"But even more terrible is that we are now up against a united al Qaeda with the Sons of Jesus. And now they have half a bomb's worth of uranium."

"Was Crawford one of them?"

"Yes. Brother Peter. The second-in-command. I only found out now."

"At least you can identify him. A crack in their invulnerability. But Greg, they'll be out to kill you."

"Well, Billy Crawford will have to hide for the rest of his pitiful life. Somewhere in Waziristan or some other hellish place like that. But we better get the word out fast."

"Okay, sir, we're done. You can put your shirt back on."

"Anyway, the main thing for now is that this Mayak heist did not succeed. At least not completely—they did get half the uranium, but not enough for a bomb. And now we know who has it. It seems that with Kolchakova and Adam dead, Mayak is unlikely to be a source for HEU in the near future. I am devastated though that you had this ordeal …"

"Thank God that we are both alive," Anne countered, turning her face towards Greg, who responded with a kiss.

Chapter 61

From Poti, the Georgian Special Forces flew Anne, Greg and Julia to an American base in Turkey, where they were all thoroughly doctored, debriefed and decontaminated. Needless to say, Greg and Anne were relieved to hand over the briefcase to the commander.

Through the local CIA representative, Anne got in touch with Interpol and a worldwide hunt for Billy and Khalid and the other half of the HEU was initiated. But Anne and Greg knew that there was not much hope of finding them. The likelihood was that the terrorists had made it to the Turkish coast and linked up with Islamic Fundamentalists who helped them hide and eventually get to Waziristan or wherever al Qaeda's main hideout was. The commander thanked them in the President's name, for foiling what had been the largest and most dangerous heist of HEU ever, and one that could have resulted in a major nuclear catastrophe. Might still, Greg thought to himself, unless Billy and the HEU are found.

From the base, via Istanbul, the three were flown to Vienna. They were relieved to be back in the West, to wash away the trauma and the travails of those few days. Greg moved in with Anne, even though her place was tiny. At least that way, Greg could help her with the slow emotional and psychological recovery and they could maximize their time together. Once he broke down and told her how he shot Adam in self-defense as his friend tried to escape with the uranium, it was her turn to console him. It had been necessary to prevent a nuclear catastrophe and in any case, Adam's evil side had totally usurped his being.

Anne did leave Greg the morning after they got back to go into the Interpol office for a debriefing—she also wanted the technicians to start working on the laptop and the radiotelephone Polyakov left behind to see what information they could glean.

And then there was the letter. Greg gently unfolded it over breakfast and Anne read Pleshkov's notes on the back. They talked about the brutal focus of the Soviet nuclear effort and wondered how many lives had been sacrificed to it. No one would ever know for sure, but the number was likely in the millions.

*****

Ten days later, after Anne and her psychologist assured him that she would be okay, Greg said good-bye and travelled back to the U.S. to wrap up his affairs. The first thing they both agreed he needed to do was to deliver András's letter to Omi, to whom it had been addressed.

Greg flew to Cleveland and went to his childhood home, where Omi still lived with his mother, Klára.

"Omi, I have something for you." He pulled out the folded letter from his briefcase and placed it into her trembling, veined and bony hands.

Klára fetched Omi's reading glasses and the old lady unfolded the yellowed paper reverently. She stared at the first page for a few moments and tears came into her eyes as she said, "I cannot believe it. No, it is not true."

And then she read it out loud, translating the letter for Greg and Klára.

A gulag somewhere near Chelyabinsk in Siberia
February 10, 1949

My dearest Lily, my beloved Klárikám:

I hope these words reach you in good health and safety. I am writing them to tell you how much I love you and long to be with you. My biggest sorrow is that I know now that I will never see you again. Lily, I implore you to build yourself and our dear child a decent and happy life, if that is possible in this new world. Marry again. Have babies, brothers and sisters for our daughter. But do not forget me, or what I write in this letter.

That night a year and a half ago, the night I was torn so cruelly from you by the brutes from the AVO, they took me to Andrássy út 60 and dumped me in a filthy solitary confinement cell. I do not know how long I was there in the dark, but it must have been a few days, because by the time they dragged me to another room, I had started to hallucinate and I was dying of thirst and hunger.

In this interrogation chamber, I was told to stand opposite a table where two officers were sitting. One addressed me as follows: 'András Bányai. You are a bourgeois intellectual. Enemy of the people. You studied in Berlin with Nazi swine. But you are a lucky man. Instead of executing you for your crimes, we have agreed to send you to a special place in our great brother nation, the Soviet Union. There you will work to advance the cause of the international proletariat. Comrade Mishkin will take charge of you from here.'

I was put in a black Volga and driven to the Keleti train station. Two guards waited with me, until eventually a freight train pulled in on one of the side tracks, carrying all sorts of industrial machinery going east. The Russians were stripping Hungary, occupied Austria and other states of whatever they could use to build their economy.

The last wagon was a cattle car and I was shoved up into it. There were six soldiers with machine guns in the wagon guarding twenty-three men, some with bruises and dried blood where they had been beaten, all disheveled, dirty and exhausted. Like the others, I was chained to a hook in the wall. We traveled on this train for five nights and four days. The guards were changed several times and we were given thin soup and allowed to go to the toilet once a day through a hole in the wagon's floor. Talking was forbidden.

Finally, from traffic noises and shouting outside, I surmised that we must have arrived in the station of some big city. Through the cracks in the wagon wall, I was able to decipher the broken sign that indicated we were in

Chelyabinsk. A city somewhere in the Soviet Union. Our wagon was unhitched and after a long wait, hooked onto another train. This train traveled for four or five hours before it stopped and the door was slid open. Our chains were unlocked and we were told to climb down. Guards led us to a brick building, where we had to wait in an anteroom, while one by one we were ushered into an office. It was in this waiting room only that I discovered that the others in the wagon were also chemists and physicists from Hungary, Czechoslovakia and Austria.

When it was my turn, I was led into a sparse room with two uniformed men and one in civil sitting at a table. The two were I think NKVD secret police and the third I recognized as Efim Pleshkov, a Russian physicist who was at the Institute in Berlin the same time I was. It was he who spoke.

'András, how good to see you. Sorry about the travel arrangements; I know they were not comfortable. Let me tell you why you are here. The highest echelons of the Communist Party, Comrade Stalin himself, Comrade Beria and General Zavenyagin, are taking great interest in developing science in the country. They have ordered that the top scientists from the Soviet Union and its brother nations be collected in special laboratories—we have come to know them as *Sharashka*—to advance this cause. The one here is working on nuclear power. As you are a bright young physicist specializing in nuclear fission, we brought you here in case you can contribute. But it is a special honor to work in these *Sharashka* and my colleagues here insist that first you prove your loyalty and reliability by helping us construct buildings for the reactors. We will call on your knowledge if and when we need you.'

I was taken away with the others from the wagon to what seemed to be a huge camp, one of those gulags we had heard about, with many wooden barracks that must have housed thousands of men who had been brought there to build the reactor complex. I was no better off than any of the others, some who were convicts, a few political prisoners from all over the Soviet Union and many former soldiers in the Red Army who had been captured by the Germans and then repatriated.

Conditions were harsh, especially once the Siberian winter set in. We worked twelve hour days, completing what we understood was Unit A of the reactor complex. On Stalin's orders, this had to be ready by June 1948, so more and more prisoners were brought to perform this construction labor. Many died from exhaustion, exposure or disease. Or accidents. Like those poor convicts who were forced to erect the one-hundred-and-fifty meter chimney of the reactor. The chimney swayed two or three meters in the wind and a few prisoners would fall to their deaths every day while they were up there building it. Many were shot on the job for sitting down to rest or for talking.

But things have gotten much worse since Unit A was finished and started operating. There are frequent accidents in the reactor during this start-up phase. This is the first one in the Soviet Union and they have no experience. They also take many shortcuts. We are the guinea pigs exposed to the problems. So little is known about radiation. It is one of my regrets that I cannot contribute to the discovery of how it works and what it does to people and our surroundings. The only thing I sense is that the dirty yellow smoke coming out of the chimney and the wastewater running into the River Techa must be very bad. Since Unit A started up, countless prisoners have died or have diseases, diarrhea, nausea. All kinds of infections are rampant in the camp and bodies are taken away daily, disposed of I don't know where.

I have seen Efim Pleshkov a few times. He looks haggard and very unhappy. Although he never told me directly, what I think is that they are building the reactors to prepare uranium so it can be used in a bomb, like the ones the Americans dropped on Nagasaki and Hiroshima to end the war. At Stalin's orders. I have the sense that Efim knows and does not want to be part of it, but he also suspects that he will be killed if he

266

does not co-operate. I think he has shielded me from the worst —at least I have not been tortured—and helped me stay alive. At least until now.

A few weeks ago, there must have been a terrible accident in the reactor. They started using us prisoners to try and set things right. Nine days ago, half the prisoners in my Block were led away and they worked long hours for six days, each day looking and feeling worse and worse. And then five days ago, I was taken to do the same work, along with the remaining prisoners in my Block: to dismantle what I think are graphite rods that have been damaged—they are corroding at the bottom where the cooling water has been in contact with them—and to remove by hand the uranium pellets from the channels inside. Of course, after months in the reactor, these pellets have been enriched and are highly radioactive and that is why we, who have been forced to do this labor, have become very sick.

It starts with vomiting and nausea. Fever, headaches, diarrhea, then faintness and disorientation follow. The worst is that I have been bringing up and defecating blood, and I cannot digest anything anymore. I think I will die very soon.

But there is more. Three days ago, or on their sixth day working in the reactor, the fifty or so prisoners in the Block who started on the shift before me did not come back. They were replaced by new prisoners brought in from another gulag. It has been five days now for me; so I think tomorrow may be my last day. I don't think they will take us to a hospital. My only hope is that I can give this letter to Efim and that somehow he will get it to you. This is a lot to ask, because no communications with the outside world are permitted and he would be risking his life.

Lily, my dear, if you do get this letter, guard it until a time when you think you can make its contents public somehow. The world must know what is happening here in these nuclear compounds in the Soviet Union, in the name of the evil pursuit of an atomic bomb.

267

Good-bye, my love, good-bye, my dearest child, think of
me often, knowing that I loved you to the last,

Your András

When she finished reading, Omi folded the letter. After a few moments of
silence while she just stared ahead of her as tears welled in her eyes, Omi
turned to Greg and said, "Thank you, my dearest Greg. I can die now in
peace."

Epilogue

Over Easter that year, Greg and Anne married in a quiet ceremony in Cornwall. They stayed in Vienna, with frequent trips to Budapest, while Greg wrote a book about his grandparents, *András and Lily*, which became a bestseller. At Anne's urging, he did finally write the story of the Adam affair and this became *Twisted Reasons,* his second highly acclaimed serious novel after *Wintertime*.

Despite Anne's diligent pursuit of Billy, Khalid and the missing uranium, they were not found. Nor has she had success in tracking Polyakov, although rumors had him surfacing in the Congo and Somalia at various times. Hetzel, too, has remained on the loose; the purchase of the Revuebar was never completed.

Julia got her job at the IAEA, as assistant to the German who took over from Adam. She has been working closely with the new Director of Mayak to ensure that such heists can never happen again.

*****

There is one more thing to recount.

Through the efforts of Anne's colleagues at Interpol in coaxing out the information stored in the laptop and radiotelephone left behind by Polyakov, and with the help of the police in Singapore, Greg and Anne were able to track down the money Billy deposited in Adam's account that fateful day in Poti. They found the entire twenty-five million dollars he had been paid as his share for the stolen HEU.

With the agreement of Adam's parents and the support of Interpol, Greg and Anne gained legal access, as trustees, to this money and with it, set up a foundation to pay for medical treatment for the children of Chelyabinsk Oblast, those affected by contamination from Mayak. By Stalin's hell.

They named it the Bányai Foundation, in honor of András and Lily.

Acknowledgements

Twisted Reasons was inspired by Graham Greene's wonderful novel, *The Third Man*, and the movie made from it. The story of Harry Lime is set in post-War Vienna; my book starts out in the former Imperial capital as well, where I had the pleasure of living for five years and where the novel was conceived and written. I thank Graham Greene for the inspiration.

The descriptions of Mayak and the very real possibility of the theft of some nuclear material, as well as the several accidents that occurred there, are largely based on William Langewiesche's *The Atomic Bazaar*, a book everyone interested in this issue should read.

The account of the February 1949 accident and the use of gulag prisoners to manually salvage the still usable uranium is best detailed in *The Unknown Stalin* by Zhores and Roy Medvedev.

I would also like to thank my parents and relatives, whose lives were in large part the models for Lily and Kálmán's story. May they rest in peace.

Finally, I thank my wife, Marcia, my daughter, Alexandra, and my son, Nicholas, who read many drafts of the manuscript and gave very useful comments and editorial advice.

And last but not least, I am grateful to Ian Shaw and the team at Deux Voiliers Publishing for taking on the work of shaping and publishing the book, and particularly for the editing done by Adriana Palanca and Norman Hall, as well as several other editors along the way who helped improve the writing. Finally, I would like to thank Lin-Lin Mao for her wonderful cover design and Arianna Scianaro for her meticulous proofreading.

About the Author

Born in Budapest, Geza Tatrallyay escaped with his family in 1956 during the Hungarian Revolution, immigrating to Canada. He graduated with a BA from Harvard in 1972 and as a Rhodes Scholar from Ontario, obtained a BA/MA from Oxford in 1974. He completed his studies with a MSc from London School of Economics in 1975. Geza's professional experience has included stints in government, international finance and environmental entrepreneurship. Geza is a citizen of Canada and Hungary, and currently divides his time between Bordeaux, France and Barnard, Vermont.

The *Twisted* trilogy was conceived while Geza lived in Budapest and Vienna and traveled throughout the former Soviet bloc. Geza has a few publishing credits (poetry, short story, translations, articles, etc.) and has published an e-thriller, *Arctic Meltdown*.

For more about Geza Tatrallyay, visit his website :

www.gezatatrallyay.com

About Deux Voiliers Publishing

Organized as a writers-plus collective, Deux Voiliers Publishing is a new generation publisher. We focus on high quality works of fiction by emerging Canadian writers. The art of creating new works of fiction is our driving force.

We are proud to have published *Twisted Reasons* by Geza Tatrallyay.

Other Works of Fiction published by Deux Voiliers Publishing

Soldier, Lily, Peace and Pearls by Con Cú (Literary Fiction 2012)

Kirk's Landing by Mike Young (Crime/Adventure 2014)

Sumer Lovin' by Nicole Chardenet (Humour/Fantasy 2013)

Last of the Ninth by Stephen Lorne Bennett (Historical Fiction 2012)

Marching to Byzantium by Brendan Ray (Historical Fiction 2012)

Tales of Other Worlds by Chris Turner (Fantasy/Science Fiction 2012)

Romulus by Fernand Hibbert and translated by Matthew Robertshaw (Historical Fiction/English Translation 2014)

Bidong by Paul Duong (Literary Fiction 2012)

Zaidie and Ferdele by Carol Katz (Illustrated Children's Fiction 2012)

Palawan Story by Caroline Vu (Literary Fiction 2014)

Cycling to Asylum by Su J. Sokol (Speculative Fiction 2014)

Stage Business by Gerry Fostaty (Crime 2014)

Stark Nakid by Sean McGinnis (Crime/Humour 2014)

Please visit our website for ordering information
www.deuxvoilierspublishing.com